2014

Rick, Tanya,
Damps   Jaru

Enjoy your heritage —
Its a "wonderful
thing"!

♡ Mom

Christmas in Scandinavia

EDITED BY

SVEN H. ROSSEL

BO ELBRØND-BEK

TRANSLATIONS BY

DAVID W. COLBERT

University of Nebraska Press

Lincoln and London

Acknowledgments for previously published material appear on pages 181–82, which constitute an extension of the copyright page. © 1996 by the University of Nebraska Press

⊖

First Bison Books printing: 1999

Library of Congress Cataloging-in-Publication Data.
Christmas in Scandinavia / edited by Sven H. Rossel and Bo Elbrønd-Bek; translations by David W. Colbert.
p.   cm.
Includes bibliographical references.
ISBN 0-8032-3907-6 (cl: alk. paper)
ISBN 0-8032-8980-4 (pa: alk. paper)
1. Scandinavian literature – Translations into English.
2. Christmas – Literary collections. I. Rossel, Sven Hakon.
II. Elbrønd-Bek, Bo, 1946–   . III. Colbert, David W., 1939–
PT7092.E5C49   1996
839'.5-dc20   95-26575
                                                      CIP

*Dedicated to the memory of
our childhood Christmas*

Contents

Preface

THIS ANTHOLOGY PRESENTS THE READER WITH A number of selected Christmas stories representing all five Nordic countries, where reading both humorous as well as more serious Christmas stories aloud continues to be a living part of the middle-class family tradition that developed during the nineteenth century. Also, teachers read aloud for the pupils in the Christmas season—and not just in the lower grades, either. *Christmas in Scandinavia* thus represents an almost two-hundred-year-old but nevertheless living literary tradition, which to be sure has been increasingly threatened since the close of the Second World War by our modern communication and media culture.

This tradition, meanwhile, unlike the vast majority of popular television series, most of them U.S. shows broadcast in the Nordic countries, is not subject to a general demand for a happy ending to the story. Many of the texts in this anthology, which are all typical of Nordic mentality, can perhaps therefore seem strange or downright abnormal compared to the traditional expectations of the U.S. public for a "good Christmas story." The editors have nevertheless seen it as our duty to provide genuine examples of Nordic literary culture and mentality. The introduction by Sven H. Rossel is oriented toward a cultural history of Nordic Christmas traditions, while in the afterword Bo Elbrønd-Bek interprets a number of selected stories seen in relation to the central Christmas message.

For necessary permission we wish to express our sincere thanks to the respective copyright holders: Albert Bonniers Förlag in Sweden, Gyldendals Forlag in Denmark, Gyldendals Norsk Forlag in Norway, Werner Söderström Osakeyhtiö in Finland, as well as Heðin Brú's heirs and Gunnar Hambræus, the author's son. For the translation we would also like to acknowledge a subsidy from the Danish Ministry of Education.

Sven H. Rossel
Bo Elbrønd-Bek

Introduction

SVEN H. ROSSEL

OF ALL THE YEAR'S HOLIDAYS AND FESTIVALS, Christmas is the favorite of Scandinavians. After the long, cold, and increasingly gloomy fall, Christmas marks for them the turning point of the year—when light begins to triumph over darkness.

Preparations begin the first Sunday in Advent, which officially opens the Christmas season. The first of four candles is lit on the Advent wreath—originally a northern German custom—made either of painted metal or wood, or of pine twigs decorated with red or purple ribbons, and in many homes a red and yellow five-pointed Advent star made of paper with an electric bulb inside is hung in the window. In Finland and Sweden an oblong holder or candlestick with four or seven candles (or electric bulbs) is more popular. Families gather to make decorations for the Christmas tree—mobiles of straw, woven paper hearts and baskets— and to bake cookies for the holidays and drink *juleglögg*, a Swedish variant of hot spiced wine with raisins, almonds and a shot of *snaps*, which Americans know as aquavit. In the morning the children can hardly wait to open the first of twenty-four windows on the Advent calendar—also a German tradition introduced as late as the 1930s. In the weeks that follow, homes are decorated with garlands, tinsel and, in Denmark, Norway, and Sweden, with cardboard Christmas elves peeking from behind picture frames and mirrors. Greeting cards and letters are written; and gifts bought, wrapped, and hidden from the children until Christmas Eve.

Until the twentieth century, superstition has been very strong in Iceland. At Christmastime, evil spirits would prowl around, especially the *gryla*, a female troll that eats little children. Her sons, called Yule-dwarfs, would visit the farms, one each day and the last on Christmas Eve. On that evening the Yule-cat would snatch and eat all those who did not get any new clothes for Christmas. Toward the end of the nineteenth century these creatures were replaced by Father Christmas, a Scandinavian version of the American Santa Claus, whose origin dates back to the celebration of Saint Nicholas on 6 December.

In Sweden, since the nineteenth century, 13 December—the date of the winter solstice before the Gregorian calendar was adopted in 1753— is celebrated as Saint Lucia's Day, a tradition that later spread to certain parts of Denmark, Finland, and Norway. A young girl is garbed in white, with a red belt and a crown of candles, suggesting a halo; her costume represents Saint Lucia, a legendary martyr from Sicily and symbolizes her innocence, her martyrdom, and her holiness, respectively. The queen of light, she heads a procession of girls carrying candles and boys carrying stars, the so-called *stjärngossar*. First the girls sing a Neapolitan popular song from about 1850, which is then followed by the "star boys" singing an old Swedish legendary ballad about Saint Stephen; the two songs are repeated until the procession has left the room.

Christmas Eve, 24 December, marks the highlight of the celebration. In Finland, at precisely noon, the "peace of Christmas" is proclaimed in the country's former capital, Turku, along with exhortations and greetings that date from the Middle Ages. Later in the day, thousands of candles are lit and shine over the snow on graves in cemeteries all across the country. In the other Scandinavian countries many families attend a church service, returning with appetites whetted for the dinner to follow. The table has been laid with a special Christmas cloth or centerpiece, with candles, and with other decorations. In olden days in the countryside, the animals were given extra fodder and a bowl with rice pudding was placed outside, in Denmark for the *nisse*, in Iceland for the *ármaður*, in Norway for the *gardvord*, and in Sweden for the *tomte*, all of them a small, solitary guardian spirit of the farm or homestead, corresponding to the brownie in Scotland except that instead of brown he would wear gray clothes and a long, pointed red cap. The traditional Danish Christmas dinner starts with a hot rice pudding made with cream and containing a single almond. The finder, usually the youngest child, wins a prize, typically a miniature marzipan pig. Various versions of this tradition can be found in the other Nordic countries. The main menu can be either roast goose or duck, stuffed with apples and prunes, or roast pork, served with candied potatoes and red cabbage. In Iceland, *Thorláksmessa* is celebrated already on 23 December with a meal consisting of cured ray with melted mutton suet and potatoes. On Christmas Eve, however, Icelanders frequently follow Danish dining traditions, often with roast lamb or smoked mutton, sausages, and crispbread as the main dish. In Finland the festive dinner may consist of a large buffet with baked ham, *lutefisk* (pickled cod), and cured salmon. This buffet is called a *smörgåsbord* in

Sweden, but it is quite different from the buffet known in the United States by the same name. *Lutefisk* is even more popular in Norway, along with boiled cod, roast goose, turkey or roast pork. In Sweden, rice pudding, *lutefisk*, headcheese, and ham were traditionally served; today the Christmas ham is a must, but by noon a *smörgåsbord* is served, again with the Christmas ham and *dopp i grytan* (bread dipped in broth) as the highlight. When the table has been cleared, everyone moves into the living room, where the candles on the trimmed tree have been lit, in most families for the first time during the Christmas season. In Sweden and Finland the excitement mounts as everyone awaits the arrival of Father Christmas himself, carrying a big basket with all the presents. In many Finnish families it can also be the Christmas Goat who brings the gifts; in twentieth-century Iceland it is the *jólasvein*, the helper of Father Christmas. In Denmark and Norway, the family forms a circle after dinner and dances around the tree, singing Christmas carols—now the gifts are unwrapped, and the children are of course told that these were brought by Father Christmas himself.

Christmas Day entails visits by friends and relatives. The Danes gather for yet another scrumptious meal with herring, cold cuts, cheeses, and other delicacies washed down with beer and *snaps*. The Icelanders enjoy their *hangikjot*, cold, smoked lamb. In Finland, Norway, and Sweden, Christmas Day is more of a quiet day of devotion, when the main activity is, or rather used to be, attending early Christmas Matins services.

As exemplified in several of the stories, Christmas and New Year are celebrated as one big Yuletide festivity in Scandinavia. In earlier times, New Year's Eve occasioned a quiet celebration, but in many homes today, especially among younger people, the holiday calls for a party with masks, streamers, and practical jokes. Traditionally, however, there is a festive meal—boiled cod in Denmark, sausage and potato salad in Finland, and smoked lamb in Iceland—after which many families, especially in Denmark, light the candles on the tree for the last time. At midnight everyone drinks a toast to the new year while the town hall or church bells ring and fireworks are set off. Icelanders light bonfires, whereas Finns play games that foretell the future from objects hidden under cups or by interpreting the meaning of melted tin.

But Christmas is not quite over yet. It lasts a total of thirteen days and ends with Twelfth Night or Epiphany. Some Scandinavians keep their tree until then; others remove it to the yard and decorate it with strings of fat and nuts for the birds. Danes used to light three candles in the living room as a token substitute for the tree, originally a tradition commemorating the Three Wise Men; in Iceland, particularly in the country, so-called "elves' parties" are held with dancing around a bonfire; in Sweden and a few places in Norway so-called "starboys" go from door to door singing and reenacting scenes from the birth of Christ, the Slaughter of the Innocents, and the flight to Egypt.

Certainly, Christmas is a Christian festival, celebrating the birth of Christ, originally around 6 January. Not until the fourth century did 25 December become the official church festival in order to oust the Roman worship of Mithra, the god of light. But the festival of Yule was celebrated long before. Yule in the Scandinavian languages is *jul* or *jól*, and Finnish has the loan word *joulu*. The etymology of this Germanic word is unclear. Perhaps it means "sacrifice" or perhaps it is related to the word "wheel," that is, a "turning" of the sun, indicating that perhaps the old pagan celebration of the winter solstice is the origin of the Yule festival.

Several Scandinavian traditions, on the other hand, hearken back to Christmas as a celebration of ancestors, the dead who during the darkest time of the year would return to their old homes. The table would be laid out for them with food, and the lights would remain lit during the night before Christmas; the beds would remain empty, the family sleeping on straw on the floor. However, the latter tradition—as well as that of hanging up sheaves of grain and placing a cake or loaf of bread in the grain bin to be distributed and eaten during spring plowing—suggests a link between the celebration of Christmas and agriculture. The holiday perhaps originally marked the end of the agrarian work year. The Christmas goat, which originally was slaughtered in gratitude for a good year, is possibly part of this tradition. Later, in Denmark, Finland, Norway, and Sweden, the term "Christmas goat" has been used about a person who dresses up during Christmas in a hide and a goat's mask. Likewise, figures of straw representing goats and old men were used for various games and contests during the holidays, and these figures are still made.

In the mid-eighteenth century, giving Christmas presents replaced the New Year's gifts that had their origin in Roman tradition. In Catholic countries, these gifts used to be given to children by Saint Nicholas on his feast day, 6 December. In Protestant Germany, this tradition was moved to Christmas Eve, reaching Scandinavia in the eighteenth century. The Christmas tree also came to Scandinavia from Germany, where its first mention was in 1605. Not until the eighteenth century was the tree decorated with candles, and from Denmark it spread to the middle classes in the other Scandinavian countries around 1820, without gaining general popularity until the 1860s.

Also, the popular Christmas elf emerged only in the nineteenth century. To a certain degree his origin is in misinterpretations of pictures of Saint Nicholas with his white beard, and he is frequently confused with Father Christmas. In fact, his history is lost in the pagan past. He has existed for several thousand years in folk beliefs, invisible or only rarely seen on the farm or in a family's house, as the ever-present brownie, a male household spirit controlling domestic fortune, helpful when respected but grumpy and even dangerous when disregarded and therefore to be bribed at Christmas time with a bowl of hot rice pudding.

Christmas as celebrated today is, of course, not identical with Christmas as it has been celebrated through the centuries. However, descriptions from previous centuries are astonishingly sparse, and not until the introduction of the features with which we today associate Christmas—such as the tree, Father Christmas, and increased secularization and materialization of the festival—do stories emerge in literature in which the celebration of Christmas is either the center or the frame. The present texts, however, offer us valuable insight into both Christmas traditions and previous social conditions. Indeed, we gain insight not only into Christmas as it was celebrated by the middle class, but also into Christmas among the lower social classes.

Idealized, romanticized, and thereby trivialized descriptions of Christmas are generally without much value. On the other hand, texts that provide insight into more general human problems—be they of spiritual, social, or psychological nature—are of great value from an artistic point of view. Only such stories have been chosen for this anthology, but this criterion does not exclude texts that, beyond their value as cultural history, are highly entertaining, as well.

Christmas in Scandinavia

An Old-fashioned Christmas Eve

« En gammeldags Juleaften »

PETER CHRISTEN ASBJØRNSEN

NORWAY 1843

*A Norwegian folklorist, Peter Christen Asbjørnsen (1812–85)
was known primarily for collecting and publishing folktales and
legends on his own or in collaboration with Jørgen Moe.*

THE WIND WAS WHISTLING THROUGH THE OLD
maple and linden trees directly across from my windows; the
snow was drifting down the street, and the sky was as somber as a December sky can be here in Christiania. My spirits were equally somber.
It was Christmas Eve, the first I had been unable to spend beside the
home fires. Some time ago I had become an officer and was hoping to
give my parents the pleasure of my company, was hoping to show myself in pomp and splendor before the ladies in my native district. But a
nervous fever had sent me to the hospital, from which I had been released only a week ago, and I now found myself in that so highly praised
state, "convalescence." I had written home for the big bay and my father's reindeer coat, but the letter would barely reach the valley before
the day after Christmas, and only around New Year could I expect the
horse to be here. My comrades had left the city, and I had no family with
whom I could feel at home. The two old spinsters I was lodging with
were indeed good-natured and kind, and they had taken care of me with
much solicitude at the onset of my sickness. But these ladies' whole manner of being was all too much of the old world, really, to recommend
itself to youth. Their thoughts were of the past, and when, as they often
did, they told me stories about the city and city life, both subject matter
and point of view called to mind a vanished time. But this old-fashioned
manner of my ladies was also in complete harmony with the house they

inhabited. It was one of those old townhouses in Tollbodgate with deep windows, long, forbidding halls and staircases, and dark rooms and attics that instinctively suggested brownies and ghosts, in short just such a house, perhaps even the very same, that Mauritz Hansen has described in his tale, "The Old Lady with the Bonnet." In addition to this, their circle of acquaintances was very restricted for, apart from a married sister, no more than a couple of tedious matrons ever came to call. The only enlivenment was a pretty niece and another batch of merry, lively nieces to whom I was always having to tell fairy tales and stories about brownies.

I tried to amuse myself in my loneliness and my despondent mood by looking at all those people walking up and down the street in the drifting snow and wind with reddish-blue noses and half-closed eyes. I began to enjoy observing the life and bustle that prevailed across the way at the pharmacy: the door was not still for one instant—servants and peasants flocked in and out, stopping to study the signatures when they came out onto the street again. Some seemed to succeed in deciphering them; but sometimes prolonged pondering and an uneasy shake of the head revealed that the task was too difficult. It was getting dark; I could no longer distinguish faces, but stared over at the old building. At that time, the Swan Pharmacy stood with its dark reddish-brown walls, pointed gables and towers with weather vanes and leaded windows as a monument to the architecture of the seventeenth century. Only the swan was then, as now, very sedate, with a gold ring around its neck, riding boots on its feet, and wings outstretched for flight. I was just about to lose myself in reflections on captured birds when I was interrupted by noise and children's laughter in the adjoining room and a faint, spinsterish knocking at my door.

At my "Come in," the elder of my landladies, Miss Mette, entered with an old-fashioned curtsy, inquiring about my health, and in a roundabout way requesting that I feel myself at home with them that evening. "It isn't good for you to sit here alone in the dark so much, my good lieutenant," she added, "won't you join us right away? Old Mother Skau and my brother's little girls have arrived—perhaps it would amuse you a bit—for you're so fond of those cheerful children, aren't you?"

I accepted her friendly invitation. When I entered, a fire blazing in a large, boxlike stove was spreading a red, unsteady light through the wide-open stove door and out into the room, which was very deep and furnished in the old style with high-backed Russia leather chairs and one of those settees intended for hoop skirts and ramrod posture. The walls were adorned with oil paintings, portraits of rigid ladies with powdered coiffures, of members of the House of Oldenburg and other illustrious persons armed cap-à-pie or in red frocks.

"You'll really have to excuse us, lieutenant, that we haven't lit the candles yet," said Miss Cecilie, the younger sister who was commonly called Sillemor, coming to greet me with a curtsy akin to her sister's; "but the children so like to romp by the fire in the twilight, and Mother Skau is also having a cozy little chat in the stove corner."

"Don't you chat me, you enjoy gossiping in the owl-light yourself, Sillemor, and then we have to take the blame," replied the old, asthmatic lady addressed as Mother Skau.

"I say, good evening, sir, come and sit down here and tell me how you're doing; by Jove, how very peaked you've become," she said to me, holding her head high above her own turgid buxomness.

I had to recount my fate, suffering in return a very long and detailed narration of her rheumatism and asthmatic afflictions, which was fortunately interrupted by the boisterous arrival of the children from the kitchen, where they had been paying a visit to the old domestic fixture, Stine.

"Auntie, do you know what Stine says?" cried an agile little brown-eyed thing. "She says that I have to go along to the hayloft this evening and give the brownie Christmas pudding. But I don't want to—I'm afraid of the brownie!"

"Oh, Stine just says that to get rid of you; she doesn't dare go to the hayloft in the dark herself, that fool, for she knows well enough that she was once frightened by the brownie herself," said Miss Mette. "But won't you say hello to the lieutenant, then, children?"

"Really, is it you, lieutenant, I didn't recognize you, how pale you are, it's so long since I saw you last," the children cried all at once, crowding around me. "Now you must tell us something funny, it's so long since you told us something, oh tell us about Butter-buck and Gold-tooth, kind sir, tell us about Butter-buck and Gold-tooth!" I had to tell them about Butter-buck and the dog Gold-tooth, and oblige with a couple of stories about the Vaker brownie and the Bure brownie, who took hay from each other and, meeting with each a load of hay on his shoulders, fought so that they vanished in a cloud of hay. I had to tell them about the brownie at Hesselberg who baited the watchdog until the master threw him out over the barn ramp. The children clapped their hands and laughed. "That served him right, that nasty brownie," they said and demanded more.

"No, you're pestering the lieutenant too much, children," said Miss

Cecilie. "Now Auntie Mette will tell a story, I dare say."

"Yes, tell us, Auntie Mette!" was the common outcry.

"I don't really know what to tell you," replied Auntie Mette, "but since we've come to talk about the brownie, then I'll tell you a little about him, too. I guess you remember old Kari Gusdal, children, who was here baking flatbread and griddle cakes, and who always had so many fairy tales and stories to tell."

"Oh yes," cried the children.

"Now, old Kari told me that she served at the orphanage here many years ago. At that time it was even more lonely and dreary in that part of town than it is now, and it's a dark and gloomy building, that orphanage. Now when Kari arrived she was to be the cook, and she was a very clever and good girl. One night she had to get up and brew, and the other servants said to her, 'Then you've got to watch out that you don't get up too early; you mustn't put the mash on before two o'clock.'

"'Why's that?' she asked.

"'Surely you know that there's a brownie here, and you ought to know that he doesn't want to be disturbed, and before two o'clock you mustn't put the mash on at all,' they said.

"'Tut, is *that* all,' said Kari. She had lots of pluck, as they say. 'I'll have nothing to do with the brownie, and if he comes to me, I'll be dashed if I don't toss him out the door.'

"The others warned her, but she stuck to her guns, and when it was perhaps a little past one o'clock, she got up and stoked under the brewing cauldron and put on the mash. But the fire kept going out under the cauldron, and it was just as if someone were tossing the logs out all over the hearth, but who it was she couldn't see. She gathered up the logs time and again, but that did no good, and the mash wouldn't brew, either. Finally, she got tired of this, took a log and, running high and low, swung it shouting, 'Get packing to where you come from! If you think you can scare me, you're mistaken!'

"'Then fie on you!' came the reply from one of the darkest corners; 'I've taken seven souls here in this house; I thought I might have had the eighth, as well.' And since that time there has not been anyone who has seen or heard of the brownie at the orphanage, Kari Gusdal said."

"I'm scared. No, you must tell us something, lieutenant; when you tell it, then I'm never scared, for you tell it so funny," said one of the little ones. Another suggested that I should tell about the brownie that danced the halling dance with the girl. That was one I was most reluctant to embark upon, since singing went with it. But under no circumstances would they let me off, and I was already starting to clear my throat in order to prepare my exceedingly inharmonious voice to sing the halling dance that went with it, when the forementioned pretty niece entered, to the children's delight and my salvation.

"All right children, now I'll tell it if you can get your cousin Lise to sing the halling for you," I said as she took a seat; "and then you yourselves can dance, can't you?" Their cousin was pestered by the little ones, promising to perform the dance music, and I began my story.

"There was a girl somewhere, I should think it was in Hallingdal, who had to take rice cream pudding to the brownie; whether it was a Thursday evening or a Christmas Eve I don't remember, but I rather think it was a Christmas Eve. Now she thought it was a shame to give the brownie such good food, so she ate the rice cream pudding herself, and drank the fat to boot, and went to the barn with oatmeal and sour milk in a pig trough.

"'There's your trough, you fiend!' she said. But no sooner had she said this than the brownie came dashing out, grabbed her, and started to dance with her; he kept dancing until she lay gasping, and when they came to the barn in the morning, she was more dead than alive. But as long as he was dancing, he sang"—here Miss Lise assumed the brownie's part, singing in halling tempo:

> *Oh you have eaten up the brownie's pudding,*
> *And you'll have to dance with the brownie now*
>
> *Oh you have eaten up the brownie's pudding,*
> *Then you'll have to dance with the brownie now!*

During this I helped out by stamping the beat with both feet, while the children gamboled boisterously and jubilantly among one another on the floor.

"I think you're raising the roof while you're at it, children; you're making such a noise that my head is aching," said old Mother Skau. "Now be quiet for a bit, then I'll tell you some stories." There was silence in the room and the matron began to speak.

"Now people have a lot to say about brownies and wood nymphs and the like, but I don't believe much of it. I haven't seen either one or the other—you see I haven't got around very much in my life, either—and I think it's all nonsense; but old Stine out there, she says she's seen the brownie. When I was preparing for confirmation she was in service to

my parents, and she came to them from an old skipper who had given up
sailing. It was so calm and peaceful where the skipper lived; they never
visited anyone, and nobody visited them, and the skipper never went farther than down to the docks. They always went to bed early, and there
was a brownie there, they said. But then there was the time, said Stine,
that the cook and she were sitting up one evening in the maid's room trying to take care of chores and sewing for themselves. It was getting on
towards bedtime, for the watchman had already cried ten o'clock. They
were getting nowhere with the sewing and darning, for every now and
then the sandman would come, and Stine would begin to nod, and the
cook would begin to nod, for they had been up early to do the washing. But just as they were sitting like that, they heard a dreadful crash
out in the kitchen—just as if someone threw all the dishes in a heap and
dashed them to the floor. They leaped up in fright, she said, and Stine
screamed, 'God comfort and help us, it's the brownie!' And Stine was so
afraid that she didn't dare set foot in the kitchen. The cook was no doubt
frightened too; but Stine plucked up her courage, and when she came
out to the kitchen, all the dishes were lying on the floor, but not one of
them was broken, and the brownie was standing in the door with his red
cap on, laughing ever so heartily. But she had heard that at times if the
brownie were told that it was quieter for him some other place, he could
be fooled into leaving. Stine had long been racking her brains to play a
trick on him, and so she told him—her voice trembled a little—that he
ought to move over to the coppersmith's across the street, where there
was more peace and quiet, for they went to bed at nine o'clock every
evening. That was no doubt also true, Stine told me, but you probably
know, she said, that the master worked and was up with everyone, both
journeymen and apprentices, hammering and making a noise from three
o'clock in the morning all day long. Since that day, Stine said, they saw
no more of the brownie at the skipper's. And he really liked it at the coppersmith's, even though they hammered and pounded all day, for people
said that the wife there put out pudding in the attic for him every Thursday evening. It should come as no surprise, either, that they got rich, for
the brownie brought them good luck, Stine said, and it's true business
picked up and they became rich, but whether it was the brownie that
helped them I couldn't say," added Mother Skau, coughing and clearing
her throat after her exertion with this narrative, unusually long for her.

When she had taken a pinch of snuff, she recovered and started afresh.

"My mother was an honest woman; she told a story that took place here in town, and on a Christmas night at that, and I know it's true, for there never came an untrue word from her mouth."

"Then we'd better hear it, Madame Skau," I said.

"Tell it, tell it, Mother Skau," cried the children.

The good woman coughed a bit, took yet another pinch, and began. "When my mother was still a girl, she would now and then call on a widow that she knew, whose name was—well what was her name now? Madame . . . no, I can't think of it, but it's all the same anyway, she lived up in Møllergate and was a woman a little beyond her prime. Now it was Christmas Eve, just like it is now; so she thought to herself that she should go to matins Christmas morning, for she was a frequent church-goer, and so she set coffee out so that she could get a little something warm to drink, so she wouldn't go on an empty stomach. When she woke up, the moon was shining in on the floor, but when she got up and tried to look at the clock, it had stopped, and the hands stood at half past eleven. She didn't know what time of night it was, but then she went over to the window and looked over at the church. There was light coming from all the church windows. She woke the maid and had her brew the coffee, while she got dressed and took her hymnal and went to church. It was so quiet in the street, and she didn't see a soul on the way. When she got to church she sat down in the pew where she usually sat, but when she looked around she thought that the people looked so pale and strange, just as if they might all be dead. There was no one she knew, but there were many she thought she must have seen before, but she couldn't re-call where she had seen them. When the pastor came to the pulpit, he wasn't any of the local ministers, but a tall, pale man she also thought she should know. He preached rather nicely, and there wasn't all that rustling and coughing and clearing of throats that there usually is at matins on Christmas morning, but it was so quiet that she might have heard a pin drop. Well, it was so quiet that she became quite anxious and afraid.

"When they started to sing again, a woman sitting next to her leaned over and whispered in her ear, 'Throw your cloak loosely around you and leave, for if you wait until it's over with, they'll put an end to you. It's the dead that are holding services.'"

"Ohh, you're scaring me, you're scaring me, Mother Skau," whimpered one of the little ones, and crawled up onto a chair.

"Hush, hush, child, she escapes unhurt; now just you listen," said Mother Skau. "But the widow was also frightened, for when she heard the voice and looked at the woman, she recognized her; it was her neighbor who had died many years ago, and when she now looked around the church she remembered well that she had seen both the pastor and many of the congregation, and that they had died ages ago. A chill ran through her, so frightened was she. She threw her cloak loosely about her as the woman had said, and began to walk out; but then it seemed to her they all turned around and grabbed at her, and her legs trembled under her so she nearly collapsed to the floor of the church. When she reached the church steps she felt they were grabbing her by the cloak; she released her grip and let them keep it, and hurried home as fast as she could. When she was at her parlor door the clock struck one, and when she entered she was almost half dead, so frightened was she. In the morning when people arrived at church, her cloak was lying on the steps, but it was torn to shreds. My mother said she'd seen it many times before, and I think she's seen one of the pieces, too; but that's all the same, it was a short cloak of pink cloth with rabbit lining and edging, the kind that was still in use in my childhood. Now it's odd to see one like that, but there are some old women here in the city and in the Institution in the Old City that I've seen in church with cloaks like that during the Christmas holidays."

The children, who during the last part of the narrative had evinced much fear and anxiety, declared that they did not want to hear more horrid stories like that. They had crawled up into the settee and onto the chairs, saying that they thought there was someone under the table who was grabbing at them. Just then light was borne in on old candelabras, and we discovered with laughter that they were sitting with their legs on the table. The candles and the fruitcake, jam, cookies, and wine soon dispelled ghost stories and fear, enlivening dispositions, and changing the subject to one's neighbor and the topics of the day. Finally, the rice pudding and the pork roast deflected thoughts toward the substantial, and we parted early, wishing one another a merry Christmas. But I had a very restless night. I don't know if the cause was the stories, the food partaken, my weak condition, or all of these together; I lay tossing back and forth and was in the midst of stories about brownies, wood nymphs, and ghosts all night long. Finally, I was riding through the air to church, sleigh bells ringing. The church was lit up, and when I entered I saw it was the church at home in the valley. There was no one to be seen there but dalesmen with red caps, soldiers in full regalia, and peasant girls with kerchiefs and red cheeks. The pastor stood in the pulpit; it was my grandfather, who had died when I was a little boy. But in the middle of his sermon he did a somersault—he was well-known as an agile fellow—

down into the middle of the church, so that his chasuble flew in one direction, his collar in the other. "There lies the pastor, and here am I," he said with a well-known phrase of his, "and now let's dance a roundel."

Immediately the congregation threw themselves into the wildest dance, and a big tall dalesman came over and took me by the shoulder and said, "You'd better come along, fellow."

I didn't know what to believe when I woke up just then and felt the grip on my shoulder, and saw the same man I had seen in my dreams bending over my bed with a dalesman's cap over his ears, a reindeer coat over his arm, and a pair of large eyes fixed firmly on me.

"You must be dreaming, fellow," he said, "there's sweat on your brow, and you're sleeping sounder than a hibernating bear. God's peace and merry Christmas from your father and those in the valley. Here's a letter from the scribe and a reindeer coat for you. The big bay is standing in the courtyard."

"But in God's name, is it you, Thor?" It was my father's head servant, a splendid dalesman. "How on earth did you get here already?" I cried delighted.

"Well I'll tell you," replied Thor; "I came with the bay, but otherwise I was with the scribe out on the headland, and then he said: Thor, he said, now it isn't far to town, you'd better take the bay and drive in to see the lieutenan', and if he's fit and can come along, then you must bring him along, he said."

When we left the city it was clear again, and we had the most splendid sledding. The bay stepped out with its nimble old legs, and such a Christmas as I celebrated then, I have never celebrated either before or since.

The Fir Tree

« Grantræet »

HANS CHRISTIAN ANDERSEN

DENMARK 1844

Known as H. C. Andersen (1805–75) in Scandinavia, this Danish writer of poems, dramas, novels, and travelogues gained world fame for his fairy tales and stories, which have been translated into more than a hundred languages. Andersen's first collection of tales was published in 1835; altogether he wrote 156 tales, among others The Ugly Duckling, The Emperor's New Clothes, The Little Mermaid, *and* The Nightingale.

OUT IN THE WOODS THERE WAS SUCH A NICE fir tree. It was growing in a good spot—it could get sunshine, there was plenty of air, and 'round about grew many larger comrades, both pines and firs. But the little fir tree was so anxious to grow up. It gave no thought to the warm sunshine and the fresh air, it didn't care about the farm children who went about chattering as they gathered strawberries or raspberries. They would often come with a whole jarful or with strawberries strung on straw, then they would sit near the little tree and say, "Oh, how nice and tiny it is!" This was not at all what the tree wanted to hear.

The next year it was a long shoot taller, and the year after that one even longer; for on a fir tree you can always tell how many years it has grown by the number of sections the trunk has.

"Oh, if only I were a great big tree like the others!" sighed the little tree, "then I could spread my branches so far out and with my top look out into the wide world! Then the birds would build nests among my branches, and when the wind blew I could nod so graciously, just like the others there!"

The fir tree took no pleasure at all in the sunshine, the birds, or the red clouds that sailed over morning and evening.

Or if it were winter with the sparkling white snow lying 'round about, a hare would often come hopping and jump right over the little tree—

oh, it was all so irritating! . . . But two winters came and went, and by the third the tree was so tall that the hare would have to go around it. "Oh, grow, grow, big and tall, that was simply the greatest thing in the world," thought the tree.

In the fall the woodcutters always came to cut down some of the tallest trees. This happened every year, and the young fir, which was now quite grown up, shuddered at this, for the magnificent tall trees fell to the ground with a creaking and crashing. Their branches were lopped off; they looked so naked, long, and skinny that you could hardly recognize them. But then they were loaded onto wagons, and horses drew them off, out of the woods.

Where were they going? What was in store for them?

In the spring, when the swallow and the stork arrived, the tree asked them, "Don't you know where they were taken to? Haven't you met them?"

The swallow knew nothing, but the stork looked uneasy, nodding his head and saying, "Well, I think so! I came across many new ships as I was flying from Egypt. There were magnificent masts on these ships; I dare say that was them, they smelled of fir. They send you their respects; they stand tall and topgallant!"

"Oh, if only I were big enough to fly across the sea, too! What is it anyway, this sea, and what does it look like?"

"Well, that's too vast to explain!" said the stork, and then left.

"Rejoice in your youth!" said the sunbeams, "rejoice in your new growth, in the young life that is in you!"

And the wind kissed the tree, and the dew wept tears onto it, but the fir tree did not understand.

When it was almost Christmas, very young trees were cut down, trees that were often not even as big or as old as this fir that was always so restless and eager to get away. These young trees—and they were precisely the very prettiest—kept all their branches; they were loaded onto wagons and horses drew them off, out of the woods.

"Where are they going?" asked the fir tree. "They're no bigger than me, there was even one that was much smaller; why did they keep all their branches? Where are they trundled off to?"

"We know! We know!" the house sparrows chirped in. "We've peeked in at the windowpanes down in the town! We know where they go off to! We've peeked in at the windows and seen them being planted in the middle of the warm room and decorated with the loveliest things, gilded apples and gingerbread, toys and hundreds of candles!"

"And then . . . ?" asked the fir tree trembling with every branch. "And then . . . ? What happens then?"

"Well, we didn't see any more! It was magnificent!"

"I wonder if I was meant for this illustrious career!" the tree shouted with joy. "That is even better than crossing the sea! How I ache with longing! If only it were Christmas! Now I'm as tall and as broad as the others that were taken away last year! . . . Oh, if only I were on the wagon already! If only I were in the warm room with all that pomp and glory! And then . . . ? Well, then comes something even better, even lovelier, why else would they decorate me so? Something even grander, even more glorious must be coming . . . ! But what? Oh, I ache! I yearn! I don't know myself what is the matter with me."

"Rejoice in us!" said the air and the sunlight, "Rejoice in your hearty youth out in the open!"

But the fir tree didn't rejoice at all. It grew and grew, standing green winter and summer; dark green it stood. People who saw it said, "That's a lovely tree." And at Christmastime it was cut down first of all. The ax cut deep through its pith, the tree fell with a sigh to the ground, it felt a pain, a faintness, it couldn't think of its fortune at all, it was distressed at leaving home, departing from the spot where it had grown up. It did know that it would never again see its dear old comrades, the little bushes and wildflowers round about, and maybe not even the birds. Departure was not at all pleasant.

The tree came to itself only when, unloaded with the other trees in the courtyard, it heard a man say, "That's splendid! It's the only one for us!"

Two servants in full uniform now came and carried the fir tree into a large, lovely drawing room. Portraits were hanging round about the walls, and by the large tiled stove were large Chinese vases with lions on their lids. There were rocking chairs, silken sofas, large tables piled with picture books and with toys costing a hundred times a hundred dollars— at least that is what the children said. And the fir tree was set up in a big tub filled with sand, but nobody could see that it was a tub because green cloth was draped around it, and it rested on a large, colorful rug. Oh, how the tree trembled! What was going to happen? Both servants and housemaids started trimming it. On its branches they hung little nets cut from colored paper; every net was full of sugar-candy; gold apples and walnuts hung as if they had grown there, and over a hundred small red, blue, and white candles were fastened to the branches. Dolls looking as lifelike as people—the tree had never seen the likes before—hovered in the greenery, and at the very top was placed a large star of gold tinsel. It was splendid, simply wonderfully splendid!

"Tonight," they all said, "Tonight it will sparkle!"

"Oh!" thought the tree, "if only it were evening! If only the candles were lit soon! I wonder what will happen then? Maybe the trees will come from the woods to look at me? Maybe the house sparrows will fly by the windowpanes? Maybe I'll take root here and stay trimmed winter and summer?"

It certainly knew what was what! But it got a regular barkache just from longing, and barkache is just as nasty for a tree as headaches for the rest of us.

Now the candles were lit. What glory, what splendor, the tree trembled in every branch at this, so that one of the candles set fire to the greenery—now that really burned!

"Heaven help us!" screamed the maids, and put it out in a hurry.

Now the tree did not even dare tremble. Oh, it was awful! It was so afraid of dropping some of all its finery, it was quite bewildered by all its splendor—And now suddenly the double doors opened, and lots of children rushed in, as if they were going to topple the whole tree. The grownups followed them sedately. The little ones were quite silent—but for only a moment; then they shouted again with joy so that the room resounded. They danced around the tree, and one present after another was plucked down.

"What is it they're doing?" thought the tree. "What's going to happen?" And the candles burned right down to the branches, and as they burned down they were put out, and then the children were allowed to plunder the tree. Oh, they rushed into it so that all its branches creaked. If it had not been fastened to the ceiling at its topmost point and its golden star, it would surely have toppled over.

The children danced about with their splendid toys, nobody looked at the tree except the old nanny, who was peeking in among the branches, but that was only to see if there were not a fig or an apple still left.

"A story! A story!" shouted the children, dragging a fat little man toward the tree, and he sat down right under it, "because then we're under the greenwood," he said, "and it'll do the tree especially good to listen, too. But I'll only tell one story. Do you want to hear the one about 'Ersy-Versy' or the one about 'Clumpy-Dumpy Who Fell Downstairs and Yet Ascended the Throne and Gained the Princess'?"

"Ersy-Versy!" shouted some, "Clumpy-Dumpy!" shouted others. There was shouting and there was screaming, but the fir tree kept quite silent, thinking, "Shouldn't I take part, shouldn't I do something?" But it had already taken part, had done what it was supposed to do.

And the man told about "Clumpy-Dumpy Who Fell Downstairs and Yet Ascended the Throne and Gained the Princess." And the children clapped their hands and shouted, "Tell more! Tell more!" They wanted "Ersy-Versy," also, but they only got the one about "Clumpy-Dumpy." The fir tree stood perfectly still, deep in thought; the birds out in the woods had never told anything like this. "Clumpy-Dumpy fell downstairs and yet gained the princess! So that's the way the world goes!" thought the fir tree, believing it to be true because such a nice man had told it. "Well, who knows! Maybe I'll fall downstairs and gain a princess!" And it looked forward to being decked out the next day with candles and toys, gold and fruit.

"Tomorrow I won't shake!" it thought. "I will really enjoy all my finery. Tomorrow I'll listen again to the story about 'Clumpy-Dumpy' and maybe also the one about 'Ersy-Versy,' too." And the tree stood deep in thought all night long.

In the morning the stable boy and the maid entered.

"Now the finery begins again!" thought the tree, but they dragged it out of the room, up the stairs, into the attic, and there, off in a dark corner where sun never shined, they dropped it. "What's the meaning of this?" thought the tree. "What am I supposed to do here? I wonder what I will get to hear up here?" And it leaned up against the wall, thinking and thinking. . . . And it had good time, for night and day went by. Nobody came up there, and when somebody finally did come, it was only to put some big boxes off in a corner. The tree was completely hidden— you would think that it had been entirely forgotten.

"Now it's winter outside!" thought the tree. "The ground is hard and covered with snow, and people can't plant me. That's why I'll probably stay sheltered here until spring! How very thoughtful! How good people really are! . . . If only it weren't so dark here and so terribly lonely! . . . Not even a little hare! . . . It was so nice in the woods after all, when the snow had fallen and the hare came hopping by, even when it jumped right over me; but I didn't like it at the time. Up here it's so terribly lonely!"

"Squeak, squeak!" said a little mouse just then and scurried out. And then came yet another little one. They sniffed at the fir tree and scurried about among its branches.

"It's terribly cold!" said the little mice. "Otherwise this is a heavenly place to be! Isn't that so, you old fir tree?"

"I'm not at all old!" said the fir tree, "there are many that are much older than me!"

"Where do you come from?" asked the mice, "and what do you know?" They were so terribly curious. "Then tell us about the loveliest place on earth! Have you been there? Have you been in the pantry where cheeses lie on the shelves and hams hang from the ceiling, where you dance on tallow candles, and go in skinny and come out fat?"

"I don't know about that," said the tree, "but I know the woods where the sun shines and the birds sing!" And then it told them all about its youth, and the little mice had never heard anything like it before, and they listened closely and said, "My, how much you've seen! How happy you've been!"

"Me!" said the fir tree and thought about all it had told. "Well, they were very pleasant times after all!" But then it told about Christmas Eve, when it had been trimmed with cakes and candles.

"Oh!" said the little mice, "how happy you've been, you old fir tree!"

"I'm not at all old!" protested the tree, "It was just this winter that I've come from the woods! I'm still in my prime, only I've been stunted in my growth!"

"What lovely stories you tell," said the little mice, and the next night they brought four other little mice to hear the tree tell stories, and the more it told, the more clearly it remembered everything and thought, "Those really were quite happy times! But they can come again, they can come again! Clumpy-Dumpy fell downstairs and yet gained the princess; maybe I can gain a princess too!" And then the fir tree thought about such a pretty little birch tree growing out in the woods, for the fir tree this was a truly beautiful princess.

"Who is Clumpy-Dumpy?" asked the little mice. And then the fir tree told the whole tale. It could remember each everlasting word, and the little mice were ready to jump up to the top of the tree from sheer pleasure. The next night many more mice came, and on Sunday even two rats; but they said that the story was not amusing, and this saddened the little mice, for now they too thought less of it.

"Do you only know the one story?" asked the rats.

"Only this one!" answered the tree, "I heard it on my happiest evening, but I wasn't thinking then how happy I was!"

"That's an extremely bad story! Don't you know any about bacon and tallow candles? No pantry stories?"

"No!" said the tree.

"Well, thanks all the same!" said the rats and went back to their own rathole.

Finally, the little mice disappeared too, and the tree sighed. "It was really quite pleasant when they were sitting around me, those nimble little mice, listening to what I had to tell! Now that, too, is over! . . . But I must remember to enjoy myself once I'm taken out again!"

But when would that happen? . . . Well, early one morning people came rummaging through the attic. The boxes were moved and the tree was pulled out. They certainly threw it rather hard to the floor, but soon a servant dragged it off toward the stairwell where the sun was shining.

"Now life is beginning again!" thought the tree. It felt the fresh air, the first sunbeam—and now it was out in the courtyard. Everything happened so quickly, the tree simply forgot to look at itself, there was so much to look at all around. The courtyard adjoined a garden, and there everything was in bloom. The roses were hanging so fresh and fragrant out over the trellis, the linden trees were in bloom, and the swallows were flying about saying, "Twitter-tweet-tweet, my husband has come!" But it was not the fir tree they meant.

"Now I'm going to live!" it shouted with joy, spreading its branches wide. Alas, they were all withered and yellow. The tree lay off in the corner among weeds and nettles. The gold paper star was still up in its top, glittering in the clearest sunshine.

A few merry children who had danced around the tree at Christmastime and had been so delighted with it were playing in the courtyard. One of the littlest ran up and tore off the golden star.

"Look what's still on the ugly old Christmas tree!" he said, trampling on its branches so they cracked under his boots.

And the tree looked at all the profusion of flowers and freshness in the garden, it looked at itself, and it wished that it had stayed in its dark corner in the attic. It thought about its fresh youth in the woods, about its merry Christmas Eve and about the little mice that had listened so happily to the story about Clumpy-Dumpy.

"Over and done!" said the poor tree. "If only I had enjoyed myself while I could! Over and done!"

And the stable boy came and chopped the tree into little pieces; a whole bundle lay there. It made a lovely blaze under the copper kettle, and it sighed so deeply, every sigh was like a little explosion. That is why the children who were playing ran up and sat before the fire, looking into it and shouting, "Bang! Bang!" But at every crack, which was a deep sigh, the tree was thinking about a summer day in the woods, a winter night out there when the stars were shining; it was thinking about Christmas Eve and Clumpy-Dumpy, the only tale it had heard and knew how to tell, . . . and then the tree was burnt up.

The boys were playing in the yard, and the littlest had on his breast the golden star that the tree had worn on its happiest evening. Now it was over, and the tree was done for, and the story too. Over and done, and so too are all stories!

Karen's Christmas

« Karens Jul »

AMALIE SKRAM

NORWAY 1885

*A prolific representative of Norwegian naturalism, Amalie
Skram (1846–1905) was drawn to the plight of the vulnerable and
powerless, be they women, children, or the poor. Her most impressive
work is the four-volume novel* Hellemyrsfolket *(1887–98; The
people of Hellemyr), in which Skram draws upon her intimate
knowledge of her native Bergen and of social hypocrisy in general.*

A NUMBER OF YEARS AGO THERE WAS ON ONE OF
the steamship wharves in Christiania an old wooden hut with a
flat roof and no chimney, about three yards long and a little shorter in
breadth. In both end walls there was a little window, the one directly
opposite the other. The door, which faced seaward, could be shut from
both the inside and the outside with iron hooks that were fastened into
cramps of the same metal.

The hut had originally been built for ferrymen so they might have a
roof over their heads in rainy weather and in the winter cold when they
would sit around waiting for someone to come and ask for a boat. Later,
when the small steamers gobbled up more and more of the traffic, the ferrymen moved on. Then the hut was only used occasionally by whomever
happened along. The latest to have made use of it were some stonework-
ers one summer, who ate their meals two at a time while repairing a part
of the wharf nearby.

After that, there was no one who took notice of the little old shack. It
stayed where it was because it never occurred to the port authorities to remove it and because no one had lodged a complaint that it was standing
in the way of anyone or anything.

Then came a night in December, just before Christmas. A little snow
was drifting down but was melting as it fell, making the sticky slush on the
paving stones of the wharf all the more wet and mushy. On the gaslights

and the steam cranes the snow lay like a grayish-white, finely fringed film, and if you came down close to the ships you could glimpse through the dark that it hung in the rigging like garlands between the masts. In the dark gray, misty air the flames in the gas lamps took on a grimy, saffron luster, while the ship lanterns shone with a cloudy red light. Now and then the glaring sound of ship bells pierced the damp atmosphere with a brutal bellow when bells were struck on board for a change of watch.

The police constable patrolling the wharf stopped under the gaslight outside the former ferryman's hut. He pulled out his watch to see how much of the night had passed, but, in holding it up to the light, he heard something that sounded like a baby crying. He lowered his hand, looked about him, and listened. No, that wasn't it. Up again the watch. The sound was there once more, this time mingled with a soft hushing. Again he lowered his hand, and again it was silent. What the hell kind of tom-foolery was this? He started to nose about the vicinity, but could discover nothing. For a third time the watch came up toward the gas light, and this time he had a chance to see that it was almost four o'clock.

He sauntered up past the hut, wondering a little but eventually thinking that it must have been his imagination, or something of that sort.

When he returned the same way a while later and approached the hut, he glanced at it. What was that? Didn't he see something moving in there? The gaslight outside cast light from both sides in through the windows, so the hut looked as if it were lit up inside.

He went over and peeked in. Sure enough. There sat a figure on the bench just under the window, a little hunched-over form bending forward fiddling with something he couldn't see. A step around the corner and he stood at the door trying to get in. It was bolted.

"Open up," he shouted, knocking.

He heard someone start with a jerk—it came as a faint, frightened exclamation, and then it was quite still again.

He knocked again with his fist, repeating, "Open up, you in there! Open up this instant."

"What is it? Good God, there's no one here," came an alarmed voice just behind the door.

"Open up. It's the police!"

"Jimini, is it the police?—Oh please, sir, it's just me, I'm doin' nothin', just only sittin' here, you know."

"Will you just see to getting the door open, or there'll be hell to pay. Will you . . ."

He got no farther, for just then the door opened, and in the next instant he was stooping through the doorway into the low room, where he could just stand upright.

"Are you crazy? Not opening up for the police! What are you thinking of?"

"Pardon me, Mr. Policeman . . . but I did open up, you see."

"That was certainly the smart thing, too," he grunted. "What kind of person are you, and who has given you permission to take lodging here?"

"It's only me, Karen," she whispered. "I'm sittin' here with my baby."

The police constable examined the speaker more closely. She was a skinny little female, with a narrow, pale face and a deep scrofulous scar on one cheek, lean as a beanpole, and obviously not fully grown. She was dressed in a light brown top, a kind of jerkin or jacket whose cut revealed that it had known better days, and a darker skirt hanging more or less in shreds below and reaching to her ankles. Her feet were thrust into a pair of leaky army boots without shoelaces. In one arm she held a bundle of rags lying across her lap. Out of the top of the bundle stuck something white. It was the head of a baby suckling her lean breast. Around her head she had a wisp of a scarf that was tied under her chin, tufts of hair sticking out at the nape of her neck. She was shivering from the cold from head to toe, and when she moved her boots squished and squeaked as if she were trodding in a mushy substance.

"I didn't think it would bother no one," she continued in a whining tone, "it's just standin' here, this shed."

The police constable had a sinking feeling. To begin with, he had considered throwing her out with some choice words and letting her off with a warning. But when he looked at this miserable child standing there with the little wretch in her arm, pressing herself against the bench and not daring to sit out of fright and humility, a strange emotion passed through him.

"But for God's sake—what are you doing here, my girl?"

She picked up on the gentler tone in his voice. Her anxiety subsided, and she began to cry.

The policeman closed the door. "Sit down a while," he said, "it's no doubt heavy holding the baby standing up."

She slid silently down onto the bench.

"Now then," said the policeman encouragingly, sitting down on the opposite crossbench.

"Oh, good God, Mr. Policeman—let me stay here," she lisped through her weeping. "I won't do no harm, not the tiniest bit . . . keep the place clean . . . see for yourself . . . no uncleanliness here . . . that *there* is bread-crusts." She pointed to a bundle of rags down on the floor. "I go beggin' in the daytime. . . . There's a dash of water in the bottle. . . . Let me stay here at night 'til I get my position back . . . if only the missus would come back." She paused, blowing her nose into her hand, which she dried on her skirt.

"The missus, now who is that, then?" asked the policeman.

"That's the one I was in service with. . . . I had such a nice place with four kroner a month and breakfast, but then I had my little accident and then I had to leave, don't you know. Mrs. Olsen went herself and got me into the Institute, she's so kind, Mrs. Olsen, and I was in service right 'til I entered the Institute for lying in, for she's alone, Mrs. Olsen, and she said she'd keep me on 'til I couldn't manage no more. But then it came up that Mrs. Olsen had to leave, 'cause she's a midwife, Mrs. Olsen, and then she took sick up in the country, and now they say she's not coming back 'til Christmas."

"But for heaven's sake, to go lugging the baby around like this while you wait for the missus. Is there any sense in that sort of thing?" The policeman shook his head.

"I got nowheres to go," she whimpered. "Since my father died there ain't nobody to protect me now when my stepmother throws me out."

"But what about the child's father?"

"Oh, him," she said, giving a little toss of her head. "There ain't no lickin' him into shape, nohow."

"But you do know that you can get a judgment against him to pay for the child?"

"Yeah, so they say," she replied. "But *how're* you gonna go about it, when he can't be found?"

"Just you turn his name over to me," the policeman opined, "then he's sure to be tracked down."

"Yeah, if only I knew it," she said quietly.

"What? You don't know the name of the father of your own child?"

Karen put her finger in her mouth and sucked it. Her head bent forward. A helpless, silly smile came to her face. "N—o," she whispered with protracted emphasis on each letter and without removing her finger.

"Well, I never in all my born days heard anything so crazy," the policeman blurted. "In heaven's name, how did you happen to get together with him, then?"

"I used to meet him on the street in the evenings when it was dark," she said, "but it wasn't long before he disappeared, and I've never seen him since."

"Haven't you asked around, then?"

"Why, I done that all the time, but there wasn't nobody that knowed where he'd gone to. He's taken a position in the country, most likes, 'cause he had to do with either horses or cows; I could tell that by the smell that came with him."

"God help me, what a state of affairs," mumbled the policeman. "You'll have to go and report for poor relief," he said louder, "so we can get matters straight with this here."

"No, I ain't gonna do it," she replied, suddenly stubborn.

"It'd be better to come to the poor house and get food and shelter, instead of what you're doing now," said the policeman.

"Yeah, but as soon as Mrs. Olsen returns . . . she's so kind, Mrs. Olsen . . . she'll take me on monthly, I know for sure, 'cause she promised . . . then I know a woman who'll take us in as lodgers for three kroner a month. She'll take care of the baby while I'm at Mrs. Olsen's, and then I'll do her chores when I come from the missus. Everythin'll be all right as soon as Mrs. Olsen comes, and she's comin' by Christmas, they say."

"All right, my lass, every grownup is his own master, but you've no right to stay here."

"If I sit here at night—is there any harm in that now? Oh, good God, please let me, I won't let the baby cry. Just 'til the missus comes . . . oh, good Mr. Policeman, just 'til the missus comes."

"But you'll freeze something fierce, both you and the baby." He was looking at her pitiful clothing.

"It's always better here than out on the open street, you know. Oh, Mr. Policeman—just 'til the missus comes."

"Strictly speaking, you should be coming down to the station right now, you know," the policeman said in a deliberating tone, scratching himself behind the ear.

She jumped up and moved toward him. "Don't do it, don't do it," she whined, grabbing his sleeve with her frozen fingers. "I beg of you . . . in God's name . . . just 'til the missus comes."

The policeman thought it over. Three days to Christmas, he figured.

"Well, all right, then," he said aloud, standing up. "You can stay here until Christmas, but not a day longer. And mind you now: nobody must know about it."

"God bless you, God bless you, and thank you so much," she exclaimed.

"But take care to be awake by precisely six o'clock in the morning, before the traffic starts up out here," he added as he was halfway out the door.

As he passed the hut the next night he stopped and looked in. She was sitting tilted back, leaning against the windowsill. Her profile with the knotted scarf was silhouetted faintly against the panes. The baby lay suckling at her breast. She did not move and seemed to be sleeping.

Later in the morning it turned to frost. During the course of the next day the thermometer dropped to twelve degrees. It was a shrill cold, the air clear and still. Onto the windows of the little ferryman's hut came a thick layer of white frost, making the panes completely opaque.

On Christmas Eve came another change of weather. It was a thaw, dripping everywhere. You almost had to use an umbrella, even though it wasn't raining. Down on the wharf all the warehouse windows were free of ice once more, and the slush was worse than ever.

About two in the afternoon the policeman came by. He had been off the last couple of nights due to a fever for which his doctor had written an excuse. He was now on his way out to talk with a fellow on one of the steamships.

His path led past the hut. Although it had already begun to get dark, he still saw at a distance of several paces something that got him to stop and made him so strangely uneasy. There she sat in exactly the same position as that night two days ago. The very same silhouette on the windowpane. He did not actually indulge in any reflection over it, only felt himself gripped by horror at this petrified sameness. An involuntary shudder went through him. Could something have happened?

He hurried over to the door; it was bolted. Then he broke a windowpane, got hold of an iron bar, which he thrust through the opening, unfastening the hook from the cramp with it. He stepped inside, quietly and cautiously.

They were both stone-dead. The baby lay up against its mother, in death still holding her breast in its mouth. Down its cheek had trickled from her nipple some drops of blood, which clotted on its chin. She was terribly emaciated, but on her face there was something like a quiet smile.

"Poor lass, what a Christmas she had," mumbled the policeman, wiping his eyes.

"But perhaps it's best the way it is for both of them. Our Lord must have his reason for this, after all."

He went out again, shut the door, and fastened the hook. He hurried down to the station to report the incident.

The first workday after the Christmas holidays the port authority had the old ferryman's hut torn down and carted away. It couldn't be left standing there as a hangout for all kinds of tramps.

Christmas Eve in the Henhouse

« Juleaften i Hønsehuset »

SOPHUS SCHANDORPH

DENMARK 1888

Danish novelist and short story writer Sophus Schandorph (1836–1901) was a strong supporter of the radical ideas of the Modern Breakthrough around 1870 and a tireless critic of the prevailing double standard in Danish society.

1

TANNER-BOLETTE IN R*** POORHOUSE HAD AN illegitimate son, named Ludvig, who lived with his mother at the poorhouse. He was considered the worst guttersnipe in town. When the "fancy" boys went swimming in the river in the summer after having disrobed on the closed bathing jetty, they were often surprised by Tanner-Bolette's Ludvig and regaled by him with some frightful dunkings. He had undressed on the open bank, paddled out and then swum underwater, falling on his prey like a shark, and before the rich boys could gather resistance, the proletarian was already on shore running stark naked up the highway with his clothes under his arm, hooting and howling. In the winter the rich boys had their chute on a hill just outside town. Often, when a rich boy's sled was at its most furious speed, its driver would notice a tug on the runners, so that he tumbled to one side and felt his face being belabored by snow that was stroked hard and flat across it. It was Tanner-Bolette's Ludvig who was once again wreaking havoc.

At the free school he never at any time knew one word of his lessons, but in the summer he amused himself with exploits like sticking a live frog or the skin of a smoked herring in the teacher's back pocket, or filling his hat with beetles.

Whippings by the teacher rolled off his back, and the teacher stopped

whipping Tanner-Bolette's Ludvig from the day that, during caning pro-
ceedings, he felt a bite on his calf, as sincerely meant as if it were a chained
dog he had come too near. But after that day the boy was not nearly so
ill-natured, and his naughtiness had a less vicious character.

His mother, Tanner-Bolette, tall as a man and stout, with a large red,
bewhiskered face, could whip her boy tender when she made up her
mind. But she was only rarely at home—she had to go out as a washing
or cleaning woman to scrape together a living. Only occasionally, when
she learned that the boy had broken a window in the poorhouse or had
wandered around town and had missed school, she would take hold of
his arm, twist it with her enormous hand, and then her knuckles would
pummel the muscles of his upper arm so that there were blue blotches
long afterward.

2

It was Christmas Eve. A thick fog hung over the town like a cloud over
a mountain. You could not see your neighbors' house across the street.
The pavement was slick. People drifted about like formless, dull, dark
interruptions in the great clammy mass that devoured all firm outlines,
all colors. The air was dank and smelled of a washhouse or scullery. In
the shops, which were filled from early morning with country people
shopping for the holiday, lights burned, staring queerly out into the fog.
The clamorous haggling and bargaining and the clinking of *snaps* glasses
sounded as if absorbed by a woolen blanket. As morning drew to a close,
the only thing that could make itself manifest in this all-encompassing
monotony was the odor of the fritters baking everywhere; later this was
varied by the odor of roast goose from the affluent houses, pork roast
or ribs from the kitchens of the middle class, dried cod from those of
humbler folks; now and then red cabbage made its contribution to the
fragrant choir.

Through this ooze below, above, 'round about on all sides, Tanner-
Bolette's Ludvig had been wading about since early morning. His mother
had not been home to the poorhouse for several days; she had had cleaning and washing to attend to, most recently at a prosperous carpenter's,
Jørgen Rasmussen, and there she had been invited to eat Christmas dinner. The boy was obviously off school. He had gone out early without
any firm plan, but he had resolved to get as much fun from his holiday
as possible.

But there were no rich boys in the street whom he could pester. His colleagues, the guttersnipes, were of less interest to him. Once he had picked a fight with three or four of them he became bored with this monotonous sport. Then he had managed to trip up a maid so that she fell with her basket, afterward exchanging some insults with her. He succeeded in placing the great filthy heel of his clog onto a dangling corner of a lady's dress train. He had afterward strolled into a grocer's yard full of farm wagons and hailed a slightly besotted farmer with the words, "Look out, look out! That wheel's going 'round," but he had not, as at last fall market day, found a man as naive as to stop and say, "What's the wheel doing?" getting down to see if there were something wrong; no, this time he only got a whiplash across the neck as thanks for his witticism, while the wagon went rushing into the fog with wheels sparking.

Tanner-Bolette's Ludvig was not in a good humor. He found this to be a lousy Christmas Eve: the year with the tiresome fog. No, in clear weather, in a shrill frost there was something to do—then there might be fun in the street. He wandered far and wide, hour after hour; by sneaking into a couple of the half-darkened shops full of farmers he got a chance to pilfer a few molded candles, a cornet of raisins, and by slipping behind a farmer's broad back into a simple tavern, to pinch four large chunks of brown sugar from a saucer, plus a box of matches standing in the window sill. For Tanner-Bolette's Ludvig, when he was bored and knew of no better occupation, would strike off matches one by one, so that time passed with at least some variety: a pop and a puff.

But, good God! Was *this* to be his last hope of Christmas Eve amusement? Last year he had, after all, eaten rice pudding and bacon at home in the poorhouse with his mother, along with sweet mead and the following extra delights: driving as an unwilling guest in a sleigh with three rich boys during the day, and at night treating the old poorhouse inmate, the ropemaker Setler, to a bottle of brandy that he had stolen from a counter, so the same dignified old man had passed through all the stages of inebriation: song, dance, mournful tears at the memory of old sweethearts and better days, a fresh outbreak of youthful courage in which he tried to thrash his colleagues in the poorhouse, assurance that this was from sheer love of them, a rattling voice and staggering legs, and, finally, a completely death-like condition.

But this year! Darkness descended while the boy was drifting about on his unsuccessful expedition, and it was soon pitch-dark outside. Light could be seen behind all the windowpanes; behind some he heard piano-playing, behind some singing, behind others boisterous talking, children laughing, glass and porcelain rattling. Tanner-Bolette's Ludvig slipped alone through the fog like a faint shadow across a wall in a half-darkened room. And how provocative they looked, all these lit-up windows! Should he hurl a stone toward a few of them? Several times he was just about to do so, had bent down and got hold of a stone, but . . . he contented himself with throwing street litter against the doors. Perhaps he suddenly became aware of the hopelessness of single combat between him and all the houses in town; it would after all end with his being taken by the police, and it would do little to shatter the Christmas merriment of the inhabitants if a windowpane were smashed.

The courage of Tanner-Bolette's Ludvig sank more and more. Into his head, completely empty of ideas for roguish pranks, there seeped with the atmospheric humidity a strange pliant timidity, something he otherwise never had known. Had he not firmly held onto the only moral emotion he had—loathing and contempt for a "crybaby" or a "sissy"— Tanner-Bolette's Ludvig would surely have sat against one of the great stones of the post office driveway portal and unburdened himself by crying, which he would then likely as not have forced up to savage bawling and howling in order to drown out some nasty thing that was hurting inside. He would have egged on his ill temper and mischievousness against this "inwardness," which was the most disagreeable of all. For it hurt just as much as the stinging pain from a burn he had got a half year ago when a blacksmith's apprentice tricked him into touching an innocent-looking piece of iron that was scorching hot. This was in revenge, because Tanner-Bolette's Ludvig had one day kicked a wagon wheel that the apprentice was rolling down the street, so that it toppled and struck him across the legs.

The boy's mother had never been tender toward him, but she was, after all, the only one he belonged to and who belonged to him. He knew she was at the carpenter's, Jørgen Rasmussen; knew as well why she would not or dared not take him along, for the reputation he enjoyed was well known to him. He was "haughty" in his own way, and he would not by any means—on this he swore a lurid oath—foist himself upon that "shaving filer" Jørgen Rasmussen or his fat wife. For all that, the boy could not refrain from constantly returning to Sankt Bendtsgade. Jørgen Rasmussen lived at its end, farthest from the square. The boy went steadily farther and farther down Sankt Bendtsgade. Not because he wanted to see or be with his mother, but . . . well, he didn't know what was eating him.

3

Without the boy knowing how it happened, he stood, despite his repeated oath about not wanting to see Jørgen Rasmussen's house, all at once in the middle of the same carpenter's courtyard. It was pitch dark, and the fog had become a drizzle.

The kitchen door was closed, but the smell of cooking filled the yard, and the boy could hear sounds of roasting and frying inside. Through the window he saw his mother's profile, saw the hairs of her beard flicker in the light as she took an enormous bite from a steaming apple fritter.

The boy was famished. That was the limit, the way they were eating in there. Something had to be done.

Tanner-Bolette's Ludvig looked around him in the yard, hunting for an idea, and found it in a hurry, as if he pulled it out of thin air. He knew that there in the yard, to the right of the dwelling, was a small annex, and that one of its rooms served as a henhouse. It might be a lark to see how a henhouse looked on Christmas Eve.

He reconnoitered the environs first. What was that?—There was a disturbance in the kitchen. His mother and the maid dried their mouths and hands each on one corner of a dishtowel, then a door was opened, and quickly the boy saw a tree all lit up, shining colorfully of gold, silver, and all kinds of colors . . . presto then the door was slammed shut. But the kitchen lamp stood burning on the table.

The boy eased up slightly the latch-bar of the door from the kitchen to the yard, streaked just as silently through it, captured some apple fritters from a plate, drank a proper gulp from a pitcher of punch, swiped a fistful of something red lying in a sieve on the chimney, and slipped both the fritters and the red, wet substance into his pocket. As he was preparing himself for a silent and rapid retreat, he saw that he had a colleague in his predatory occupation. A big, black tomcat, having come through God knows which opening, stood licking milk from a bowl on the kitchen table. This cat immediately gained the boy's sympathy. Taking a pitcher of cream, he poured its contents into an empty bowl in order to ease the cat's opportunity for farther regaling itself, after which he once more slipped out into the yard.

Just in time. Tanner-Bolette and Jørgen Rasmussen's maid, who had been dancing around the Christmas tree, reappeared. The cat's dastardly deed was discovered, and the malefactor was chased out into the yard with a broom amidst a succession of invectives, of which "dirty dog" and "lousy pig" were both the least logical and the least indecent.

The boy had just got the latch of the door to the henhouse lifted; then he ducked suddenly, startled by the feeble light seeping out from the kitchen door into the yard, and just then he saw his friend the cat.

That cat could be a very funny companion to have in the henhouse that evening. He began to coax the cat, whispering softly, "Kitty-cat!" He could see it in the form of a black lump rubbing against a wall. It approached with hesitation, stopping to reconnoiter the dark with sparkling eyes.

At the same time, it found perhaps a sort of spiritual affinity between itself and the boy; it let itself be enticed by his muffled, affectionate calling; he soon felt its back arch warm and soft under his stroking hand. With the other hand he lifted the latch of the henhouse door, opened it ajar, and the cat and the boy streaked into the henhouse.

Only a faint, immediately ceasing cackling disclosed that one or two of the chickens sleeping high up on perches had suffered a fleeting disruption of their sleep. Everything quieted down instantly in the brooding darkness. The cat eluded the boy's reach; he no longer felt it, he did not even see its eyes shining in the dark. Well, for the time being the boy had no use for the cat. He had a fierce hunger and wanted to tackle some of his booty: the rock candy and the raisins. He did not begrudge the cat a bite, too, but he realized that an invitation to such a meal was purposeless, and said half aloud, "No, I suppose you're not wild about this kind of food, Pussy-cat!"

The boy felt a well-being akin to that of going to bed tired in the evening. In the poorhouse or at the free school he was not accustomed to fresh or good air. The cloying, sultry atmosphere of the henhouse, its warmth in contrast to the drizzle outside, and even the stillness made him feel cozy for a few moments while he sat munching the rock candy and raisins.

But he felt like having something wet; he began to get thirsty. Tanner-Bolette's Ludvig was a boy with resources. For the cat it was no problem; it had had both milk and cream.

He struck a match and lit one of the stolen molded candles. The cat spat in surprise—and a rooster began to crow. It was enthroned high up on a perch in the middle of a row of hens sitting with their heads ducked down among their tailfeathers. The rooster's red eyes stared out with infinite stupidity, but its hackle gleamed like delicate gold embroidery on a ground of red silk.

It is a well-known fact that there is but insignificant egg production at this time of the year. Only specimens few and far between were to be found; this the boy knew. But he had been in chicken coops before; he knew how to find eggs. Four eggs! What a treat, to eat raw egg yolks with his rock candy. Surely Jørgen Rasmussen's bandy-legged Peter and red-haired Elvine hardly got anything more delicious. "Eh—you shaving-filer's brats! You needn't be so stuck-up!"

"You've got a light up there in the front room! Eh—I can light up, too."

He lit a second candle. He had difficulty placing the candles firmly; several attempts at getting one of them bored down into the dirt floor were unsuccessful. The dirt was too dry. The candle toppled and went out, singeing some straw in the fall.

The boy bored into himself, and the wellsprings of invention bubbled over. There were plenty of nails on the henhouse walls, and the spotted cotton scarf he was wearing was not worth a string of beans. He loosened it, tore it in two, tied the remaining half around his neck—it was really just as much use as it had been in conjunction with its severed half—this was halved again, and from each quarter the boy made two loops; he tied the lower around the molded candles, the upper he hung on the nails. These were improvised bracket lamps, the candles hanging rather askew, dangling and dripping tallow liberally onto the floor, but so what? Tanner-Bolette's Ludvig was positively haughty about his invention. He thought that it looked like some gewgaws with candles in them that he had once seen one morning at city hall, when the ceremonial room had been decorated for the evening's ball and his mother was mopping the floor together with the jailkeeper's wife. This was before Ludvig's reputation had become so bad that people only took on Tanner-Bolette with the stipulation that her boy stay at home.

Wow, what fun! How bright it was in the henhouse! While the boy was eating eggs and sugar, the chickens woke up, looking about with astonishment—and the rooster crowed as if it were daybreak. The hens cackled slightly, and the cat, whom the boy had forgotten, took a clamber up the wall's timber frame post and sent the big rooster some searching, suspicious, sidelong glances, which were reciprocated in the same spirit. The rooster remained seated on its perch, the cat on the sill of the hatch, adopting that attitude of armed neutrality that the cat and the inhabitants of the henhouse always observed during times when there were no chicks, for in the chick period there prevailed a hostility that, if not open, was nevertheless quite vigilant.

The cat arched its back, the rooster raised its head and ruffled up its hackles; the cat yawned, the rooster shook itself: there was a continual correspondence in their movements on each side. Every single hen kept its eye on that individual of another species that had intruded into its preserves; the boy did not seem to interest them particularly.

Now that he had finished his egg dish, he felt quite good, and he took on a benevolent disposition as full people usually do, finding that the chickens and the cat ought to have fun, too.

In standing up to prod the awakened but bashful or nervous chickens down from their perches, he noticed something damp on one of his thighs. It came from his pocket. He reached into it, got a whole fistful of something damp. . . . Oh! That was the red stuff he had stolen from the sieve in the kitchen.

Maybe it was jam? Let's taste it. . . . No, it was a blend of sour and strong! Actually it tasted nasty. God knows if the chickens would eat it?

"Shoo! Hey—hullo! . . . Down you go! Hey, you big rooster . . . down with you and all your ladies! . . . Cat! . . . down with you, you rhinoceros!"

The cat spat and drew back into a corner of the window-hatch. The rooster and hens cackled and cried out, twitching as they fluttered down to the floor . . . and threw themselves voraciously, contending among themselves for the food, on the red substance that Tanner-Bolette's Ludvig had scattered over the straw.

Ooh—how they ate, ate, and ate! And the more they ate, the more racket they made. The boy cackled, crowed, and squealed apace with the chickens, running around among them like their buddy; only the cat remained sitting with its back arched, glaring down on it all with a Mephistophelian look. If it had been able to sing a part in Gounod's *Faust*, it would have transposed the bass part in feline treble and sung, "Now the devil leads the dance!"

The chickens became merrier and merrier. The rooster became erotic; indescribable episodes took place amid the savage dance. It was the first time that Tanner-Bolette's Ludvig gained the impression that chickens were birds, such did they fly with a flapping of wings and a hullabaloo. He played tag with them, at times managing to pull a wing feather out, at times grasping the big rooster by the leg—oh, how the rooster or hen squawked—the cat meowing at fortissimo. The chickens that were not at the moment part of the wild hunt were partaking of the red substance.

The boy was intoxicated by the commotion, the noise, the savagery! He screamed and squealed, drowning out all the crowing and cackling, running about as if possessed, grabbing into what was lying on the floor, flinging it every which way, laughing and singing

And that is why I'll fight
As gallant soldierboy.
Hurrah, hurrah, hurrah!

He suspected nothing, sensed nothing; he and the chickens were equally possessed by the infernal Christmas play-party he was leading.

What now?

A hammering at the door.

"Keep hammering, I'll hammer back!" And the boy hammered a drumroll with both boot heels on the inside of the henhouse door, continuing to irritate the chickens into fluttering and running about.

"Who's in the henhouse?" came a deep voice from the other side of the door.

The boy recognized the voice. He realized that it augured a boxed ear and a thrashing. But he was so lyrically inspired that he considered such everyday matters as trifles.

"Good evening and merry Christmas, Tanner-Bolette!" he bellowed out through the door.

From outside came, "Well, as long as I've lived and 'til I leave this world, I've never known such a stupid ass!"

The boy shouted, "Thanks, Ma, thanks, the same to you!"

"I'll thrash you to within an inch of your life!"

"Thanks, Ma! Only wait 'til we get frosty weather, then it'll warm so nicely."

"Will you open up, you pig-noodle?"

"By all means, Ma! . . . So, good evening! It's Jørgen Rasmussen's Trine! Good evening, Trine!"

Tanner-Bolette and the maid Trine had heard the unusual commotion in the henhouse from the kitchen, seen a streak of light through a chink in the door, and Tanner-Bolette had immediately suspected that if there were anyone in the whole town who could create such a ruckus in Jørgen Rasmussen's henhouse, it had to be "Lawdvi."

Trine and Tanner-Bolette entered. The boy opened the door for them.

"Oh—say, you know what, Bolette," said Trine, "there are so help me bracketing lamps on the wall. Look—Bolette! . . . look at the chickens, how they're carrying on! Look at the big rooster . . . hee-hee-hee! Hey, Bolette . . . look how it—ugh!—it's . . . what? It's . . ."

"Shut up, Trine! There's a child present!"

"Tush . . . someone like Lawdvi! He knows just as much about such things as the rooster."

"Shut your trap, Trine!"

"Well, there's something to it, Bolette."

"Hurrah for Trine's two children!" the boy shouted.

"There, you can see for yourself, Bolette!" said Trine.

"You are a beast," Bolette said to her son. . . . "But you, Trine—how the chickens are carrying on! How they gad about! Chickens, that are otherwise such sleepy critters! And they're staggering, Trine—God help me if they're not staggering! They're drunk, Trine!"

"They're gobbling down something red, Bolette! Hey, Lawdvi! What is it they're gobbling down?"

"It's just some jam, Trine," said the boy.

Trine reached into the red stuff, smelled it, and said, "Bolette, honest to God! It's those black currants that were in the brandy, the ones I threw out this morning. It's them that the chickens have got drunk on. . . . But how did those currants get down here?"

"I pinched 'em," said the boy. He couldn't restrain his pride.

Trine said, "I say, Bolette! If that boy isn't a genius, then I'd never . . ."

"Have had two children," bellowed the boy, "one with the teamster Herman Petersen and . . . one with . . ."

Trine socked him one across his neck. His mother wished to complete the punishment by boxing his ear, but the boy quickly stuck two fingers into an eggshell, holding it before him like a miniature shield.

The chickens cackled loudly, staggering about, inebriated as they were from the highly alcoholic residue of black currant. And Tanner-Bolette's shocked surprise blunted her quick thrust. She said to Trine, "He's been eating eggs, that dog's tongue!"

Big Trine broke out in a tremendous roar of laughter, pinching the equally big and even stouter Tanner-Bolette in the arm and stammering out the words, "Well, now I've lived to see that, too, before I die! That's a regular comedian, that boy!"

"And God's death, here's the cat," said Bolette.

"Well, damned if it's not the cat," seconded Trine, still laughing aloud.

"Say, Bolette, I'll bring some punch and some fritters down here, then we'll sit down, too, and have some fun just like the cat and the chickens and the boy. . . . Eh, Bolette? There's nobody who provides any other amusement than what we provide ourselves."

The festive atmosphere infected the solemn charwoman. Trine brought the promised items; she, Bolette, and "Lawdvi" shared the delicacies, the cat and the chickens got their portion of the fritters; the punch affected the humans as the currants had the chickens; Trine, mother, and son danced in a row among the staggering and mincing chickens, while Trine sang

In wintertime we ride our sleighs
Until our noses turn Turkey blue.

Plop! The candle-ends fell out of their loops onto the floor. The smoking snuffs were put out in a hurry under the weight of clog-heels.

With darkness came consciousness.

"If 'upstairs' heard it," said Bolette.

"By golly! That'd make things miserable for me," mumbled Trine.

Everyone sneaked up into the kitchen. The family was still awake, with the exception of the carpenter's octogenarian mother-in-law, who occupied a room facing the courtyard. Its window was closed, the lights out, and the curtain was rolled down.

Tanner-Bolette and her boy walked back to the poorhouse together. The boy received neither a thrashing nor cross words, for Tanner-Bolette conceded inwardly that the boy had provided her with a merry Christmas Eve.

4

Old Mrs. Brask, Mrs. Rasmussen's mother, whispered at the coffee table Christmas morning with a mysterious look, "What a hullabaloo in the henhouse last night!"

The carpenter shrugged his shoulders. The old lady was after all in her second childhood and saw and heard what nobody else saw and heard.

"There were lights, and singing and dancing down there," continued Mrs. Brask.

"Sure, I suppose so," said the carpenter and left the room mumbling, "Balderdash!"

Mrs. Brask whispered to her daughter, "In my day we put a little food out for . . . for the little people on Christmas Eve. Now everyone has to be so enlightened. But I've been in the henhouse this morning, and there were four empty eggshells and two candle-ends in the straw. And then you still say that nothing else exists but what you can grasp with your hand. Who do you think has kept the Christmas feast there? And the chickens couldn't be roused."

Christmas Matins in Finland's Barkbread Country

« En julotta i barkbrödets Finland »

KARL A. TAVASTSTJERNA

FINLAND 1894

The poetry and prose of Karl A. Tavaststjerna (1860–98), Finnish author writing in Swedish, made him the leading exponent of realism in late-nineteenth-century Fenno-Swedish literature. His novel Barndomsvänner *(1886; Childhood friends) is regarded as the first critical portrait of Finnish petty-bourgeois society of the times.*

ANTTI METSÄNTAUSTA IS LYING ATOP THE oven in his smoke-blackened settler's cabin, thinking the fleeting thoughts of the backwoodsman about the present and the future without being disturbed by the children, who are busy on the black floor with a kind of game. The game, called "eating," is played with bits of wood instead of bread and an empty tankard of beer.

Antti Metsäntausta has been lying on his oven since early morning, when his wife set out for the nearest town, about three miles from the homestead by the shortcut through the forest. She should have been back already, and to make his waiting less tiresome, Antti climbs down from the oven, goes to the fireplace, and lights afresh from the fire the burned-out sediment in his short-stemmed pipe, after having put new firewood on the embers and blown life into them. The children's game becomes for a moment less boisterous, but when the scraggy figure in dingy, coarse linen clothes again disappears into the gloom up on the oven, it starts up once more. They see a glowing spot gleaming out of the dark up there and hear the reluctantly burning tobacco remnants rustling in the pipe. Immediately after, regular and deep breathing begins, with a slight snoring now and then.

The room is illuminated partly by the faint, white daylight of winter working its way through the ice and the pine slats of the window, partly by the two dying chunks of firewood on the hearth that slip all the while down into the embers. The illumination reaches up about two yards from the black floor, then peters out: soot takes over, with an occasional shiny reflection where walls and timbers have been polished bright by clothing and hands grazing past. Lining the walls, shiny, massive benches; above them a wall cupboard, some articles of clothing, a new, white sheepskin coat, a leather cap, a flintlock rifle. A third of the room is occupied by the large oven plastered across the front with lime, whose whiteness has long since vanished under soot. Another third contains the empty dining table under the window. It is the only white thing in the log cabin, illuminating it with its great, desolate pine top, worn by the sand of the scouring cloth. The final third of the room has been adopted by the four children for their play; the littlest is in the cradle, but eagerly participates from there.

The room speaks of relative prosperity: the soot is black without smudging, like a purposely used natural oil paint, the household goods are tidy, and the children are not excessively ragged. This impression is farther confirmed by the distant, muffled mooing of a cow, coming from the little outhouse. For more than sixty miles around the log cabin lies Kuusamo—the ancient barkbread district; and there are other cabins that do not have fireplace and chimney and outhouse, but where the cow, the sheep, and the chickens share the room with the inhabitants. A horse is still a distant desideratum for most, a daring dream that will be realized some time in a succeeding generation, in a century or so.

In this relative prosperity only one thing is missing: bread. That is why the children play at eating with bits of wood and an empty tankard, and that is why the master of the house lies dozing on the oven. All at once the children stop their playing and listen. Footsteps approach, crunching outside in the cold, a pair of soft feet rub the snow off against the icy doorstep, a hand grabs the door. It is drawn open, creaking, and amid a biting cloud of cold winter air a woman steps like a revelation into the room, wrapped past her ears in a hoar-frosted garment. She quickly closes the door behind her, the cloud dissolves, the children cluster around her, and the youngest, who cannot walk yet, gropes instead out of the cradle and tumbles to the floor, raising an outcry with all his might. The woman takes him up with a practiced motion, pressing him to her hoar-frosted breast to lull him to sleep, unconcerned by the even shriller scream the little one gives off. Then she goes quickly over to the oven, staring up at it looking for her husband, discovers his light gray linen clothes in the dark, and says harshly, "Now then, Antti, there's nothing for you to do now but to get up and shove off on your way to the church town!"

"There, there," comes his reply, "it isn't getting too hot for me to handle here. Why all the rush? I can't very well set out on a trip to the church at night!"

"Rush! Is there really so much difference between hunger and fire? If one or the other pesters you it's really all the same. But I come with good news from Pusula, I do. They've all gone to the church town, for there the high crown itself is distributing flour to the needy at Christmas. And now you, too, are going there like all the others, Antti, so we'll have at least fresh bread for the holidays!"

Up on the oven Antti rolls over and sticks an unwilling, rugged face out from the darkness. Looking as if he were listening to another voice, he shakes his head and runs his sinewy fingers through his forelock.

"Oh, is that so—nothing less will do, that I have to go out and beg!"

"What else does any good? Haven't we had to live for the fourth day now on the drop of milk that wretch of a cow leaves us, and aren't the children screaming for food, and aren't you starving yourself, and aren't I starving? And how long can we keep up like this?"

"All right, all right, I guess it's like you say . . . if only you weren't in such a goddamned hurry!"

"Lord God almighty, are you cursing about it, as well? What have you done so that we might be spared starving? You've been lying there stretched out on the oven all autumn and into winter waiting for the forest owners to come and offer us food. But they haven't come and probably won't come at all this year. There's too little snow lying in the woods for towing timber, and that's why we'll have to starve to death. You know all that yourself. And if I hadn't gone and borrowed the bare necessities from the neighbors in these last weeks, then we'd have done so already. You, you don't budge from the spot, but only want us to slaughter the cow-critter, even if we have plenty of hay for the animal, and even if we have it to thank for there still being a thread of life in us. . . . But now, you see, now it's over with help from the neighbors! They've had to go to town themselves and take from the crown—as if you can call it begging when it's the czar who's treating! Even the master of Storgård doesn't have anything to give away, he told me that today. And I got no more than a mouthful of bread for me and this here for the children!"

She puts a hard piece of black barkbread out on the living room table, while the children greedily gather around the morsel.

"Have you said enough?" Antti waits to put in when his wife draws her breath and begins to remove her overclothes. She doesn't listen to him, going anxiously over to the cradle with the littlest and preparing to give him her breast. Then Antti climbs down from the oven, stretches himself as if waking up, takes a few steps toward his wife to say something to her, pulls up with it, and instead goes out hunched over. A cold mist drifts far out into the room along the floor, since Antti does not take the time to close the door. His wife calls after him, "Would you have us freeze to death, too?"

At once the door is shut. Anna turns toward the children, satisfies the littlest, and then takes a bowl half filled with milk from the cupboard, lowers the black barkbread into it to soak, and with the ravenous children about her—they have not tasted a bit of food for a day—she prepares a celebration for them. While this feast is going on, Antti comes in again, dragging his skis with him. He cannot keep from casting a furtive and greedy glance at the banquet, with the back of his hand stroking his mouth and swallowing when it waters. Then he lights a pine splinter, sitting down in the falling winter twilight by the fireplace to repair his skis. His wife looks silently at his activity, gentler features come into her face, and she says half turned away from him, "Couldn't you get a ride from Pusula? There's always somebody there with a horse who has Christmas business in the church town."

"I don't care for their horses when I can go myself."

"But it's forty miles to the church, and you haven't eaten a proper meal in a week . . ."

"I always have as much strength as I need to glide a few miles on good skis."

"But you'll have to make it up hills, and then you'll have to carry the flour sack home on the way back . . ."

There is no answer, not even grumbling. Anna, who thinks she has cautioned and advised her husband enough, puts the children to sleep, takes out her spinning wheel, and begins drawing out her interminable thread, which all autumn long has not come to an end. The spinning wheel whirs, the pine splinters emit sparks now and then, burn out, and are succeeded by new ones. Not a word is exchanged. Anna silently reproaches herself for having spoken so forcefully to her husband because, all things considered, he really wasn't the cause of their distress. She tries to force out some conciliatory words, but they stick in her throat.

Antti is at length finished with his skis, he takes them out to the en-tryway, comes back, and brusquely asks his wife to get their biggest and whitest floursack ready. Then he goes up onto the oven to lie down.

"When are you going to start?"

"Don't you worry about that! The only thing you have to concern yourself with is whether I bring the flour home properly."

A little later Anna tries to appease her husband by laying her hand appealingly on his arm where he lies pretending to sleep. But it is left lying there.

The next morning, so early that the morning star has not yet risen, Antti glides in the bitterly cold, still, and star-twinkling night, silent as a shadow, down the forest path leading to the charcoal rack and so on to the neighboring village. He had arisen and made ready for the journey without disturbing his family's sleep. Only his stomach growled against his will so loudly that he feared that it would wake his wife. But then he put on his short, new, white sheepskin coat, buckled his belt tightly around his waist, cut apart the last remnant of his leaf tobacco as victuals, lit his pipe, and left. He selected his largest, iron-tipped ski pole, for this year the wolves were running in packs already before Christmas.

When the winter twilight falls on the evening of the same day, a bent, hoar-frosted figure with an empty sack on his back and a short-stemmed pipe in his mouth glides in along the village street in the church town Kuusamo. Forty miles in twelve hours, without interruption, straight through the woods, has Antti done, and now he has reached his destination. There are no sportsmen taking down his record amid applause, he glances half ashamed about him, stopping outside the general store, where there are horses and people waiting.

"Is this where the czar is distributing flour for Christmas?"

"You get flour here sure enough, but it's not said to be the czar who's giving it out."

"Whatever." Antti steps into the shop, waits a long while to get up to the counter, and when his turn finally comes he unties the sack from his back and hands it without a word to the shopkeeper. He and his help are busy shoveling flour from bales into the sacks of the needy under the supervision of a distinguished woman. All of them are white with flourdust right up to their eyebrows. Then the interrogation begins.

"What's your name?"

"Antti Metsäntausta."

"Where are you from?"

"From Metsäntaka croft beyond the village of Pusula."

"And you want some flour?"

"Yes, they told me you could get flour here for nothing."

"Do you really need the flour?"

"I don't reckon I'm begging for the fun of it, and I don't reckon I've skied forty miles since this morning for the fun of it."

"Are you starving, then?"

"Well, I haven't eaten one bite of real bread in a week."

"And still you've got a new coat, and have the strength to ski forty miles since this morning?"

"Yes . . . hmm . . . what else could I do?"

The shopkeeper examines him with a suspicious look, turns toward the lady, and says, "This here fellow is too healthy and too well-dressed. He's not one of your customers, believe me!"

The interrogation begins anew: "Can you prove that you need the flour?"

Antti looks about the shop, perplexed; there is not one familiar face. He pales with shame mixed with indignation and stammers out uncertainly, "Well, you see, it's like this, that I'm from up there in the depths of the wilderness beyond the town of Pusula, and I have so few acquaintances. We don't often have occasion to come here to the church and make acquaintances . . ."

"Is there anyone here from the town of Pusula who could certify that you're in need?"

There was nobody. One voice remarks that the village community of Pusula had fetched its flour already days ago in order to be able to transport it the long way home by Christmas!

"Why, then, do you come so late and so alone?" the shopkeeper asks abruptly. Antti loses his composure: he has so much to say but stumbles over every word.

When his explanation comes to nothing, the woman kindly interrupts him: "You see, we must know that we give out public help to people who really need it. Surely you can easily get a certificate that you are needy from the parson or parish clerk. Come back tomorrow when you've got it. We have to be conscientious about it."

Antti straightens himself up, casts a queer look at the shopkeeper and at the flour bales, pulls his cap down in front, and leaves without a word.

The following day, the morning of Christmas Eve, Antti presents himself in the shop in good time, this time accompanied by a hand from a farm in the vicinity. In his need Antti has remembered him from grammar school days, searched for him for several hours last evening, found him, been recognized and believed, had a good square meal and a bed to sleep in, and now the farm hand has accompanied him in order to certify his need. Antti now gets his sack filled to the brim without difficulty, but when he says that he still has to carry it forty miles on his back today, the shopkeeper begins to empty it again.

"No, no," says Antti, "just let it stay full, I'll manage for sure!"

"But it weighs five stone, and that's more than a man can carry, that."

"Yes, but I have a wife and four children who have been starving for two weeks, and I reckon we need everything we can get, for the forest owners are probably not coming with work for me right away."

"Why didn't you say anything yesterday about having a wife and four children who are starving?" asks the woman.

"I didn't want to in front of all the people . . . you see, I get embarrassed damned easily . . ."

They couldn't help it—they had to laugh. Antti gets his full sack, bows in general gratitude to the relief committee off in Helsinki, and offers the lady his coarse fist as a special token of favor. As he is about to leave, he turns around in the door and says to the shopkeeper, "Sir, couldn't you please give me a batch of leaf tobacco on credit until spring? See, it's like this, that if I can just smoke, then I don't feel the worst of the stomach pains. It was the tobacco that helped me here yesterday, but now I haven't got any for the return trip."

The shopkeeper laughs and shows himself to be generous in the presence of others, placing two large packs of leaf tobacco on the counter in front of Antti. That was because he did Antti an injustice yesterday, he said.

"But you'll get payment for sure come spring," Antti assures him, getting chummy in his delight and offering him, too, his hand in parting. As he goes through the door he jovially turns his head once more. "Well, it's like this," he says, "I haven't always been poor and doubtless won't stay that way forever, either."

Next he takes leave of his friend the farm hand, stops his pipe, latches himself to his skis, and with smoke puffing around his mouth disappears in the bend of the road, scarcely bent under his five-stone load. It is not far into the morning yet, he makes reckless speed under the influence of the tobacco and his successful mission, and in his confidence reckons to be home before midnight. The surface is good for skiing and there is not much loose snow lying in the woods. The slight stiffness in his legs after the strain yesterday should also go away if only he could get into the right stride.

The day is milder than the previous one; the low sun shines forth above the forest in the south, and he becomes warm under his sheepskin coat. So he pulls it off, rolls it up, and lays it on the sack, continuing on his way in his shirtsleeves. He digs up a lumberjack song, singing it in time to his long paces, and when it is finished he starts a hymn. When the sun has set and the stars light themselves in the twilight, the forest opens up upon a large, ice-covered lake, and now Antti knows that he has covered more than a third of the way. He is not so pleased any longer: he has made poor speed, and still he feels fatigue sneaking into all his joints, so that he would have liked most of all to throw himself down into a snowdrift and fall asleep away from it all. To refresh himself he gets full speed down the shore slope and onto the ice. There a cold puff of air comes blowing through him. With the twilight the cold has sharpened, and his sweaty shirtcollar has frozen stiff and is chafing him in the neck. The flour sack weighs insufferably and the ropes are cutting painfully deep into his shoulders.

Far on the other side of the lake he sees a light twinkling from a solitary farm. For a moment he stands magnetized by the thought of stretching himself out in the warmth and resting a minute before moving on in the night, but in the next he has restrained himself, loosens the load from his back and pulls on his cold coat—it is getting too chilly to spend Christmas night in shirtsleeves. He sweeps the ice under his feet free from snow and chops a hole in it with his iron-tipped pole, so that the water rises up. Then he carefully takes some fistfuls of flour out of the sack, mixing it into a gruel in the water, and slurps his lonesome Christmas Eve supper. Next he hikes up his sack, lights his pipe, picks up speed again, and aims in a straight line diagonally across the gloomy, white bay, while the Christmas stars twinkle in the cold and the first quarter moon rises, a little piece above the dim horizon only to disappear soon behind it again. He is no longer thinking about the twenty-five miles of desolate moor that he has to cross before he is home; he again dreams the backwoodsman's fleeting dreams, quite as if he were lying at home on the oven.

At Metsäntaka homestead Anna is already waiting for her husband at dusk, figuring that he has set out from the church town just as early in the morning as he did from home. She has shared yesterday's milk among the children without allowing a drop for herself, confidently keeping up her spirits all day. She is pleased that the cow, due to extra Christmas feeding, gives an unusual quantity of milk, which she bears in silent triumph to the cabin, putting the milk pail away in the cupboard where she keeps her birchbark pans ready to bake the soft, fresh bread as soon as Antti comes home with the flour. In her thoughts she revels in the magnificent Christmas feast, stroking the children's hair more fondly than usual.

Already before dusk she fires up the sauna in order to be able to offer Antti a hot bath immediately upon his return from his strenuous journey. There is, thank goodness, no lack of firewood, and when the sauna is fired up she heats up the cabin's large baking oven for baking Christmas bread and to get a real Christmas coziness for the evening. Then she bathes herself and the children clean for the holiday, each moment expecting to hear Antti stamping the snow from his skis in the yard. And evening comes and darkness comes—but Antti does not come. It is already bedtime, and the children, who have been held in suspense, noticing that something unusual was up, will not go to bed willingly. They want to have Christmas, they say, since Mommy had said that it would come this evening.

"It comes only when Daddy comes," she answers.

"Then when is he coming?" ask three inquisitive mouths.

She calms them, but cannot calm herself. When she prevails upon them to go to bed, she takes out her spinning wheel in her anxiety, begins drawing out her interminable thread, singing a hymn to appease God for working on such a festive evening. Without work she cannot stand the waiting. But her thoughts nevertheless flutter bitter and anguished around Antti and their separation yesterday half in animosity. She wrings her hands in silent remorse, blaming herself for Antti freezing to death in the forest. When it is getting on toward midnight she goes out, walks off a distance from the cabin so as not to wake up the children, and cries out in the darkness quite softly with a shrill voice full of anguish, so that she is ashamed of herself, "Antti, Antti! . . . Why are you not home yet?"

". . . not home yet!" comes the echo from the pine grove scornfully in reply.

She stands outside until she starts to freeze, then goes in again with her head bowed, and bursts into tears. Her conscience is suffering, and her tears do not relieve her. She half suffocates in her sighs and moans under her breath, "My Lord, almighty God who art good and wise, why did you let me chase my husband out into the winter night—why? It would have been better if he had stayed at home, so we might have died together . . . !"

The oldest girl is awakened by her wailing and, astonished, creeps over to her mother. When she finds her crying, her tears begin to flow, too. But her mother impulsively tucks the seven-year-old girl in to her, wets her hair and cheeks with the tears of her immense grief, and vehemently rocks her to and fro, wailing incessantly, "Now we've nothing else to wait for but death . . . let's just hope it comes soon!"

"Death? What's that?" asks the girl.

Instead of answering, the mother carries her oldest child to her bed, bowing her head and her heart before the Almighty and praying long and ardently for her husband, for her children, for herself . . . for the whole sinful world.

Later in the wee hours of the completely silent Christmas night, a very sharp ear can discern a gentle rustling sound, which in slow and weary rhythm approaches Metsäntaka homestead. Suddenly the cold fires off a salvo of joy in the cabin corner. Anna awakes in the cabin, a happy presentiment takes possession of her, she runs in her bare chemise to the door, pulls it open, and in the uncertain snowlight sees an entirely white figure gliding into the yard.

"Good God! . . . Antti! . . . Finally!"

Antti is unable even to clear his throat for a gruff answer. He mumbles something, steps with difficulty out of his skis, which are left lying there, and staggers up to the door. The hoar-frost, snow, and flour dust in combination have whitewashed him to a shining Christmas angel. Anna drags him into the cabin, where he sinks without a word down onto the bench and sighs deeply and appreciatively. With a splinter flare in her hand Anna relieves her husband of the flour sack and his coat, examining him anxiously to see if he has been frostbitten, but calming down when she feels that he is bathed in sweat. It is the final effort to make it home that has had this effect.

"And now you must have a sauna at once, Antti! There's still heat left and it'll be easy to make more!"

Antti allows himself to be treated as his wife wishes. She leads him to the sauna, heats it anew although it is warm enough, prepares hot water and birch twigs for bathing, and has no time to notice that Antti is not wearing a shirt next to his body. She leaves him alone only when he has staggered up onto the ledge and she has stretched him out there, when his skin begins to redden and his joints soften to the salutary effect of the water vapor.

She rushes back to the cabin and lights a flaming fire in the baking oven. The children wake up and are told that Christmas has arrived with Daddy from the church town. She dresses them in their best clothes and tells them that now they will soon have enough to eat.

Jubilation!

Only after an hour does she get Antti from the sauna; he is so weary that he can scarcely walk without support, but nevertheless he props his skis up against the cabin in passing. Inside the log cabin everything is as if transformed. A splendid log fire burns in the fireplace, a white tablecloth is spread over the pine table, the splinter flares sparkle in wall chinks and in brackets—and four magnificent, large, steaming birchbark pans with fresh bread baked from flour and milk stand in the middle of the table. The children are seated according to age 'round about it without touching the belly cheer, and Anna takes the youngest out of the cradle to her breast.

"So come now, dear Antti, and let's bless the Christmas bread!"

When grace is finished, Antti, in helping himself, speaks his first words since coming home. "I had to bury half of the flour down in a sandpit six or seven miles from here, otherwise I'd never have had the strength to make it. I expect I can find the way there some other day to fetch it."

"But then it'll be mixed with sand," says Anna.

"Oh no, love—I put it inside my shirt . . . !"

When their worst hunger is appeased, Anna considers that elsewhere people are going to matins at this time, and she brings out her hymnal.

"We should find a hymn we know by heart," says Antti.

The hymn, which the starving denizens of the wilderness knew by heart, is

> *All the world, rejoice ye early*
> *In the Lord with heart and soul . . . !*

The children join in with the songs they know, each piping his own lay. This does nothing to disturb the devotions, all the more as the parents hold the dominant with the hymn beat.

Before the
Candles Go Out

« Før lysene slukner »

HANS E. KINCK

NORWAY 1901

*The novels and short stories of Norwegian Hans E. Kinck (1865–
1926) explore the class and cultural tensions between the people of
rural Norway and government officials as well as their longing for
community and harmony in a threatening and fragmented world.
Kinck's psychological mastery and love for tradition are particularly
noticeable in his numerous short-story collections. Involved in
assimilating dialect words into Dano-Norwegian, Kinck thus
contributed to the revitalization of Norwegian language.*

THE SCHOOLTEACHER SLIPPED DOWN THROUGH
town. He was out rather late, indeed; he had to get a Christmas
tree for his four-year-old daughter, who still had to stay in bed a while
following that gastritis. And now it was late afternoon on Christmas Eve.
He walked as older teachers so often do—with no neck, his head shoved
down into his shoulders, as if he were swallowing a stubborn conviction
that wanted to come up again—and arm and cane held in a straight line
slanting out to the side like a buttress against an old church. People were
brushing past on their way uptown and downtown. Never did people
walk so fast in Christiania as on the afternoon of Christmas Eve; there
were footsteps close on every side, as if they were Parisians or Romans.
Then you might also see many a bellicose thirteen-year-old brother walking without bashfulness with his grown sister on his arm chatting eagerly,
for darned if they couldn't think of a present for Mama! And from a doorway sailed an unbridled mother alone, darting bewildered through the
streets, for darned if she hadn't also quite forgotten a present for the maid!
. . . It is somehow the only day of the year that people do not cast severe

small-town eyes on each other or think that something is unpleasant.

Sheaves of golden grain rustled past the schoolteacher on the sidewalk, and there was a swishing of dark fir trees with quivering branches. But at the coal merchant's on the corner there were still a couple of trees, and on one open lot there was quite a little forest left—but these were the scraps, and the lot was full of little boys and girls taking advantage of the afternoon fall in prices to dicker the trees down to half price before taking them. And one or two had saved their tree stands from last year's Christmas tree and wanted a twenty-øre discount for them. And they finally got their discount, too. Because it was, after all, so late in the afternoon on Christmas Eve.

And one quiet snowflake or another was falling, as snowflakes are wont to do on Christmas Eve . . .

The slag of autumn drudgery was melting within him, and was, as it were, dripping loose shiny little drops of silvery joy within his breast. He was thinking back to the holidays in his home, when he was a child, how they were spoiled by ill humor. For his parents got so somber on those days, so strangely irascible, dragging out the account that they had not had the time to settle between themselves in the week's workdays. For rest is a thing of beauty—but they seemed to feel that there was not a shred of beauty left in them for the holidays—and then they angrily dragged out their account just as well. He certainly never forgot one such afternoon on Christmas Eve. Now it reemerged today as he was out here looking for a little Christmas tree:

. . . He had come rushing into the room, then, where Dad and Mom were lighting the Christmas candles; the children had been lured into the servants' quarters and were not supposed to find out, for it was supposed to be a surprise, the tree was. Still, they didn't notice that he had entered the room—as animated as they were, for he came rushing into the middle of something they were talking about. His father was standing on a chair and lighting up at the top.

"Why didn't you send the maid with the brace of grouse to the parson?" his father said.

She answered sarcastically, "Sure, so he'd construe it as prompt receipt for the ham that he sent us!"

"It's strange," his father said after a while, "how long it stays with you when a woman like you has once been motherless and left to the stableboy and milkmaid as a child . . ."

She replied, "You're crude, Berg!"

He reached up, unperturbed. "The barnyard smell hangs around so long.... For milkmaids and stableboys certainly never give presents away unless they get something in return."

"You're downright callous!"

He calmly struck a match for the Christmas candles, whistling as he reached up. "Your kind heart will never unfold, you know. Because your whole life becomes such a perpetual guard against relapse, and a flight away from your memories.... Prompt receipt! Just barn-smelling panic! Just barn-smelling panic!"

She hissed, "Now you've found a rather nice slogan: Barn-smelling!" And she laughed silently at the phrase.

... He sneaked quietly out of the room again and took a place by the wall of the house, taking furtive joy in Christmas. He was facing south, but the sky had already darkened; one snowflake or another was falling out there, as they are wont to do on Christmas Eve. The two parents were arguing inside.... Word was sent over to the servants' quarters for the children that the Christmas tree was now lit! But he stayed outside looking at a star until they had been calling for a long time. And later he went back outside, taking up his place by the wall of the house ...

And that is why the schoolteacher now wanted to protect his child's joy, placing the sparkling Christmas candles around it and kindling their powerful gleam right into her eye. For this furtive joy in a child was no doubt so infinitely beautiful; it was more beautiful than everything else— it was like a solitary lily shedding its fragrance for itself out in a wilderness. But it was so dearly bought. The furtive joy had evil consequences; throughout an entire life it became a poison for all that was shining, which people called good humor.

It was, after all, as if it were always a workday at home in the schoolteacher's rooms, too. And he couldn't deny it, nor could she. They were first cousins and had got married; there were no new worlds to go discovering, and they knew one another. And perhaps they were a little old when they got married. But they now had a four-year-old child all the same. And sometimes they thought it incredible just thinking about it. For he was almost fifty and she over forty when they got married. They had had their reasons for postponing it; they had both one and the same reason: they had learned from childhood that Christmas candles went out in that kind of life together.

The schoolteacher finally found a tree on a lot and bought it, having it cut off way up near the top so it became a tiny tree. For it had to stand on a board on the bedspread right in front of the little girl and forcibly shed joy directly into her eyes. He also bought *Hansel and Gretel* at a bookstore.

And then he hurried home.

But at home his wife sat polishing a candlestick and had almost nothing left to do for Christmas. The child was still taking her afternoon nap within.

She was thinking of almost the same thing he had been thinking about—about her childhood holidays, how they so invariably loomed like a bank of heavy clouds; the sight of a tired mother—that was her festival day. That was when father was in chapel, for when he preached in the parish church Sunday was a workday like the others and she had to make an appearance in the rectory pew before the congregation. And still! *Sunday*—just name the word and it was still shining like sunshine on white birch trunks. But for her mother it was as if her busy fingers couldn't stand to rest and therefore had to scratch on that day. First the gloomy book of sermons came out after the week's six busy days, demanding devotion on the seventh, a certain atmosphere: all the workweek's white lies, all the unsettling affairs, all the little oversights, and then the dodges afterward in order to divert the attention of Father or the domestics, the crafty silence in order to look perfect, the tacit setdowns—this was to be cleansed away in atmosphere! . . . Oh, the counterfeit eyes of a pastor's wife! . . . Then Mother grimaced within, and she defiantly locked herself in her room with her night jacket, washing and "making herself up," as it was called, for half the day; and when she then came out she kept silent, going about with clenched mouth all day long, and at times angrily humming a hymn. And the cup for whipped egg yolks and sugar was left all day long prosaically on the buffet after Father emptied it on his way to the chapel, in order to lubricate his voice with something good and to help the word of God resound in church!

It was this vision of her mother that had come over her and spellbound her so the first time they had kissed, she and the schoolteacher, he asked what she had cried about. "Oh, it's frightful! . . . I can see her slogging away as if it were yesterday!" And they told each other everything, so that they could be on their guard together and salvage the holidays and the shining gold of good humor.

She had salvaged something, too; she bore a little vision around inside her of what Sunday was; it lay there glittering: Sunday was sunshine and white birch trunks!—but like a ship in distress it lay . . .

She was in the dining room rubbing the candlestick. She was tall. She had brownish eyes; they were in any case so dark that they didn't appear blue. She had dreamed such an outrageous dream in the night that it had left her with a heavy heart.

But Sunday was going to be sunshine and white birch trunks for her four-year-old girl. The child was now beginning to understand—and she must never see the cloud bank of bad moods rising!

She was thinking: . . . All of life's many Sundays—hmm, that was hopelessly many. . . . But in any case all its Christmas Eves, they ought to be salvaged!—and there weren't so many of them, anyway, in a lifetime . . .

There was a rattling in the hall lock. The schoolteacher was home with the little fir. He put the tree on the living room table. He looked into the dining room. She looked up with the bashful, guilty look that people get when they are unhappy, rubbing a few quick strokes across the candlestick. In a lightning-quick pang they felt each other's apprehension that for God's sake Christmas Eve might still be salvaged.

That incited them. And delight in persecution rushed strangely into them both at the same time.

"What is it you're afraid of?" he said.

"What is it you're angry about?" she said.

"I'm not at all angry."

"What are you, then?"

"Do I need to tell you all over again that there's something called Christmas Eve memories?"

"Now I have to laugh!" she said; and it was the silent, scornful laugh that she remembered from her mother, as if in its first clumsy beginning.

"You need that. You don't laugh that often."

"What a mean attack!"

"I never attack. It's against my nature. I only parry."

"No, that's right, you don't attack. You're too cowardly."

"Call it what you like.—In any case it's against my nature to attack." And with this the little girl woke up within.

"Isn't the Christmas tree coming soon?"

"Yes darling, now the Christmas tree is coming soon," they both said at once—but their voices had lost their tone, and they gasped for breath.

She went into the kitchen. He trimmed the tree. He put the candles firmly into clips. And carried it in, placing two packages at its foot. And then he lit the candles. And on top of the bedspread he put the largest board in the house and then placed the tree on it. The candles twinkled in the girl's pale, sick eyes, and she was embarrassed at the festivities, sticking her whole hand into her mouth and chewing her fingers.

"Here's a package for you!" he said.

She opened it. And there was *Hansel and Gretel*. He showed her the pictures and told her about the poor parents that had no food for their children, and they talked about setting them out in the forest. He read:

> *At first their father, who is kind,*
> *Says no, but must consent,*
> *For Mother has made up her mind*
> *And never will relent.*

The little girl stuck fingers of both hands into her mouth to keep from crying, and gulped, "But why do they have to be so mean to Hansel and Gretel?"

"But everything turns out fine in the end," her father said. "But here are more packages!"

She shouted, "Mama, come here and see!" They were packages with toys in them.

And he stood up at the shout and went into the living room, where the mother was still sitting, polishing a new candlestick.

"You're coaxing the child away from me," she said, remaining seated.

But the little one shouted once again, forgetting that it was her mother she had called for. And her father went in again.

"Didn't *you* have any toys when *you* were little?"

"Yes, indeed. I had boats. I had lots of boats and ships. And then I dammed up a huge pond out in the woods. I would lie there alone all day long, waiting for puffs of air up in the trees, if they wouldn't come down and start blowing a little in the sails for me. And I would lie in wait for the wind in the blades of grass and position my ships correctly, so they could sail . . ."

The child was not listening and spread the toys out over the bedspread, shouting, "Look! Mama!"

Her father rose from his chair at the shout; but slowly, so the child would not think anything was wrong. He retreated, continuing to narrate as if pleased with his memories: "The wind was blowing! The boats rocked and waited. They tugged impatiently at their little lines. The wind struck the sails. And they were off!—they were off! Far out to sea, out to the edge of the sea where the stars are." He was already in the living room door. "And I would lie in the grass sailing with them, far, far away!"

Her mother stood up. "I dare say there's something tugging just like that in your will to live." And she whispered close to him as she went by, " 'Out to sea!' seems to say it. Away from all the misery here at home!"

"Yes it *does*. You're standing in the way of what's vivacious in me!"

She sighed painfully, as if for a flock of children that had died on her: "Zest for life . . . will to live . . . wanderlust! . . ." She looked despondently at him as she moved into the bedroom to the child. "Now your thought is darting past me . . ."

"So now *you've* got to tell me something!" said the little one.

"What should I tell you about? I've got nothing to tell you about—know nothing about stars and about the sea . . . Well, I dreamed such a queer dream last night. It seemed like there was a horse race on a vast plain outside a large foreign city." And her mother forgot the child as she narrated: "I don't know where I was standing, for it seemed as if there were two fiery steeds that were led out of the stable and past me—they had to go in behind a board fence and be hitched up and start there. And it was as if I couldn't see them anymore during the whole race because of the board fence—I had a bad seat, I imagine. More horses were led past. But I only noticed these two and remembered them, because they were so glistening brown, and happy, and bold. . . . Awhile later loud, ugly shouts were heard from the judge's stand. I peeked over the board fence: Away off down the road, far out on the plain, two horses appeared, came galloping with a yellow, heavy streetcar after them . . ."

The schoolteacher was standing in the doorway. "A streetcar?" he said, trying to laugh through his nose.

"Yes, a streetcar. A heavy streetcar with small, narrow, cast-iron wheels under it, which were sinking in right to the axle, . . . and then there were no carriage shafts to pull it with, but only ropes, so it was running to the side, constantly getting stuck, then unexpectedly getting loose and just about to hit the horses' hocks. The lieutenant was whipping away—it was all a joke!—a race with streetcars—a crazy whim, a bet, I dare say! . . . The two horses were led on past me; they were loose-bellied, trembling, dripping wet, whipped to pieces. I thought it was strange that two fiery steeds could be ruined in so short a time . . ."

"Look here, Mama! When I do like this, then the doll can stand."

And her father said in the living room, "It's some really frightfully meaningless things one can dream up, too!"

But she suddenly said, getting up, "Oh! how people struggle, have a hard and heavy time of it! . . . Just because of a joke! . . . Because of a crazy whim! . . . For the sake of nothing at all!"

And when she was standing in the living room again, he reached out to her, holding her head between his hands.

"You're so nice, you are," she said gently and smiled.

But he pondered her smile—for there seemed to be the small, sparkling point of an awl lying there. "How's that?" he said warily, feeling out the meaning of her smile.

"Ohh, nothing; . . . you're just so nice, you are . . . take it from me . . ."

"And so are you, too!" he said more firmly.

And it was then that the sharper meaning of the smile drew near: "I almost think that I've become your bad conscience, I do," she said willfully and quietly, "when your wanderlust comes and tugs at the little lines, as you say."

And he said the same; but he patted her head as before. "It's not *my* fault that you are!"

She turned around cheerfully, speaking casually so as to pretend that she would rather broach a new subject; but she said it quietly: "It's not my fault either, you know. It's his who has caused ours—it is!"

Then they parted silently. She sat in the living room. He sat far away, in the dining room. The child was playing with her new doll on her bed.

They sat like this a while. Then the mother said, groaning, "You never *help* me!"

But he kept silent in there; for her awl-sharp smile was still alive in him and somehow stabbing.

"*Say* something. . . . Ohh!"

Just then the child shouted, "Papa, come here!"

He came through the living room, going past the mother and sitting down on the edge of the bed in the little one's room.

"Come, we'll row out fishing!" she said. And took her father by the hand. And they carefully rowed out to the fishing shoals; for her stomach could not stand very much motion yet.

"Mama, come here!—hurry, before the candles go out in the Christmas tree!" Her father started to get up; but she held him firmly, rowing gently to the fishing shoals. . . . "And then you were *alone* up in the woods with your boats? Your mama and your papa, didn't they come along?"

"No."

"Hurry, Mama, before the candles go out!—Sit down on the edge of the bed—*there*!" And her mother sat down bashfully farthest down at the foot of the bed beside her husband. "Why didn't *they* come along?"

"Because."

They lost themselves staring into a child's eye, where there was no lightning-quick glint of fear that the holidays might be wrecked. And it was as if it lit up. And suddenly he laughed: "Because Mama and Papa weren't friends—have you ever heard anything so crazy?"

"Why weren't they friends?"

"Because of nothing at all! Have you ever heard anything so crazy?"

"And I'll row out fishing with my doll a while. And now you and Mama must row out fishing—hurry, before the candles go out!"

And the two adults had to take each other in both hands and row out fishing.

"Do you know where that wanderlust comes from?" he said.

"From that furtive joy out by the wall of the house on Christmas Eve." And then he had to tell about that time, while he was rowing.

But he didn't get far. Then he said, keeping stroke with the rowing, "My wife is nice."

She answered in time, "My husband is nice."

And the child fell asleep in the meanwhile with her doll on the bedspread. And the last candles crackled in the fir needles. But the two only rowed out to the fishing shoals.

"My wife is nice."

"My husband is nice."

"My wife is nice."

"My husband is nice."

"Why, you're young!" he said. "Why, the skin of your hands is on fire."

"Your words are like snowflakes in my hair and eyebrows . . . Christmas Eve snowflakes . . . so quiet . . . insinuating . . . flattering . . . delightful . . . *Say* something—ohh!"

"You're so young, you are!"

Christmas Peace

« Julefred »

JOHANNES V. JENSEN

DENMARK 1904

In 1944, Danish poet and prose writer Johannes V. Jensen (1873–1950) received the Nobel Prize in literature. Jensen is regarded as one of the most significant twentieth-century Danish authors. He is best known for his historical novel Kongens Fald (1900–1901; The Fall of the King), *poems, various collections of myths, and three volumes of stories from Himmerland, his native region in northern Jylland.*

NOWADAYS THERE ARE PEACEFUL CONDITIONS in Jylland, and especially at Christmas the peace goes beyond all understanding. But a mere two generations ago, Christmas was still that time when peace was proclaimed in preference to the rest of the year, when security was not as great. Was it not strange then, that precisely Christmastime was often so troubled in days of old? Again and again we are told about outbreaks of ancient resentment, about showdowns between mortal enemies, about atrocities—and these were on Christmas Eve, or it was Saint Stephen's Day in the church itself! For some people no doubt thought that they would take advantage of the opportunity while everyone was thinking of peace and good will, while others took their peace when it was denied them, securing their own Christmas peace by capital offenses.

There was a man living on Sønderup Heath whom they called Peat-Christen; people shrank from him, although he was harmless: he was an honest, humble person who owned a miserably tiny small holding out on the moor and otherwise earned his living as a day laborer. But he was a murderer. Peat-Christen had stabbed the Tinker to death one Christmas Eve. He was fully acquitted, to be sure, but there remained a boundary of reticence around his name; there was blood on his hands.

The Tinker was a thief and a prisonhouse slave who lived in the vicinity; even today they talk about his transgressions. It is said that he was one of the itinerants from Hole. In spite of his thus coming from a rotten lot and of people being afraid of him, still there is some of the rude warmth of the old days clinging to his renown; people were amused by him, he was a crafty rascal—many a time he committed offenses from sheer caprice; there was fun in him. He seems to have been one of those loony birds who are ultimately perhaps nothing more than errant and wasted talent. There were many stories about the Tinker going around. His forte was breaking out of jail; he thought up the most incredible things, and he was not to be detained. Tradition asserts that he had unusually small hands and feet and that the jail warden never realized that he could slip off his shackles. However he may have managed it, and whatever new tricks he thought up, regularly every year they had him on the loose in the vicinity. His wife and daughter lived in a hovel on Sønderup Heath, you see. Not far off lay Peat-Christen's house.

A yawning social abyss separated the two families, although their circumstances were just about equally wretched. To this must be added a personal hatred emanating from the Tinker and kept alive many years. And you can almost understand him. When he who yearly broke out of prison and workhouse with unspeakable trouble and came home to his own like a forest beast with the dogs at his heels, should he have Peat-Christen's poor but patently innocent little abode to look at first thing from his own despised windows? There lived Peat-Christen, that dirt poor apostle who eternally guarded himself against seeking conflict with those who had something, who in his modest and unpunishable conduct never infringed on another and could never live quietly enough and never let himself be shaken in his contempt for dishonest people! There went the three children Peat-Christen had acquired, toddling around his hut like some angels from God's Kingdom, while Peat-Christen ground himself crooked with his spade on his plot of heath. The Tinker was ill at ease from a yearning to tar the magnanimous poorling and light a fire in his top and transform him into a flaming saint! Every time he was home he made a point of inviting Peat-Christen to quarrels, but the staid small holder minded his own business and harbored no desire to compete with the Tinker in any sort of contest skill. At last the Tinker longed to come home just as much for Peat-Christen's sake as for his family's: he hated him and had it in for him. And the day came when he could no longer control himself.

On the gray, light-forsaken day before Christmas, the town of

Sønderup was startled in every nook and cranny by a half squadron of Randers Dragoons resounding through town, and not a soul suspected mischief; darkness had begun to fall, and the simple, sweet Christmas peace began to hang over the village. Every sound became so intimately discreet, every thought of a world outside had perished, and then a countless troop of cavalry in blue with helmets and cold cutlasses came rushing through town! There was a splattering of slush and muck up around them from the road. They came galloping like a dreadful apparition through the winter fog. Old folks' knees shook in fright. They recalled another Christmas that they had seen the dragoons in the town of Sønderup. That was many years ago now. The occasion then was that the parish bailiff himself and four other men had gone out onto the moor, where there were trash living then, too, a man with a wife and two sons who had long been shearing the sheep on the fields at night and making the district unsafe in other ways. Sønderup folk wanted some peace from them during that Christmas, and to that end forced their way into his cottage and wiped out all four inhabitants with ax-blows. But this was a mistake on their part; it could not be argued as self-defense, and they were all five executed in return.

Meanwhile, it was soon learned why the dragoons were coming this time; the Tinker had broken out again and under worse circumstances than usual, in that he had happened to give the jail warden a knock that he had not survived. Consequently, so much force was put to having him rearrested; and now they meant to nab him from the bosom of his family on Christmas Eve.

The dragoons split up when they got out onto the moor, drawing together at a run around the Tinker's house, and had it surrounded in a hurry. But the Tinker was not there. They hunted and searched right to the ridge of the hovel, they interrogated his wife and daughter, they turned over every straw, but did not find the Tinker. When they had ridden off again without any success, the Tinker crawled up out of a hole under the dirt floor that had been well trampled up over him and concealed with peat litter; he was too sharp for them.

Two hours later the church bells in Sønderup tolled in the holy day. It became so silent, so hushed under the darkness. Only the bell in the church tower put in a word, babbling with its peculiar voice into the night thaw over the low, timorous town lying so alone in the broad landscape. The wind drifted back and forth, water seeped and dripped in the ditch full of slimy snow. The church bell spoke, now weary, now in a singing tone, dejected and happy, up and down like an old man with experience. And at length it held its tongue with nodding emphasis like an old, old man. It grew clear under the night sky, the stars were lit beneath the deepness of space, hanging crackling cool and small. Crumbling sounds were sown out over the earth, the water seeped more silently, cold rose against the night. Then the anxious ice-sound of the water fell silent, too, with solitary faint creaks as in sleep; it froze, and the frost held.

Everyone was now home, indoors. Only a man from Sønderup, who out of necessity had been out of town, was coming across the moor in the evening. And he met to his unspeakable horror the Tinker, who was coming with a tar can in his hand.

"Good evening," said the Tinker, as it appeared in an excellent mood. "You needn't fear, little Knud, I won't do you no harm. I'm going down to light a fire in Peat-Christen's hair. God go with you, and happy holidays!"

Within Peat-Christen's living room Christmas had begun. It made itself known by a growing silence. Peat-Christen's wife was putting things in order as if for strangers. The three children had to take turns undergoing an agonizing minute before the three-legged stool with wash basin and soap. Jeppe and Laurine, the two eldest, with great force of will let themselves be washed: they had a grasp of the deep significance of the holy vigil that was approaching. Jeppe, five years old, and Laurine, four, were already knowledgeable about many things. They had once been to the town of Sønderup, where they had been seen wandering hand in hand. That was the richest episode of their young lives. They had viewed the wicket to the churchyard and the other mysteries of the village, a large, deep garden from which arose a tree with fat pears; they had viewed a wooden crate full of lapping ducks somewhere near a fine house, and after having next breathed in the air outside the rectory gate and caught a glimpse of strange flowering plants in the clear windows farthest in, they wandered again hand in hand out of town, arriving home at nightfall. Karen Marie was only two years old and too little in every respect; she cried for that reason as she was being washed. Jeppe and Laurine were way past her in every regard. They had experience from the outside world in which they had moved; they knew the moor's plants and insects, knew all about the value of rushes and the shiny seeds of the sedge, about red, round stones and colorful shards. They plucked the tiny cones of the bog myrtle and played with them as cows, they patted cakes from the mash outside the house, and sailed woodchips in a puddle. In the long summer they played outside in the winding sunken road, where the fine black sand in the ruts warmed and ran between their little toes. Winter had now cooped them up for time out of mind. They had been able to extend a thin hand out of the door to catch the drip from the eaves, and they had tasted the bitter water that ran down the windowpanes when they thawed. The bench under the window was their winter hangout; at night it opened its well-known and cozy feather embrace for them, the day they spent on its shiny, well-worn lid. Their things they kept in the window sill: Jeppe's chattels, valuables excavated from the earth, nice stones and the like, and Laurine's hoard of woolen yarn drums and chicory paper. Karen Marie, who was so little, of course owned nothing.

When the children had now been washed and combed and had their Sunday blouses on, their mother started to lay the table with a white cloth, and they had to be so well-behaved that one could hardly imagine, so as not to throw anything into disorder. The porridge, which today was quite white, of another finer and costlier kind of grain than the daily barley groats, burbled so richly in the pot and went "Puff," as if it were making the utmost effort to be good. And their mother was so quiet and gentle. When Peat-Christen came home from work and bent his tall, stooping figure under the low ceiling, he saw his three offspring sitting in a row on the bench behind the white table, three pairs of tiny wooden shoes sticking straight out, three soap-blushing solemnities, three shocks of yellow hair in the dimly lit room.

Silence descended over the room. While the food was being prepared the three little ones were witness to their father washing himself, and he even washed his face—he too suffered for the holiday, consecrated himself to the indescribable. Next they ate, first the fine porridge and afterwards roast pork and boiled potatoes. They felt so good. Somewhere, above or below, something radical had happened for everyone, so that it became brighter in every room, be it ever so narrow. Peat-Christen's portion had been three children with diamond clear eyes sitting each with his piece of fat-spewing pork in his little fingers and eating ever so. The room got cozier. His wife had a surprise behind the closed damper of the stove; they heard it seething and browning in there. The tallow candle on the table yellowed the room, which was full of modest peace.

Then one of the windowpanes came shattering in. The splinters fell into Laurine's hair. The wife broke into a wail. Peat-Christen looked up and noticed a glint off the blade of a peat spade in the broken window. He stood up, tall and deathly pale in his stubby face. Outside was heard the Tinker's loud, quite everyday voice, "Now you'll be tarred or I'll be damned, you holy Boniface . . ."

Peat-Christen had long ago made himself a spear, because the Tinker had threatened his life before. He took it down from the beam and went to the door.

The battle took place in the little entryway. The Tinker had got the front door open and wanted to come in, but Peat-Christen threatened him with the spear through the doorway. The Tinker heaped a hailstorm of insults on him, but could not reach him with his peat spade. For a long time nothing more happened. Then the nimble little Tinker saw his chance and fetched a blow at Christen with the sharp spade. It was maliciously meant, and Peat-Christen, who was a heavy and clumsy man, evaded it with difficulty. He had, after all, not thought that the Tinker was serious. He began to tremble.

"Beware!" he said weeping. And when the Tinker seemed to want to strike out again, he warned him, full of sorrow, "Beware! Or I'll stick you in your gut!"

"You wouldn't dare, you prophet!" teased the Tinker. He was mouthing off, but now there came a strange heat into his eyes, and he was tripping over his tongue so he could not speak properly. All at once he fell silent, and instead of scolding and using a foul mouth, he drew himself closer sidelong, on the lookout with his spade . . . and then Peat-Christen felt that the Tinker was getting too dangerous. His brains started to reel and whiz in the back of Peat-Christen's head. The clear frosty sky out there, the door under siege by a malevolent person with blood in his eyes, the room behind him lying in a whirl of terror and children wailing, all of it was spinning around, was seething through him. And when the Tinker, grimacing like a butcher, made a sudden move and leaped forward, Peat-Christen bent his heavy weight forward and stuck him straight through the chest. The Tinker's life blood spurted out like warm soup along the shaft of the spear, scalding Peat-Christen's hands. After a short, violent death struggle, during which he growled like a sheep and wrapped his hands around the shaft of the spear and, lying on his back, tried to move his feet as well up to the sharp iron, the Tinker was dead.

When it was done, Christen sighed and blinked the tears from his eyes. After having thought it over a bit, he dragged the corpse a distance from the house before he went in to the others. An hour later he was standing in the parish bailiff's hall reporting himself. He was taken to town and put in jail. But after having been interrogated he was, of course, acquitted.

The Legend of the Christmas Roses

« Legenden om julrosorna »

SELMA LAGERLÖF

SWEDEN 1908

Selma Lagerlöf (1856–1940), Swedish writer of world renown, received the Nobel Prize in literature in 1909 and became, in 1914, the first woman elected a member of the Swedish Academy. Her debut novel Gösta Berlings saga *(1891;* The Story of Gösta Berling) *was also her breakthrough work. It was followed by bestsellers such as* Jerusalem *(1901–2) and* Nils Holgerssons underbara resa *(1906–7;* The Wonderful Adventures of Nils). *The latter contained an abundance of fairy tales and legends pointing to another genre by which Lagerlöf gained international fame: the legend.*

THE ROBBER'S MOLL, WHO LIVED IN THE ROBBER'S den up in Göinge Forest, had one day set out on a begging expedition down to the flat country. The robber chief himself was an outlawed man and dared not leave the forest, but restricted himself to lying in wait for travelers who ventured within the forest belt. But in those days there were not many travelers in northern Skåne. Thus, if it happened that the husband had no luck with his hunting for several weeks, his wife would set out rambling. She had five young ones with her, and each youngster had tattered skin clothing and birchbark shoes, and carried on his back a sack that was just as long as he was tall. When she stepped inside a cottage door, nobody dared refuse to give her what she asked for, for she did not regard herself too good to return the next night and set the house afire if she had not been well received. The robber's moll and her youngsters were worse than a pack of wolves, and many would have liked to put spears through them, but this was never done because people knew that the man stayed behind in the forest, and he would no doubt have known how to get revenge if anything had happened to the children or the woman.

As the robber's moll went from farm to farm begging, she came one fine day to Öved, which at that time was an abbey. She rang at the abbey door and asked for food, and the porter lowered a little hatch in the door and handed her six round loaves of bread, one for her and one for every single one of her children.

While the mother was standing still at the door, her youngsters ran about. And now one of them came and tugged at her skirt as a sign that he had found something that she should come and see, and the robber's moll immediately went with him.

The entire abbey was surrounded by a high and solid wall, but the youngster had been able to spy out a little back gate that was standing ajar. When the robber's moll got there, she immediately pushed the gate open and stepped inside without asking for permission, such was her habit.

Öved Abbey was governed at this time by Abbot Hans, who was a man well-versed in horticulture. Within the abbey walls he had laid out a little garden, and it was into this that the robber's moll had forced her way.

At first glance the robber's moll was so startled that she stopped at the entrance. It was high summer, and Abbot Hans's garden was so full of flowers that it glittered before your eyes with blue and red and yellow when you looked into it. But soon a delighted smile spread over her face, and she began down a narrow path running between many small flower beds.

In the garden a lay brother was going about, clearing weeds. It was he who had left the door in the wall half open in order to take goosefoot and couch grass to the rubbish heap outside. When he saw the robber's moll coming into the garden with all five youngsters after her, he ran at once toward them and ordered them to go away. But the beggar woman walked on as before. She cast glances to every side, looking now at the stiff, white lilies spreading in one plot, and now at the ivy climbing high up the abbey wall, and she pretended not to see the lay brother at all.

The lay brother thought that she had not understood him. He was about to take her by the arm in order to turn her toward the way out, but when the robber's moll sensed his purpose, she gave him such a look that he started back. She had been walking with her back bent under her beggar's scrip, but now she straightened herself to her full height.

"I'm the robber's moll from Göinge Forest," she said. "Now, touch me if you dare!" And it was evident that when she had said this she was just as certain of being allowed to go in peace as if she had told him that she was the Queen of Denmark.

But still the lay brother made so bold as to disturb her; although now knowing who she was, he spoke amenably with her.

"You must know, robber's moll," he said, "that this is a monastery and that no woman in the country is allowed to come inside these walls. If you do not go away the monks will be angry with me because I forgot to shut the gate, and perhaps they will drive me from both the abbey and the garden."

But such petitions were wasted on the robber's moll. She continued, approaching the little rose garden, looking at the hyssop blooming with mauve flowers, and at the honeysuckle laden with clusters of yellowish red flowers.

So the lay brother knew no better remedy than to run into the abbey and call for help.

When he returned with two sturdy monks, the robber's moll saw at once that they meant business. She stood with legs wide apart on the path and began to shriek about all the frightful vengeance that she would take out upon the abbey if she were not allowed to stay in the garden as long as she wanted. But the monks figured that they did not need to fear her, thinking simply to drive her out. Then the robber's moll raised shrill screams, throwing herself upon them and scratching and biting, and all the youngsters did likewise. The three fellows soon felt that she was their superior. There was nothing else for them to do but to return to the abbey for reinforcements.

As they were running through the passage leading into the abbey, they met Abbot Hans hurrying up to find out what the row was about in the garden. They had to confess that the robber's moll from Göinge Forest had entered the abbey and that they had not been able to drive her out, but needed to secure relief.

But Abbot Hans reproached them for having used force, forbidding them to call for help. He sent the two monks back to their work, and although he was a frail old man, he took along only the lay brother to the garden.

When Abbot Hans got there, the robber's moll was walking about as before among the flower beds. And there was no end to his astonishment at her. He was convinced that never before had she seen a garden. All the same, she was walking among all the little plots, which were sown each with its species of foreign and unusual flowers, looking them over as if they were old acquaintances. It appeared as if she were familiar with both periwinkle and sage and rosemary. At some she smiled, and at others she shook her head.

Abbot Hans loved his garden as much as it was possible for him to love anything that was worldly and corruptible. As savage and frightful as the strange woman may have looked, still he could not help liking that she had fought with three monks in order to look at the flower garden in peace. He approached her and asked meekly if the garden pleased her.

The robber's moll turned violently toward Abbot Hans, for she expected only ambush and assault, but when she saw his white hair and his bent back she answered quite peacefully, "When I first saw it I thought that I had never seen anything lovelier, but now I see that it doesn't come up to another I know of."

Abbot Hans had certainly expected a different reply. When he heard that the robber's moll had seen a flower garden more beautiful than his, a faint blush spread across his wrinkled cheek.

The lay brother, who was standing close by, at once began to reprimand the robber's moll. "This is Abbot Hans," he said, "who with much labor and industry has himself collected the flowers for his garden from far and wide. We all know that there's no more abundant flower garden in the whole province of Skåne, and it's not for you, living all year round in the wild forest, to criticize his work."

"I don't want to make myself out to be a critic either of him or of you," said the robber's moll, "I'm just saying that if you could only see the flower garden I'm thinking of, then you'd pull up all the flowers planted here and throw them out like weeds."

But the garden hand was hardly less proud of the flowers than Abbot Hans himself, and when he heard these words, he started to laugh derisively. "I can see that you're only talking like this to tease us," he said. "It must be a fine flower garden that you've arranged for yourself among the pines and junipers of Göinge Forest. I'd dare to swear away my soul that you've never before been within the walls of a garden."

The robber's moll turned red with outrage at being so distrusted, and she exclaimed, "It may well be that until today I've never been inside the walls of a garden, but you monks, who are holy men, surely ought to know that every Christmas Eve the great Göinge Forest transforms itself into a flower garden to commemorate the hour of our Lord's birth. We who live in the forest have seen it happen every year, and in that flower garden I have beheld such glorious flowers that I haven't dared lift my hand to pick them."

The lay brother wanted to answer her, but Abbot Hans motioned him to silence. For ever since childhood Abbot Hans had heard talk about the forest clothing itself in festive attire on Christmas night. He had often longed to see it but had never succeeded. He now fervently began to implore the robber's moll that on Christmas Eve he might be allowed to come up to the robber's den. If only she would send one of her children to show him the way, he would ride there alone, and he would never betray them, but instead reward them as well as it stood in his power.

The robber's moll refused, at first, for she was thinking of the robber chief and the risk he might run by her letting Abbot Hans come to their den. But then her desire to show the monk that the flower garden she knew of was finer than his nevertheless overcame her, so that she gave in.

"But you get to take no more than one companion with you," she said. "And you mustn't set any trap or ambush for us, as sure as you're a holy man."

This Abbot Hans promised, and with this the robber's moll left. Then Abbot Hans commanded the lay brother that he not for anything reveal what had been agreed upon. He feared that his monks would not allow as old a man as he to travel to the robber's den if they realized what he was undertaking.

Nor did he intend to reveal his plan to a living soul, either. But then it happened that Archbishop Absalon of Lund came visiting to Öved and stayed the night. When Abbot Hans was showing him his garden, he came to think of the visit of the robber's moll, and the lay brother, who was going about working there, heard the abbot telling the bishop about the robber chief, who for many years had lived as an outlaw in the forest, and requesting a letter of protection for him, so that he once more would be able to lead a respectable life among other people.

"As things now stand," said Abbot Hans, "his offspring grow up to be worse malefactors than he is himself, and you'll soon have a whole gang of robbers to contend with up there in the forest."

But Archbishop Absalon replied that he would not let that evil brigand loose down among the honest folk on the plain. It would be best for all if he stayed up in his forest.

Then Abbot Hans got worked up and took to telling the bishop about Göinge Forest, which every year was decked in Christmas attire. "If these robbers are no worse than that God's glory appears to them," he said, "surely they couldn't be too evil to experience human mercy."

But the archbishop knew well how to answer Abbot Hans. "This much I will promise you, Abbot Hans," he said smiling, "that the day you send me a flower from the Christmas garden in Göinge Forest, I will give you a letter of protection for as many fugitives as you would want."

The lay brother perceived that Bishop Absalon believed the robber moll's tale as little as he did himself, but Abbot Hans noticed no such thing; instead, he thanked Absalon for his good promise and said that he would send him that flower.

Abbot Hans got his way, and next Christmas Eve he was not sitting home at Öved, but was instead on his way to Göinge Forest. One of the robber moll's wild youngsters ran before him, and as a companion he had the lay brother who had spoken with the robber's moll in the garden.

Abbot Hans had greatly longed to make this journey and was now very glad that it had come about. But it was an entirely different matter with the lay brother accompanying him. He held Abbot Hans very dear, and he would not have liked to leave it to another to escort him and watch over him, but he did not in the least believe that they would get to see any Christmas night garden. He thought that it was all a trap laid by the robber's moll with great cunning so that Abbot Hans should fall into her husband's power.

As Abbot Hans was riding northward toward the woodland, he saw preparations being made everywhere to celebrate Christmas. In every farming village a fire was lit in the sauna, so that it would be warm for bathing in the afternoon. Quantities of meat and bread were carried from storehouses into the cottages, and from the barns men came with large sheaves of straw that were to be strewn over the floor.

As he rode past the little village churches, he saw that the priest and his sexton would be busy decking them in the best tapestries they could find, and when he came to the bypath leading to Bosjö Abbey, the convent's poor itinerants came with loads of large loaves of bread and long candles that they had procured at the abbey gate.

When Abbot Hans saw all these Christmas preparations, his haste increased. He imagined that a feast awaited him that was greater than that any of the others would celebrate.

But the lay brother moaned and complained when he saw how they were making ready to celebrate Christmas in even the smallest farm. He grew increasingly anxious, praying and beseeching Abbot Hans to turn around and not voluntarily put himself in the hands of brigands.

Abbot Hans continued the journey without minding the complaining of the lay brother. They left flat country behind them and came to desolate and wild woodland. Here the road worsened. It became more like a stony path strewn with needles, and neither span nor footbridge helped the travelers across rivers and streams. The farther they went, the colder it got, and presently they came upon ground covered with snow.

It was a long and difficult journey. They turned off onto steep and slippery side paths, traversed bogs and marshes, made their way over wind-fallen trees and through thickets. Just as daylight was beginning to fail, the robber boy led them across a woodland meadow surrounded by tall trees, both conifers and bare hardwoods. Behind the meadow rose a rock face, and in the rock face they saw a door of thick planks.

Abbot Hans realized that they had now arrived, and he dismounted. The child opened the heavy door for him, and he peered into a shabby mountain cave with bare stone walls. The robber's moll was sitting at a log fire burning in the middle of the floor. All along the walls were beds of fir twigs and moss, and on one of these the robber chief lay sleeping.

"Come in, you out there!" the robber's moll shouted without rising. "And bring the horses into the room, so that they won't be harmed by the night cold!"

Abbot Hans now boldly entered the den, and the lay brother followed him. It was poor and wretched there, and nothing had been done to celebrate Christmas. The robber's moll had neither brewed nor baked, she had neither swept nor scrubbed. Her children sat on the floor around a cauldron, eating, but they were treated to no better food than weak water gruel.

The robber's moll spoke as proudly and authoritatively as a well-to-do farmer's wife. "Sit down here by the fire, Abbot Hans, and warm yourself," she said, "and if you've got food with you, then eat! For the food that we prepare in the forest, I don't think you'd want to taste. And if you're tired after the journey, lie down to sleep afterwards on one of those beds there. You don't need to be afraid of oversleeping. I'm sitting here by the fire keeping watch, and I'll wake you so that you can get to see what you've ridden out to see."

Abbot Hans obeyed the robber's moll, taking out his meal bag. But he was so tired after the journey that he scarcely had the strength to eat, and as soon as he got to stretch out on the bed he fell asleep.

The lay brother was also shown a bed to rest on, but he dared not sleep because he thought he ought to keep his eye on the robber chief, so that he would not rise up and take Abbot Hans prisoner. Little by little fatigue nevertheless gained power over him, too, so that he dozed off. When he awoke, he saw that Abbot Hans had left his bed and was now sitting by the fire conversing with the robber's moll. The outlawed robber was also sitting beside the fire. He was a tall, thin man who looked listless and gloomy. His back was turned to Abbot Hans, and it appeared as if he did not want to let on that he was listening to the conversation.

Abbot Hans was telling the robber's moll about all the Christmas preparations that he had observed underway, and he reminded her of the Christmas feasts and merry Christmas games in which she no doubt had participated in her youth, when she was living peaceably among other people.

"It's a shame for your children, who never get to dress up and run through the street, or romp in the Christmas straw," said Abbot Hans. The robber's moll had at first replied shortly and abruptly, but little by little she became more hushed and listened more eagerly.

Suddenly the robber chief turned toward Abbot Hans, holding his clenched fist up in front of his face. "You miserable monk, have you come here to entice wife and children away from me? Don't you know that I've been outlawed and can never leave the forest?"

Abbot Hans looked him fearlessly straight in the eye. "My intention is to obtain a letter of protection for you from the archbishop," he said. He had hardly said this before both the outlaw and his wife started to roar with laughter. They well knew the kind of mercy forest robbers could expect from Bishop Absalon.

"Well, if I get such a letter from Absalon," said the robber chief, "I promise you that never again will I steal as much as a goose."

The lay brother was annoyed that the robber folk dared to laugh at Abbot Hans, but the abbot himself seemed quite pleased. The lay brother had seen him scarcely more peaceable and gentle when sitting among the monks at Öved than he now saw him with the savage robber band.

But suddenly the robber's moll stood up. "Here you sit talking, Abbot Hans," she said, "so that we're forgetting to look at the forest. Even now I can hear from here the Christmas bells ringing."

This was scarcely spoken before everyone sprang to their feet and ran out. But in the forest they found dark night and cold winter still. The only thing they were sensible of was a distant ringing of bells carried there by a light southern breeze.

"How will this ringing of bells be able to awaken the dead forest?"

thought Abbot Hans. For now that he stood amid the winter darkness, he thought that it was far more impossible that a flower garden might arise here than it had seemed to him previously.

But when the bells had been ringing a few moments, a sudden dawn went through the forest. Immediately after, it was just as dark again, but then the light returned. It came on as a luminous haze among the dark trees. And it gained enough for the darkness to pass into a faint daybreak.

Then Abbot Hans saw that the snow was disappearing from the ground, as if someone had pulled back a rug, and that the earth was beginning to turn green. The ferns poked up their shoots, rolled up like bishop's crosiers. The heather growing on the stony slope and the bog myrtle rooted in the moss had suddenly clothed themselves in new green. The tufts of moss swelled and rose up, and spring flowers shot up with swelling buds that already had a tinge of color.

Abbot Hans's heart was beating hard when he saw these first signs that the forest was beginning to awaken. "Then will an old man like me get to see such a marvel?" he thought, with tears pressing against his eyes.

Sometimes it became so dim that he feared that the night darkness would prevail once more.

But soon a new wave of light came bursting forth. It brought with it the murmur of brooks and the rush of cataracts released. Then the leaves burst out on the hardwood trees as swiftly as if a swarm of green butterflies had come flying and flocked on the branches. And it was not just trees and plants that awakened. The crossbills began to hop on the branches. The woodpeckers hammered against the tree trunks so that wood chips went flying about. A procession of starlings heading upcountry swooped down into the top of a fir tree to rest. They were splendid starlings. The top of each little feather shone bright red, and when the birds stirred they glittered like gemstones.

Again it darkened for a while, but soon came a new wave of light. A strong, warm south wind blew, sowing out over the forest meadow all the little seeds from southern lands that had been brought to this country by birds and ships and winds, which would not grow elsewhere due to the severity of the winter, and they took root and sprouted in the same instant that they reached the ground.

When the next wave of light came rushing in, the blueberries and cowberries blossomed. Graylag geese and cranes called up in the sky, and chaffinches built nests, and the young squirrels began to play on the tree branches.

Everything now began to go so fast that Abbot Hans did not have time to consider what an extremely great marvel was happening. He only had time to use his eyes and ears. The next wave of light that came rushing brought with it the scent of newly plowed fields. Far off, shepherd girls were heard calling the cows and little sheep bells were tinkling. Firs and pines were decked so thick with little red cones that the trees shone like mantles of purple. The junipers grew berries that changed color each moment. And the wildflowers decked the ground so that it turned white and blue and yellow.

Abbot Hans bent down to the ground and picked a wild strawberry flower. As he straightened himself up the berry ripened. The fox came forth from her den with a large litter of black-legged cubs. She went up to the robber's moll and scratched at her skirt, and the robber's moll bent down over her and praised her cubs. The great horned owl that just now had begun night hunting, turned home, frightened by the light, sought out its cleft, and settled down to sleep. The cuckoo called, and his hen sneaked 'round the nests of smaller birds with its egg in its mouth.

The moll's youngsters gave off chirping screams of joy. They ate their fill of the wild berries hanging, as big as pine cones, on the bushes. One of them played with a flock of wild hares, another ran races with young crows that had hopped from the nest before their wings were ready, a third picked up the viper from the ground and wrapped it around his neck and arm. The robber chief stood out on the moss eating cloudberries. When he looked up, a large, black beast was walking alongside him. The robber chief broke off a willow twig and hit the bear on the nose. "You keep your distance!" he said. "This is my turf." Then the bear stood aside and lumbered off in another direction.

New waves of warmth and light washed over them, and now they brought with them quacking ducks from the forest tarn. Yellow pollen from the rye fields swarmed through the air. Butterflies arrived, so big that they looked like flying lilies. The beehive in a hollow oak was already so full of honey that it was dripping down the trunk. Now also those flowers began to blossom that had grown out of seeds from foreign lands. The prettiest roses climbed up the rock face in a race with the blackberry. Out of the forest meadow sprang flowers as big as a person's face. Abbot Hans thought about the flower that he had to pick for Bishop Absalon, but still he hesitated in picking it. One flower grew up lovelier than the next, and he wanted to choose the prettiest of all for him.

Wave after wave came, and now the air was so shot with light that it glittered. All the delight and splendor and happiness of summer smiled around Abbot Hans. He thought that the earth could not bring greater joy than that which was welling up around him, and he said to himself, "Now I don't know what sort of splendor the next wave that comes can bring with it."

But the light continued to come pouring in, and now it seemed to Abbot Hans that it brought with it something from an infinite distance. He felt that celestial air surrounded him and, trembling, he began to expect that since the delights of the earth had now arrived, then the delights of heaven were close at hand.

Abbot Hans noticed that everything became quiet: the birds were silent, the fox cubs played no more, and the flowers ceased growing. The bliss that was drawing near was such that the heart would stop, the eye wept without the mind knowing, the soul longed to be able to fly away into the everlasting. From far off, faint harp tones were heard, and celestial song reached them as a rustling whisper.

Abbot Hans clasped his hands together and sank to his knees. His face was bright with bliss. Never had he expected that it should be granted him already in this life to taste the joy of heaven and hear angels singing Christmas carols.

But beside Abbot Hans stood the lay brother who had accompanied him. There were dark thoughts going through his head. "It cannot be a true miracle, this, which is appearing to evil malefactors," he thought. "This cannot have come from God, but originates in evil. It has been sent here through the devil's malicious cunning. It's the might of the wicked enemy, bewitching us and compelling us to see that which does not exist."

In the distance could be heard angel harps sounding and angel song resounding, but the lay brother thought that it was infernal spirits drawing near. "They wish to entice and seduce us," he sighed, "we'll never get out of this in one piece. We'll be enchanted and sold to the infernal pit."

The heavenly host was now so close that Abbot Hans glimpsed bright figures through the tree trunks. And the lay brother saw the same as he did, but he was only thinking of how wicked the devil was to practice these arts during the night when our Savior was born. For this was merely to bewitch the miserable humans all the more certainly.

All this while the birds had fluttered about Abbot Hans's head, and he had been able to take them in his hands. Of the lay brother, on the other hand, the animals had been afraid: no bird had settled on his shoulder, no serpent had played at his feet. But then there was a little stock dove.

When she noticed the angels approaching, she plucked up her courage, flew down onto the lay brother's shoulder, and placed her head against his cheek. Then it seemed to him that the evil enemy came quite close to him in order to tempt and entice him. He struck after the dove with his hand, shouting in so loud a voice that it thundered through the forest, "You go to hell, where you come from!"

Just then the angels were so close that Abbot Hans felt the fanning of their large wings, and he bowed right down to the ground to greet them. But when the lay brother's words rang out, their singing was abruptly broken off, and the holy guests turned to flee. And the light fled, too, as did the mild warmth, in unspeakable horror at the cold and the darkness in a human heart. The night sank down over the earth like a cover, the cold came, the plants on the ground shriveled up, the animals darted off, the rush of cataracts ceased, and the leaves fell from the trees, rustling like rain.

Abbot Hans felt his heart, which had just been swelling with bliss, now contract in insufferable pain. "Never," he thought, "can I survive this, that the angels of heaven were this close to me and were driven away, that they were about to sing Christmas carols for me and were put to flight."

In the same instant he remembered the flower that he had promised Bishop Absalon, and he bent down to grope among the moss and leaves to try to pick it now at the very last moment. But he felt the ground freeze under his fingers, and the white snow came drifting back over the ground.

Then his heart gave him even greater torment. He couldn't straighten up, but fell to the ground and remained there.

When the robber folk and the lay brother had groped their way in the deep darkness back to the robber's den, they found Abbot Hans missing. They took brands from the fire and went out to look for him, and they found him lying dead on the snow cover.

And the lay brother began to weep and wail. He understood that it was he who had killed Abbot Hans, by having snatched from him the cup of joy that he had so longed to empty.

When Abbot Hans had been taken down to Öved, those who took care of the dead man saw that his right hand was clenched fast about something that he must have grasped as he was dying. When they finally got it opened, they found that what he held firmly with such strength was a couple of white tubers that he had pulled up from the moss and leaves. And when the lay brother who had accompanied Abbot Hans saw these tubers, he took them and put them in the ground in Abbot Hans's garden.

He tended them all year long, expecting that a flower should come up from them, but he waited in vain during spring and summer and fall alike. When finally winter had come and all the leaves and flowers were dead, he gave up paying attention to them.

But when Christmas Eve came, he was reminded so powerfully of Abbot Hans that he went into the garden to think about him. And lo, when he walked past the place where he had put down the bare tubers, he saw that out of them had grown up luxuriant, green stems supporting beautiful flowers with silver-white petals!

He summoned all the monks of Öved, and when they saw that this plant blossomed on Christmas Eve when all other plants were dead, they understood that it really was picked by Abbot Hans in the Christmas pleasure-garden in Göinge Forest. The lay brother asked the monks for permission to bring some of the flowers to Bishop Absalon.

When the lay brother was admitted to Bishop Absalon's presence, he handed him the flowers, saying, "Abbot Hans sends you these. They are the flowers that he promised to pick for you from the Christmas pleasure-garden in Göinge Forest."

When Bishop Absalon saw the flowers that had arisen from the ground in the dark of winter and heard his words, he turned quite as pale as if he had met a dead man. He sat silently a moment, and then he said, "Abbot Hans has kept his word well, so I shall also keep mine." And he had a letter of protection drawn up for the wild robber who had been outlawed to the forest ever since his youth.

He handed the letter to the lay brother, and the latter set out up to the forest and found his way to the robber's den. When he entered there on Christmas Day, the robber approached him with a raised ax.

"I'll cut you monks down, every last one!" he said. "It's got to be your fault that Göinge Forest hasn't decked itself in Christmas attire tonight."

"It's my fault alone," said the lay brother, "and I'll gladly die for it, but first I must bring you a message from Abbot Hans." And he brought forth the bishop's letter and spoke to the man about his being granted protection. "Henceforth you and your children shall play in the Christmas straw and celebrate Christmas among other humans, just as Abbot Hans wished," he said.

Then the robber chief stood pallid and speechless, but the robber's moll said in his name, "Abbot Hans has kept his word well, so the robber chief shall also keep his."

When the robber and his wife went away from the robber's den, the lay brother moved in, living there alone in the woods in constant prayer that his hardness of heart might be forgiven him.

But Göinge Forest has never since celebrated the hour of our Savior's birth, and of all its splendor only the plant that Abbot Hans picked remains alive. It has been called the *Christmas rose*, and every year it sends its white flowers and green stems up out of the soil at Christmastime, as if it has never been able to forget that it once has grown in the great Christmas pleasure-garden.

A Farm Owner's
Christmas Eve

« Erään talollisen jouluaatto »

FRANS EEMIL SILLANPÄÄ

FINLAND 1924

*Finnish novelist Frans Eemil Sillanpää (1888–1964) received the
Nobel Prize in literature in 1939. Sillanpää gained international
recognition with the naturalistic novel from the bloody Finnish
civil war of 1918,* Hurskas kurjuus *(1919;* Meek Heritage*). His
following novels are characterized by a more poetic mood. They
are set in the countryside, and the narrative, often focusing on
love and sexuality as the ruling forces of human life, is framed by
sensitive descriptions of nature.*

VISTI-MINA, AN ELDERLY WIDOW AND MISTRESS
and owner of the freehold farm Visti, assessed at 0.003 of a holding, had been awakened by the cat's mewing, and in letting it out she
noticed that it was rather cold in the room; even without looking she
could tell that the water was frozen in the water cask by the door. And
how might the poor little girl be doing, then? But she was still sleeping
soundly in the middle of the bed under half the quilt. It had been necessary to move her sleeping space farther down, away from the right side of
the bedstead. If Mina had her lying right alongside her, then she would
kick all night against Mina's sensitive midriff. She is Ida's daughter, Mina
is the child's maternal grandmother. God only knows where Ida herself
is gadding about . . .

These dry sticks and twigs up in the chimney vault were really true
treasures on a winter's morning; they were almost like edible delicacies.
When you put them on the hearth under the trivet, they caught fire at
once, and with their help you could then also get the damp firewood smol-
dering. And the coffee simmered, its fragrance filling the room, which

was warmed bit by bit. The windowpanes, which just now were coated with a thick crust of ice, were already beginning to thaw on their uppermost edges; while the coffee was settling Mina could peer through the thawed-out spots to the yard, where a reddish-yellow December morning had just dawned. From the farms the smoke was rising straight up to the sky, and she thought she heard the crunch of sleigh runners. Now look how long I've slept.—Well, and then it's Christmas Eve, too, by golly!—Up with you in a hurry, lass!

From under the covers two lively little eyes were opened and aimed at the room and at Mina, whose familiar features quickly dispelled the memory of the tangled splendors of the child's dreams. The blazing fire in the fireplace, the frozen windowpanes, and the confidently puttering old woman gave the child's mind full compensation, auguring a long, clear day with thousands of adventures.

The woman shuffled over to the bed and gave the child a drop of coffee from her own cup while chattering incessantly, ". . . and I didn't notice that I'd slept half the day, and then it's Christmas Eve at that, and we haven't got hold of anything for Christmas. Now get dressed, and then we'll go and find out if we can get a little pork or some other vittles at Tiura . . ." These last words had a cautionary tone.

This announcement was most welcome to Saima, the little girl. While she was putting on her warm rags she chattered just like the old woman, trying to persuade herself that at Christmas you needed no more than any other day. And after a little pause the girl closed her monologue with, "And then the farm is, of course, freehold."

There had really been cause to take care what you said in the girl's presence: she repeated your every word just like a phonograph. Not because of that—it wasn't really dangerous, but—now, for instance, this bragging about the farm being freehold. Imagine if she should blab it out at Tiura. There was no reason to remind her of it on the day before Christmas—even though, it might well occur to her otherwise to say it, if anyone were at all too uppity toward her. There's nobody who's going to come and order me about in my own house and on my own property; I'll go to my grave just as well from it as from any other larger farm.

This freehold thing was a bit of a double-edged affair for Mina. Sometimes she almost regretted having bought the place, and other times it made her breast swell with pride and instilled pithy words in her in case anyone by force of habit reminded her of their charity. Also, Mina had previously been fairly well off. She lived on the outskirts of town in her cottage, which was as old and rotten as any hovel in a picture book. Past her cottage ran the road to the town's outlying common lands, and there she met farmers and their hands both winter and summer and had a chance to offer them a cup of coffee. And even the master of Tiura, a rather stingy old codger, had always come with a load of firewood at Christmas, "so that the coffee will be brewed next year, too." And the farm wives used to stick something edible in her bag. So there was no reason for Mina to complain about her earlier existence.

Since then conditions had changed little by little. Ida came home with this girl when she had been divorced from her husband and—so they claimed, although Mina knew nothing, but they said so—had begun loose living; but Mina did know that her husband was a drunkard and turned vicious in his cups. In any case, she couldn't refuse to take the child in when Ida asked her, even paying a little for her in the beginning. But the farmers were of another opinion. All needs and wants were felt more, now, so Mina was sometimes obliged to come right out and ask for a pinch of flour or a little salt when Ida had not written. Then one of the farm wives had hinted that it really didn't pay to support that kind of Bolshevik spawn—why, she could betake herself to the land of ideals in the east—that would surely suit her better. Mina had taken this much amiss and replied by asking who it was that during this spring strike had gone and helped out with the milking and therefore had to put up with the strikers' insults on the way home, and, by the way, what was it really like the time the Whites assaulted the town . . . ?

"I remember it well, and for my own part I've had to pay for it, but who was it over in Riitiala who set the Reds on the farmers here in town? It was Ida herself and her sweetheart, and she's now left to become one of them . . ."

"Good day to you, and don't think I'd lend you a hand again," screamed Mina and went off, and when she was out on the highway her head and face muscles still had difficulty gaining composure, continuing to jerk and twitch angrily.

That freehold thing originated with this incident, even though Mina's cottage was not situated on the farm in question. But when in the very same week Ida came on a visit to Mina and Saima and had melted their hearts with large, welcoming gifts, Mina told her about the farm wife's abuse. And Ida always had a ready answer—it was only a shame that the old cow couldn't hear her herself. Then this freehold thing cropped up, too—or rather Mina had already seen and heard that larger holdings could become freehold, but she had never believed that it would apply to someone like her. Ida simply laughed at her, saying that the state would probably put up the purchase price, and afterwards Mother could pay bit by bit according to means and opportunity—by the way, Ida would probably pay herself when the time came. Not because there was any danger now of eviction, but you could get a higher price for the cottage later on.

"Oh, Lord! Do I really have to sell it?"

"No, just listen"—and Ida explained what she meant.

Uh-huh, Mina certainly understood that—when she's dead, Ida will inherit. But she uttered with some ardor in her voice, "Remember that it's Saima who's going to inherit from me if there's anything left, Saima's going to inherit from me if I don't end up in the poorhouse before I die."

And so it came to pass that when the small holdings under Tiura estate could be bought according to the new law, Visti-Mina's papers were also among the applications. And the estate owner had nothing particular against it, either—what good would that do, anyway, in such a clear case? Over at the corner of the fence he had tried to move the boundary a little, but the master of Hirvo, who was chairman of the board of tenants, was of the opinion that there was no use bothering about such trifles—after all, that bit of land was not a piece of serge that could be measured out by the centimeter. Afterwards, the whole company, even the master of the estate, had coffee at her place. But after that day he has not visited her on his own initiative, and the usual Christmas firewood failed to show up.

Saima had been with Mina at Huikku the time that the farm woman called her a Bolshevik spawn, and she had also listened to Ida's and Mina's conversations about the freehold thing. So it was not so strange that the girl was interested in the affair.

Since outsiders had now dwelled so much upon this freehold thing, she had not really wanted to admit even to herself the small and almost imperceptible changes that went with it. Thus, for instance the master of Tiura had indeed been just as polite as before when Mina after insistent importunity once offered him a cup of coffee, but when he had drunk his coffee he took out a one-mark coin and put it on a corner of the table—and the Christmas firewood never showed up, either. Close to her cottage there was a forest belonging to Tuomola, and Mina had now without special permission collected a little fuel that was lying on the ground there—she had taken it with a private fear of the consequences. Now that it was getting on toward Christmas she had several times also written a letter to Ida, but there was no answer, and this first Christmas as a freeholder was thus threatening to become a rather lean one for the old woman and the little girl.

Christmas Eve morning nevertheless seemed promising; the refreshing winter weather, the village with its rising smoke, and the well-packed road filled the spirits of the two wanderers with the best Christmas cheer. Their morning coffee warmed their bellies, and they were thinking that soon they would be sitting in the kitchen of the first farm—maybe they would get more coffee with a good, fresh roll there. Nobody can resist the magic of Christmas Eve.

The first farm was none other than Tuomola. It was warm and spacious there, and a peculiar fragrance was noticeable, which was not to be found in their own cottage. It came from the Christmas ham, which the housewife was just about to turn.

Now at this farm Mina had never succeeded in getting anything that was worth talking about; it always used to be that the woman happened not to have anything. "I'm sure I'd open a meat shop if I had meat left over," the housewife had once assured Mina when she asked her for meat. But now there was that firewood. . . . Mina did not think she could pass the farm by without mentioning it.

"I would indeed like to buy a little meat from the missus, but my real errand now is more for the master of the house."

"Well, well. So Mina suffers from desires of the flesh in her old age.— There is certainly meat in the house, if it only would roast properly.—I see, desires of the flesh, indeed . . ."

With this she called the maid and admonished her children. It was quite apparent that for her sake Mina and Saima could sit there right to Saint Stephen's Day.

But then the master entered, as if in a bit of a hurry and with the familiar wrinkled brow. He was talking about firing up the Christmas sauna, which he feared that all this roasting and baking would delay. He did not take any notice of the pair on the bench, either, until Mina said, "I'd like to talk to the master about a little firewood from the woods behind my house, but does the master have time to think about this now on Christmas Eve?"

The master looked at Mina a little from the side—he heard better in one ear—but said nothing right away. Mina was about to repeat her words when his wife burst out with "Why, that firewood has long since been in your cottage, so now you can talk about the ashes."

"Yes, what have you been thinking, anyway—that you've started running riot in our forest?"

"You see, good sir, it went like this, that that firewood from Tiura ran out before he came with more, and then one day I said to Saima . . ."

"Sure, sure, Mina can certainly always talk, but it's still not right for one freeholder to take from another's forest, even if it's right behind the house; there are penalties for that sort of thing."

"Oh, dear sir, people make such a fuss about my being a freeholder— it's not something I thought up myself, but I've said that Saima is going to inherit from me if there's anything left to inherit, and then I thought that maybe later on she could get a little more for the cottage . . ." Mina wept.

And so it went at that farm. They did come to an agreement about the firewood; for the exacting housewife Mina would spin a large batch of cowhair, together with coming to sweep the farmyard in the spring. She could indeed sell some meat, why not, fifteen marks a kilo. Good Lord, no, Mina owned no such sum. Well then, look here—the housewife was well acquainted with Mina's affairs—she gave them each a bite of ham and a piece of potato pancake to eat. Blushing and bashful they devoured their booty and thereupon continued their tour.

Now they turned into Tiura, their "own farm."

There they were already farther along with Christmas. The farmhand came in with an enormous Christmas tree, and the housewife and children followed him into the drawing room, only the cook staying out with Mina and Saima.

The cook inquired after Ida, and Mina instinctively spoke to her in just as obliging a tone as if she were talking to the housewife. Or as if the housewife had been listening from behind the door. She happened, moreover, to criticize her own child a bit, yet the housewife did not show herself. Just look, she's staying away, thought Mina and also said something of the kind.

"She certainly doesn't stay away from you, but maybe she's a bit annoyed with you."

"I see, she's annoyed—I see—she's annoyed."

When the housewife returned to the kitchen a little later, she stood alongside the cook and watched Mina and Saima leaving the farm, and the cook described how subtly she had dismissed the uninvited Christmas guests. The housewife then went back to the drawing room, and on the farm the real Christmas spirit spread all the more. The milkmaid came in and announced that the sick cow had already begun to eat and chew its cud. The master of the house was just then off driving the veterinarian home.

Even Mina and Saima felt the Christmas spirit spreading, as they stood there on the highway. The weather had become slightly overcast since morning; here in the middle of town you thought you smelled the scent of Christmas preparations even out on the road. Eager and hopeful, Saima tried to guess Mina's intentions. Just then, however, Mina felt somewhat encumbered by the girl's presence—if she had been alone, she would have wandered off to Peltoniemi after these unfriendly receptions and would have talked aloud to herself the whole time. But if she now said as much as one word, Saima would have joined in the conversation at once with her childishly trusting remarks or added her own reflections to Mina's protest.

If Ida could see them now . . . she who—though God knows where—was rolling in plenty.

As Mina was now thinking about Ida and regarded Saima, it seemed to her that the child also stood on her side against her own mother. She muttered something to herself, and when Saima asked what she said Mina growled, "Nothing that concerns you," and walked on.

Saima guessed that they were going to Peltoniemi, which Mina had always talked about, and whose mistress she had always praised. It was rather a long way there, but for Saima the main thing was that they were not going home yet.

So there lay Peltoniemi, a remotely situated farmstead with dark-trodden paths to stable and barn, with nice and cozy buildings in which there prevailed an atmosphere distinctive to this farm—an atmosphere of prosperity and homey disorder both in parlor and bakehouse. Mina had known the wife ever since the old days. She had always been a kind-hearted person; she would pour their cups brimful of good coffee, and slice the white bread as thick as a hand. Sometimes she would even ask Mina to go and take something, and she would chat and laugh and discuss town gossip with her exactly as with an equal. And whenever Mina praised her former beauty, she would break into a broad laugh that already sounded a bit hollow.

However, this time she was not so fortunate, in that the mistress was sick in bed. And incidentally it was already a little too late on Christmas Eve for visits of this sort. It was as if the festive hour were approaching with ever increasing haste. Everyone on the farm was preparing for the Christmas sauna.

Mina was admitted to the bedroom of the housewife, who between sighs and moans tried to revive her former friendship with Mina. But everything still got a bit confused. At first she said to the maid that Mina should have some yeast bread, but as her pains worsened she failed to say how many loaves it should be. When the pains again let up she asked about something quite unimportant from town, but was hardly able to listen to Mina's eager answer. The conversation stalled hopelessly. Mina looked hesitantly at the invalid, who asked, "Have you already bathed? I do believe the sauna is ready . . . just go in and tell Mari that she should give you and Saima something to eat . . . oh, dear."

Mina and Saima bathed in Peltoniemi's sauna, after which they were amply treated to Christmas fare, and at length they set out for home. The housewife had fallen asleep, so they could not even say goodbye to her. Before leaving, Mina reminded the maid about the yeast bread, and the maid gave her . . . *one* loaf. That is how things go when a farm is without its mistress.

One paltry loaf of yeast bread was the only booty the poor pair brought with them as they slowly toddled home in the evening twilight. The cold worsened, and the crunch of the snow beneath their soles reminded Mina that her room was cold and the firewood damp. Saima marched on bravely, trying now and then to prattle about the delicacies she had eaten on the tour, but Mina almost shouted that there was not much to be said for what was already eaten, and how would Christmas go now, when they had nothing at home but herring and potatoes and this paltry yeast bread?

"Why do we need more at Christmas than on other days?" Saima said, repeating Mina's own words.

"Hmm, well, it may be that we don't, but your mother could still care enough about her child to send something for Christmas Eve, at least— she's the one who's always screaming about bourgeois wickedness—then I wouldn't need to beg from them and disgrace myself as a farm owner."

"Well, they obviously haven't given you very much."

The voice came from the door of the woodshed, where they could make out the form of a woman, who on closer examination turned out to be Ida. Mina played offended, pretending not to see how the little one ran up to her mother. But Mina had nevertheless concluded from Ida's first words that she had not come empty-handed this time, either. Whenever she finally came home she usually had a bundle full of the most incredible welcoming gifts, her bragging mouth full of big words.

There was now no lack of food nor, God have mercy, of drink, either, for Ida had brought a bottle with enough of the strong stuff to warm up Mina's old blood. Mina had tears in her eyes as she explained for her daughter that Christmas was still common to all, that there was not any special bourgeois Christmas—even if imperfect people now and then hardened their hearts.

Saima listened in wonder to their conversation while she played with the new, unusually splendid doll that Ida had brought with her.

At the Bottom of the Snow Ocean

« *Paa Bunden af Snehavet* »

GUNNAR GUNNARSSON

ICELAND 1929

The Icelandic writer Gunnar Gunnarsson (1889–1975) lived in Denmark from 1907 to 1939 and wrote in Danish during this period. His first literary success was the four-volume novel Borgslægtens Historie *(1912–14; Guest the One-Eyed), a monumental vision of his native country, its people, history, and nature, and the first Icelandic book to be made into a movie.*

LIKE A ROARING SURF THE BITTER BREATH OF THE Arctic Ocean, whose moisture has glistened into ice, stands inshore toward the valley. Like angry spray-whipped waters it inundates the stone-frozen terrain, where the huddled-up, downy-legged grouse lets itself be snowed over, in order to save its life in its snow hollow by the warmth of its own blood. Like frenzied forces of nature in unbridled outbreak, the frothing snow howls around every stone, every hill, every house, every crag in the landscape.

Tonight there is no mercy. Everything that is out and about must die.

The little cots in Grundarkot stand quivering under the hideous grip of the storm. Like a monster that is out to waste life, it squalls its senseless song outside the windows. The children have crawled from their bed over into their mother's, lying squeezed up against her. A heavy silence prevails in the little room with a stove. Only once has little Guðny whispered out into the dark, "God is angry. . . . " Nobody has answered her. Her mother has her own things to think and worry about. And Árni, who is nine years old, four whole years older than his sister, has thought to himself that it probably wasn't God raging out there. But he contented himself with thinking it. Guðny, the mother, says, "Go to sleep, good children . . ."

Then there is silence again in the stove room. But there is no sleeping.

On such a night there is no sleeping many places on Héðinsfjord—this fjord lying open to the north, open to the evil spirits of winter—this fjord, which rocks the blood of the midnight sun on its waves at midsummer. The solstitial storm raging out there—a storm that can come a little earlier, a little later, but never fails to come—comes rushing over naked, frightened hearts under cottage roofs, comes rushing over minds stretched to the breaking point.

Through the bitter experience of centuries it is implanted into the race that on such a night something is happening. Evil forces are afoot; the country's harsh gods are holding a sacrificial feast. Tomorrow—or perhaps in a week, perhaps not for a fortnight—it will become apparent who is affected this time, and how severely. One thing is inevitable: something evil will happen. A terror as yet unknown will grow from this night devoid of mercy. This knowledge lies hidden in everyone's blood—passed down, continually revived, ineradicable. If someone speaks of a housemate who is absent, it usually occurs in a lighthearted tone—but with ominous pauses. Perhaps there is weeping only in the event that the man comes home safe and sound. Then a tear may fall. But provided the danger is obvious, the absent one is spoken of reluctantly. Even little Guðny has this in her blood—it was only later in the night that she asks, "Mama—do you think Papa has reached land—before the storm?"

And then she breaks into tears.

What can Guðny, the mother, answer her? She gives no answer. She is content to dry her daughter's tears in the dark, a child's profuse tears. And to kiss her. It is Árni, now the man of the house, who says, "They must have had an awfully good wind towards the fjord, just before the storm broke out!—So if they had got out in good time . . ."

Árni here voices his mother's only hope: that the boat in which her husband sailed might have been out of Héðinsfjord and past the headland before it started blowing in earnest. In that case it has probably made land somewhere in Siglufjord.

"I dare say you'll make a good sailor, Árni," his mother says in order to say something after all, stroking his hair—how she recognized the stubborn cowlick over his forehead!

"I'll sail them to pieces, just like Papa does!" an animated Árni brags. "I'll. . . . It was Papa, the time they caught the big flounder, who thought of cutting the heads off all the codfish, so that the enormous fish could come on board without sinking the boat. Papa always finds a way! It was also Papa, the time the old boat was about to slip apart out in the middle of the fjord, who cast a rope down around the keel and hauled taut!"

"But the best was still the time that Papa rescued the five horses from an avalanche!" little Guðny bursts in.

"Is that so!" Árni scoffs in older-brotherly tone. "The best I'd say was the time he got himself out of the avalanche, little blockhead!"

"Yeah—but I forgot all about that," little Guðny admits complaisantly.

"Papa has probably made it to land this evening, too!" Árni finally dares to predict—still, something in his voice contradicts the certainty of his words.

Incidentally, his mother thought so, too. Høskuld was a man without fear. And a man without fear has ten expedients where others have one—or none. Høskuld had once tumbled down into a gorge in the snow and dark of night and come away unharmed. Another time he had twice one frosty night gone into the water up to his neck, only to make his escape toward early morning into a sheepcote, where he kept warm by wedging himself between the ruminating animals. He had, however, been worse off the night that, practically without clothes on his body, he had been overtaken by a snowstorm and had roamed about astray until daylight broke—his cap had been sitting like a clump of ice in his hair, so it all had to be cut off. . . . His shirt had iced up on the inside. But he had been smeared in syrup. And had pulled through. Høskuld seemed immortal. But still—fearless folk can run into bad luck, too. Guðny carried a hard-earned knowledge in her blood about the conditions for all life here in the most rugged region in the country. She hoped. But she was prepared.

Her greatest fear stemmed from Høskuld's unusual eagerness just this once to get off together with the other farmers from Héðinsfjord—to fetch flour, he had said. Perhaps he had also thought a little about it being only twelve days until Christmas—and that this might be the last opportunity. However, he had not spoken about it. Nor had Guðny spoken about it, either. Nor the children, either. It was the thought of this travel haste of his that most disquieted Guðny. It has been seen before that people ran breathless after death. Leaped with blind zeal into an open grave!

Christmas was being thought about at Grundarkot, even if so far it was not talked about. Little Guðny, still young and loose-mouthed, whispered to her mother toward early morning, "So today there's only eleven days 'til Christmas—isn't there, Mama?"

She received no answer.

It had become so calm out there. So strangely calm. So unreasonably calm! . . . The way the storm had set to, it was beyond comprehension that it could be over already. Guðny listens. . . . She cannot hear anything. But it's as if she senses a storm far off. It's calm out there. But the calm won't sink into her. When the cow under the stove room floor gently reminds her that it's time for morning feeding and therefore must be six o'clock, Guðny says to the children as she gets out of bed, "Just crawl together and try to fall asleep, good children. As calm as the weather has become, maybe we'll get to see Papa before evening, already."

Guðny gets dressed as she usually does, without lighting a lamp. That she knows her few clothes well and knows where to find them means that she doesn't drain the lamp that long. When she is dressed she gropes for the train-oil lamp. And with lamp in hand she creeps down the stove room stairs and out along the passageways to the cookhouse, where ash-covered embers preserve the humble hearth's extinct fire. She lights the lamp, covers the embers again, gives herself plenty of time to feed the cow and the sheep—all the while thinking of Høskuld.

Ten years ago they took over Grundarkot as a derelict farm, she and Høskuld—newlyweds. Høskuld built up every bit of wall in these buildings with his own hands, thick and cozy walls, four to six feet thick—built them up from choice flat stones and well-dried chunks of turf. Likewise, every piece of timber, and most of it from imperishable driftwood, he fitted himself, with saw and ax, nailed together and rigged—rafters, beams, posts—all of the heaviest and most solid quality. Every smallest thing in this farm is Høskuld's work—from the cow's stall under the stove room floor to the bedsteads. Even to the table flap under the window. The horn spoons they eat with, the wooden buckets for milk and water—these, too, are his handiwork. That is why it's dreadful not having him around the house. He belongs here. They cannot do without him.

With a shudder in her heart Guðny recalls how the sifting snow had obliterated him as he was going toward the fjord yesterday morning. Wiped him out! She had stood looking at him—anxious as always whenever he left home. And as so often, often before, at a loss to understand the apparent ease with which his legs carried him away from their farm. She had had to dry her eyes, and not just from tears. The snow had wiped him out.

But it seemed inconceivable that he would never again return to their little place, where he had arranged everything so well, where he had seen to it that through cozy passageways you could get to even the hay barns and sheep houses, where every tiniest thing was well thought out and well executed. Even the brook, which previously flowed a fair distance off, was with ingenuity and industry given a new course, so that it now fell right past the buildings. And not only that—he had built a hut over it, so that you didn't need to shovel snow and chop ice every time you had to fetch water in the wintertime. And even this little wellhouse was connected by a passageway to the rest of the farm. When on a calm day—like today—you went past this passage, you could hear the water gurgling in there, alive and alert—gurgling and trilling softly in the little waterfall that Høskuld had made so that it was easier to fill a pail. Ah—Høskuld. . . . Everything here was painstakingly arranged. And well arranged. How like him, that yesterday morning he had been so sorry about not having yet brought the peat bricks indoors. As if it were any matter for her to fetch the little bit she needed during his absence the ten steps from the stack! This morning it would indeed have been nice if she had not had to go outside to fetch peat—that would probably take some deep digging! But for the time being the children could get warm milk from the cow. If they hadn't fallen asleep—the poor little tykes. In that case she wouldn't wake them up.

No—the children weren't asleep. Two pairs of shining eyes met the red glare of the train-oil lamp as their mother shined it across the bed. And it was with an exceedingly alert voice that Árni asked, "Why isn't there any dawn at all today, Mama?"

Guðny halted. Already several times this morning she had felt a strange uneasiness flooding over her—a shivering through her body produced by this extraordinary calm. A calm that with a suffocating chokehold seemed to want to arrest her breathing. But it was for only an instant—she stood uncertain, listening—then she calmly said, "Now Mama's going to go out and see about getting the snow brushed from the windows, good children!"

Árni was down on the floor in an instant. "I'll take care of that, Mama . . ."

He intended to get a good deal more done in the course of the day—fetch peat, carry water to the cow and the sheep, muck out! . . . He ran on about these and other contemplated feats while he was getting dressed, between taking long gulps from the bowl of warm, still-frothy cow's milk.

Mother would surely help fetch the peat—although for the meanwhile the two got no farther than the farmyard door. It opened out and couldn't be budged.

There must have come a snowdrift up against it—even right over it! Mother and son laughed at these hardships. For there was fortunately another outside door—the door to the sheep house. And it opened in! However—when they got it open, they stood there, too, before a wall of snow. Then they laughed even more. They were snowed in! . . . Árni was already looking forward to how much they now had to tell his father. They thought it was a priceless situation, that they were shut in like this by snowdrifts as tall as a man. What a storm there must have been!

"There's nothing else to do—I'll have to crawl out through the smoke hole!" Árni laughed.

But how to get up there?

First they got hold of a long pikestaff. They wanted to try boring a hole in the drift outside the sheep house door to measure how thick it was.

For a long time they stood poking in every direction, even at an upward slant, but the drift seemed to be thicker than they had reckoned—it seemed to be very thick, indeed. Not even when they peeked down the holes the pikestaff had made could they see the faintest glimmer. Guðny gradually began to reach her own conclusions.

But Árni was still carefree and cheerful. They tackled the farmyard door afresh. Guðny pushed it off its hinges. But the drift was not to be penetrated here, either. Guðny found a shovel and all of a sudden started digging—vehemently—outward and upward. . . . Soon the sweat was pouring from her, and her hair hung tousled. Árni held the train-oil lamp up for her—following her with frightened eyes. Guðny just dug away. Throwing large shovelfuls of snow into the little entryway. Suddenly saying angrily, "Stomp the snow down and make some room! Do something, boy!"

Whimpering a little, Árni started tramping the snow down—now and then switching the train-oil lamp from one numb hand into the other. His mother paid him no heed. Just dug.

Meanwhile, her thoughts were busy. And bit by bit she grew calmer. She had several times experienced large drifts that had lain up against a farm's doors and windows. But she had never seen drifts that were so thick that they entirely blocked out the daylight—that from the inside the snow looked like a dark, sparkling wall. She suddenly threw down the shovel and ran into the cook house. . . . No—not even from the smoke hole could be seen as much as the mere hint of a glimmer.

Guðny stood still for a moment in the darkness, trying to get used to the thought that she really was snowed in. That the snow ocean had simply closed down over the little farm. Drowned it! That the storm might still be raging out there—up there above the rooftops. And could continue to rage, for as many as two or ten—or even twenty days!

As long as the storm lasted, nobody would come by the farm—that much was certain. And when the storm subsided and people realized that the farm was lying at the bottom of a snow ocean that perhaps filled the valley—would they then perhaps try digging their way down to it? But even if they tried—would they find it? . . . They could keep on digging all winter in vain, in case the snow had settled really thick and smooth in the bottom of the valley. Looking for a farm through the snow would be like dragging for a sunken ship in the depths of a murky ocean. Well, even more hopeless and more difficult. . . . In other words, her position, and the children's, was as serious as ever it could be—alone at the bottom of this dark, white abyss of death. Alone—and without fuel. The little bit of water in the brook would no doubt also disappear—this she had seen before in harsh, snowy winters. And then when the thaw came, the water would force its way in from all sides—filling the buildings. . . . But since she and the children were in such dire straits, Høskuld must be alive! She suddenly felt convinced of this. For it was part of the race's premonitions and traditions that it wouldn't go hard on everyone at once. . . . Høskuld was alive!

Guðny walked with firm strides to Árni, who was standing motionless where she had left him staring at the darkening snow hole, took the lamp from him and patted him on the head. "I guess we're snowed in, little Árni—and of course that's bad enough," she said with a firm and calm voice. "But now Mama knows that Papa's alive—do you hear that? Mama knows! And we two—we're sure to dig our way up through the drifts, even if we have to dig from now 'til New Year!"

His mother had such a confident voice that Árni at once abandoned his fear and calmly began discussing the matter with her. What should they do with the snow? Stow it away in the storehouse and the other outhouses where there was room. And stomp it down good? Yes, there's no other way. . . . But the fuel? Why, they could cook neither porridge nor meat, could cook nothing, had to eat cold food. . . . And they couldn't bake bread.

"First of all we'll dig a passage out to the peat stack," Guðny decided.

They got down to work on this passage to the peat stack at once. When they had been working on it for four days and had made it twelve yards long, they realized that they must have gone in the wrong direction.

In the meanwhile they had nothing to eat except sour blood sausage and then the drop of milk from the cow. Their spirits sank. Down here in the darkness and the dead silence it was like being in a grave. Mother and son mostly moved about silently in the flickering glow from the smoking train-oil lamp. Árni betrayed his understanding of the situation by being most obliging—not by any other means.

The train-oil lamp burned day and night. If it went out they would be hopelessly doomed to the dark. For the hearth fire had now gone out. Guðny lowered the little flame with trembling heart in the evening— pulling the wick so far down into the oil container that the light was just alive with a little red core in a bowl of blue. This drained the oil supply alarmingly. She hardly dared sleep for fear that the lamp might go out. Just one little accident—and they would be consigned to darkness and futility.

One morning she noticed that the roof of the stove room was beginning to give way. . . . For a moment she sat on the edge of her bed, dying within—abandoning hope. But then she suddenly thought of the ceiling in the storehouse. There were boards there! . . . and Guðny got busy tearing out this ceiling, splitting the boards, making diagonal struts for the sinking roof of the stove room. She didn't dare think how deep they must be buried, since the roof was giving way. That sturdy roof! Nor did she have the time to think about it. . . . Other roofs had to be propped up, too, as time went on. The heavy rafters were bent like taut bows. Slowly, death sank down over the little house. Sank and sank. Cold and icy, and with ominous dripping of the snow that was melting slightly from the warmth emitted by the livestock.

But Guðny did not give up. Høskuld was alive! Of this she remained convinced. And, provided it was in any way possible, she intended to save the children, save the cow, save the sheep—save the little farm and herself. Provided it was humanly possible!

Her terribly desperate situation gave her a resourcefulness that no one previously had known her to possess. From the flimsy brace boards she created an entire wickerwork that increased their bearing capacity— throwing them together in crosses and frames, she was continually on the go and everywhere, keeping watch with an all-seeing eye over every single weak point. She didn't get much sleep. But when she did sleep, she slept like a log.

Christmas Eve arrived. . . . Guðny and the children sat down by the cow—for the sake of company. Creeping up into its byre and against one another. And then sitting there singing Christmas carols. They also sang other hymns—all the hymns they knew. Finally, they sang folksongs and nursery rhymes—giving their hearts a good rest in melancholy and nourishing forbearance. The cow rested safe and satisfied, chewing its cud, laying its muzzle in Guðny's lap, letting itself be petted. And when they fed the sheep tonight they must have forgotten to shut the door, for suddenly the little stall was filled with braying lambs, at first shy, huddling together and tumbling over each other, but later so secure that they examined the cow's crib and sniffed at Guðny's and the children's hands to see if they might smell of bread or something else good to eat.

Guðny and Árni spent every spare moment digging the tunnel upward to the surface of the snow—their stairway to life. They stamped each knee-high step down hard and firm. After that they bored their way farther upwards. They had reached ten steps skywards and were already a fair distance up above the roofs of the farm, but there was still no glimmer of light to be seen through the snow. No tidings of day. The thought crossed Guðny's mind that the world might well have foundered—that all settlement, all land, could be snowed under mountain-high glacial heaps! They might dig and dig as long as they still had something to nourish them—but if they reached up through the layer of snow one day, it would perhaps only be to survey a desolate, a deserted earth where no life could thrive anymore.

She dismissed the thought irascibly. Árni and she continued to work with the shovel—regularly inspecting the weighted-down roofs—repairing the support posts where they threatened to give way—digging every spare minute on the stairway. Bearing up against the horror and just digging, digging.

The water in the brook began to disappear bit by bit. Soon there was no more water than what they could easily collect as it flowed by. They always kept a pail or tub under the sparse waterfall, which was now only dripping. Nothing must be wasted.

It had been a long time since the sheep had had any water to drink; they had to be content with eating snow. Guðny also tried to train the cow to eat snow for its thirst. But they noticed it in the milk, which neither flowed as amply as before, either. The springs were about to dry up—including the springs of courage.

Árni hinted one day at whether they should not try to find the peat stack, after all. But should they look for it to the left or to the right of the passage they had dug in vain? They didn't know which!

On the other hand, they knew that someplace up above their heads there must be light and day and sky as before in the world. For surely there must be! The snow ocean, at whose bottom they were toiling: it must have a surface, mustn't it?

On New Year's Day they broke through. New Year's Day! . . . It was as if they had never known before what a New Year was. It was fresh air like this in your lungs, it was sun and ice-blue sky.

Thirteen steps up the snow had grown brighter. When this dawned on Guðny, she broke down—sitting down and having to hold her heart. It was threatening to burst her breast. But she sat for only a moment.

When her only attack of weakness was over, she put her back into it again, working like a maniac. Working as on the first day—scooping the snow downward and speaking harshly and curtly to Árni, who was toiling to get it away. Suddenly they stood in a flood of light from a clear blue sky—fifteen tall steps led up to a sheet of snow that stretched undulating and finely fluted beneath the sparkling sky-blue heaven, outward and inward, toward a snow-blue heath to one side, and day-blue fjord to the other. Gliding into slippery mountainsides.

Guðny rushed down to get little Guðny, wrapping her in a wool shawl, running with her squeezed in her embrace up the steep, slippery steps—Árni was already standing up there, light flooding about him, staring with a hand above his half-blind eyes toward a darkening line in the landscape over which many men were coming into sight. A whole party!

One of these men suddenly began to run, breaking away from the others and approaching at a heavy trot across the ice-hard sheet of snow. Guðny knew, even before she could recognize him, that it must be Høskuld . . . Høskuld!

Then she burst into tears, squeezing little Guðny to her and weeping in short gasps. Already before Høskuld reached them she had dried her eyes—she stood smiling, just a little bashfully proud, awkwardly meeting his kiss.

Høskuld stopped, staring down into the snow shaft. Staring. He stood with his back turned to them a long time, with eyes blinking. Guðny let him be.

When Árni thought that the silence had now lasted long enough, he said—and his voice faltered, like a bird fleeing before a squall, "We've had an awful lot of hard work, Papa!"

Høskuld put his hand on the boy's head. Then he turned to his wife with downcast eyes.

"We were able to get outdoors for the first time yesterday. I—I came here this morning. . . . We would never have found you, I'm afraid."

Guðny had noticed some round little clumps of ice in his beard. She had seen the same kind of ice clumps there that winter day when Høskuld had driven one of their children on a hand sled to a distant church. In a little coffin. She looked away quickly, wrapping little Guðny tighter into the wool shawl.

Høskuld cleared his throat. "When were you snowed in for good?"

"The night after you left . . ?"

Høskuld strokes his forehead, saying with a faraway stare, "Eighteen days . . ?"

But now the men that Høskuld had brought for help from the village, twelve in number, come closer. The little group becomes agitated. And amid this agitation little Guðny suddenly asks—with her clear, inexperienced child's voice, frail but still full—a voice as if from another world, "Isn't God angry any more, Mama?"

Nobody hears her. Nobody answers her. With large eyes she stares at all these strange grownups talking about things that are of no interest to her.

A Legend

« Legende »

JAKOB SANDE

NORWAY 1935

*A voyage to South America provided the Norwegian writer Jakob
Sande (1906–67) with material for the volume* Fra Sunnfjord
til Rio *(1933; From Sunnfjord to Rio), which contains humorous
sailors' songs as well as grotesque descriptions from Norwegian
village life, features which characterize Sande's subsequent works.*

IT WAS DUSK AND CHRISTMAS EVE. THE SNOW WAS
coming down quietly and steadily from a heavy and wool-gray
sky. The small seaside town huddled up in the snowstorm, little and low
under black slate roofs, two or three solitary streetlamps glowing dimly
through the dusk.

The windows in the church tower stood open. A sooty membrane
lantern hung swinging from the tower beam, casting a faint and flickering
gleam into the darkness. The bell ringer came into view in the window.
Silent and still like a dark shadow, he stood there waiting for the hour
when the holiday should be rung in.

The streets lay empty in the semi-darkness. Only some delayed office worker or laborer hurried homeward, loaded down with baskets and
packages. Outside Mr. Aronsen's shop stood a flock of poor youngsters
gaping wide-eyed at the Christmas finery hanging and glittering behind
shiny plate glass windows. Inside by the counter stood a flock of work-
ers and fishermen finishing their holiday shopping. In the back room
they could dimly see Mr. Aronsen. He sat rotund, leafing through heavy
ledgers with a satisfied smile on his chubby face.

It was then they saw the stranger. Nobody could say where he came
from. It was as if he had been standing in their midst without their
knowing it. Conversation came to a standstill. They moved aside and
made room at the counter, half frightened and half humbled. Not that
the stranger was fearful to look at, or acted self-important. Rather to the

contrary. But there was a power emanating from him that nobody could explain but which everybody felt. Did it come from his eyes? They were irresistibly black, shining out of a pale face encircled by blue-black hair and beard.—Or did it come from the way he behaved? He was somehow master and servant at the same time, strong, but unassuming.

It didn't look as if he would buy anything. He walked right through the astonished crowd and into the back room where Mr. Aronsen was sitting. What did he want from Aronsen? They held their breath and bent their ears. There came his voice, calm and firm, as they had thought it would. He had a foreign accent and was not easy to understand. But this much they discerned, that he requested room and board for the holiday.

Mr. Aronsen looked sharply up from his figures, minutely examining the stranger with his eyes. *His* house was no inn, it came coldly. That was farther up the street, if he wanted to know.

The stranger turned around to go. Then it was as if Aronsen thought of something. He grabbed at his vest pocket with his paw, rooting about until he got his hand on a half-krone piece. "Look here," he said, tossing the coin onto the table.

But then something happened that put these people of modest means in the greatest amazement: the stranger wouldn't accept it. He remained standing a moment, looking at Aronsen, sadly and sorrowfully, then turned around and walked right through the gaping crowd and out. And before they could come to their senses and look for him, he was gone. Nobody knew which way he went.

But the stranger walked on in the snowstorm, slender and hunched down in his jacket collar. Where the little main street turned into flat farmland, he stopped in front of a large white house with surrounding garden. It was the rectory. He stood a moment looking up at a warm light in the second story before going up and knocking on the door. A young girl with a white apron opened up. She looked straight into his black shining eyes, and a weak and strange feeling came over her. She wanted to say something, but it was as if the words withered on her tongue.

The stranger asked for the pastor. With knees shaking, the girl preceded him up the stairs to the second story, where the parson sat preparing his Christmas sermon. A cheerful and friendly voice answered when she knocked. The stranger took his hat under his arm and entered. But the girl remained standing at the door, listening, her heart pounding in her breast.

She heard the strange voice requesting room and board for the holiday and felt that as far as she herself was concerned she could never say no. There came the parson's voice, cheerful and warm. It was good he came *here*, he said. For in *his* parish nobody should go around freezing and starving on Christmas Eve. *He* had seen to that. Now look, he said, down by the shore there was a warm and comfortable shelter just waiting for such poor down-and-out creatures as he. And this evening they would hand out milk soup. Free of charge. Warm, steaming milk soup from whole milk and rice and raisins. Almost, really, a pudding. The parson's voice was warm and trembling with emotion. Besides, he could get a bed at the same place. Twenty-five øre. At that price, the bed was almost free, too. And in case it was a matter of twenty-five øre, then. . . . She heard him rooting through the bentwood box of change on the table.

But suddenly there was silence—as if all living things were holding their breath. The door opened, and the stranger came out with pained features. She caught a glimpse of the pastor standing and looking after him with open mouth. Slowly and unobtrusively the stranger went downstairs, and the door slammed behind him. The girl wanted to run after him and get him to come in again. Invite him into her room and please him a little. She felt as if the pastor had incurred a great sin, but she couldn't lift a finger to make it better. Pale and trembling she stood at the door, sadly holding her hand to her breast.

The stranger stood a moment outside the gate, looking sorrowfully up at the warm, friendly light. Then he turned up his jacket collar and headed for the harbor.

He stopped in front of a low and tumbledown hut, where the faint gleam of a tallow candle glimmered forth through broken glass. With hat in hand he knocked on the ramshackle door plank, and stepped in.

The room was cozy and warm, but the air was stuffy, and the burned-out cooking stove reeked of raw firewood. In the wicker chair at the end of the table sat the head of the household himself, Zakarias Olsen, a worker—or, rather, past worker—at the mill. Now he was unemployed and got a few kroner from poor relief, enough to struggle by. At the stove stood his wife, skinny and worn from work, stirring something in a steaming kettle. Close to the oven was a flock of youngsters who were playing with some sticks of firewood. The oldest looked as if he could be twelve or fourteen, but the smallest had not learned to walk.

They looked wide-eyed and astonished at the stranger. Modestly and humbly he remained standing at the door, his eyes shining strangely in the half-light. It was as if he were looking at each individual simultaneously, deeply, and imploringly.

Could he get room and board for the holiday, he asked quietly, looking down.

"I reckon we can find a way," replied Zakarias Olsen himself, looking inquiringly over at his wife.

"I reckon we can, sure," replied the wife mildly, swinging the kettle from the fire.

A while later they were seated around the table, each with their plate of steaming rice pudding in front of them. The wife went around with a wooden butter dish, laying a goodly lump of butter in every plate. But the smallest got only a little bitty dab in his little teacup. The stranger had been given the place of honor at the upper end of the table, and he was given the wicker chair to sit in. And to show him real honor he had been given the silver spoon—a costly possession and a wedding present—to eat with. The others had only simple tin spoons.

There was not much talk in the stranger. And it was hard to grasp what little he said, too. The youngsters sat, stealing uncertain glances at him, and didn't really dare let themselves relax. Indeed, even the oldest, named Jan Edvart—an enterprising lad with smart, lively facial features—kept quiet. But his eyes came back time after time to the stranger, taking notice of his face with a pondering and slightly suspicious expression.

Even Zakarias Olsen himself felt a little uncertain. He had half a bottle of alcohol in the cupboard and had thought of brewing himself a little toddy, since it was Christmas Eve. But every time he looked at his guest he completely lost his nerve. What kind of fellow was this, he wondered. It wouldn't surprise him if he were a man of God. A *great* man of God, at that.

It was best to be careful. And instead of the bottle of alcohol, Zakarias Olsen took out the hymnal, and kept up singing all evening. Now and then the stranger sang along. His tune was the usual one, but they understood nothing of his text. A curious man! Just looking at him was like reading the Bible and hearing strange tales from the Orient.

The hymn singing became a bit monotonous in the long run, and Zakarias Olsen and his household went to bed early. Their guest got to sleep with Jan Edvart in the loft above the bedchamber. They slept well and peacefully until morning light, as people usually do when they have a good conscience. But in the morning the stranger was gone. No one had seen him, and no one had heard him. He was like one big riddle that no one could solve, and the whole of Christmas Eve was like a strange dream.

There was much talk about the stranger afterward in the little town.

Every one of them had seen him, and every one had something to tell. That it was no *ordinary* man, all were agreed upon, and he became more and more extraordinary as time passed. Finally, there was someone who figured it out. It was a tanner in Klokkarsmoget, no less, who belonged to the Free Church.—It was the Lord himself who had visited their town in order to test their kindheartedness. And they all saw it at once. They dug up old pictures of altarpieces and such, and compared them. There was no doubt! The same eyes and the same forehead, why, his very hair and beard, fitted to a T.

But how had their town received the Savior? They recalled Mr. Aronsen, and crossed themselves. Plenty of them had heard how he dismissed him like another hobo. Nobody did business with a man like that! In his distress Mr. Aronsen took to the bottle, and things went downhill all the faster for him. Within a year he was dead broke and left town, in steerage.

And then the pastor! Didn't the Master himself have to leave the rectory without getting either food or drink! And such a man was supposed to be a parson! Nobody listened to a man like that. Complaints against him were lodged with both dean and bishop, and the pastor was discharged in great disgrace. Afterwards it was learned that he had ended his days as a poor tutor someplace up north.

But Zakarias Olsen! Poor, unfortunate Zakarias Olsen! He had received the Lord, just like the poor fishermen in Galilee had done, and shared his paltry bread with him. Everybody wanted to help a man like that. And before the new year had passed he was foreman at the mill and could move into a fine, white house on the outskirts of town.—The Free Church bought his old house as a meeting house, calling it "The Christmas Manger."

Not until the family moved did it come to light that the silver spoon was missing. It had probably been lost during the chaos of the move, they thought. Oh well, there was surely the possibility of a new silver spoon, now—one or even two, for that matter.

But when little Jan Edvart thought it over, hadn't he heard a curious creaking in the stairs on Christmas night? And cautious steps on the floor over to the cupboard where the spoon was kept? But he was not altogether certain whether he had dreamed it or not, and so he decided that it was best to keep quiet.—For little Jan Edvart was a smart lad, as mentioned.

Little Jan Edvart, indeed. A lot of man came out of him, in due course. He became both highly respected and rich, and the owner of the large flour mill, Zakariasen & Co. But sometimes when he was sitting in good company, he took much amusement in telling the story of the Italian thief who turned their town topsy-turvy, laying the foundation for the flour mill Zakariasen & Co., because he was craftier than most people, and bore a certain resemblance to the Master, such as he is found painted on old altarpieces.

The Christmas Basket

« Julkorgen »

FRITIOF NILSSON PIRATEN

SWEDEN 1936

The Swedish writer Fritiof Nilsson Piraten (1895–1972) became immensely popular with his two humorous novels, Bombi Bitt och jag *(1932; Bombi Bitt and I) and* Bombi Bitt och Nick Carter *(1946; Bombi Bitt and Nick Carter), detective stories set in the village milieu of southern Sweden.*

CHRISTMAS EVE BROUGHT A THAW AND FALLING icicles.

My sister Marianne—my big sister, two years older than me—rolled up the window shade in the morning. It was still only half-light. We crawled up onto the windowsill, rubbing peepholes in the vapor on the pane and looking out. We became as overcast as the winter sky. For we had decided on a Christmas Eve with frost and fine sledding. And the reality: meltwater was purling in the downspout, the snow on the outside window sill was densely perforated by water drops, and the road was already turning brown with gravel and horse droppings.

However, our expressions brightened immediately, for, frost or thaw, it was still Christmas Eve.

We dressed in record time that morning—I'm afraid that washing took a backseat. I pulled on my wooden-soled boots at once. Actually, they were forbidden indoors (which Marianne did not fail to point out), but they were my first boots and thus the most important detail in my toilette.

We slipped into the parlor, where we spent a long, silent devotional hour before a well-locked wardrobe door. We had been practicing these morning devotions for the past week. In the wardrobe were Christmas presents that had been locked up. Finally, Marianne laid her ear to the door. Then she said, "I think I hear a clock ticking in there. It must be for me. You're too little, Eli!"

I felt my littleness and cried a piece. It was obvious the clock was for Marianne! But then I grew bolder and attempted a retort.

"Hey," I said with a secretive and momentous air, "I've got something that nobody knows about, not even you! And I'm not telling what it is, not for a hundred kronor!"

The retort did not sink in. Marianne's interest in the matter was much cooler than I had expected. I still couldn't keep my secret to myself. When I confided to Marianne that I had four live wood-lice and a cartridge case of real brass in a cardboard box under my bed, she turned up her nose with disgust at the wood-lice. And as far as the cartridge case was concerned, she had thrown it away herself over a month ago. Marianne was so grown-up.

By and by we betook ourselves from the parlor and sought out Mother to pester her with packing the basket for Mother Calla. She was a poor old rag weaver who lived alone in a cottage far out on Tosterup Common. It was the custom that every Christmas Eve she got a basket with food and other good things, and this year it had been promised that Marianne and I would take her the basket. We held great expectations of this expedition. Mother was sitting at the dining-room table ruffling tissue paper. Marianne and I placed ourselves on both sides of her, pulling at her dress and going on about the basket for Mother Calla. Mother cast a look through the window.

"Calm down, children," she said. "It's barely light yet."

But no, we wouldn't calm down. And when we had harassed Mother a while longer, she had to rise from the table and put down paper and scissors. We followed close on her heels into the kitchen, where old Boel was standing by the stove watching over the ham that was boiling in the iron kettle.

The big arm-basket was taken out, and Mother began selecting tidbits from the pantry. Marianne officiously helped out with the packing and saw to it that I wasn't in the way. In the bottom of the basket was put a loaf of Swedish rye, several loaves of browned white bread, and a loaf of sifted rye. On top of this came the garnish: headcheese, smoked pork, flank of mutton with onion and thyme, cured sausage smelling of juniper, liver sausage glistening with fat, and a thigh-thick piece of blood sausage whose cross section was a mosaic of diced apples and lard. To this Mother added a nice chunk of Christmas cheese. Then came bags with pastry twists, almond mussels, and gingersnaps plus—most important of all—coffee and sugar lumps. Marianne demanded more sugar lumps, since after all Mother Calla dunked her lumps, and Marianne got her way: the sugar bag was stuffed full. Finally, Mother fetched a package of Liljeholmen's Stearin Candles from the linen cupboard in the drawing room. Old Mother Calla mustn't go without candles on Christmas Eve.

Mother spread a dishtowel over the contents of the basket, while Marianne and I put on our jackets, rolling our pointed wool caps down over our ears and pulling on our mittens. Mother sent us out through the kitchen, sending Christmas greetings to Mother Calla and giving us many good admonitions for the trip.

Outside we were met by a southwest thawing wind that blew away all admonitions in the same instant the door was shut behind us.

We took the path through the garden, carrying the arm-basket between us. As soon as we had gone behind the ice stack, Marianne stopped.

"Do you hafta switch arms already?" I asked scornfully.

But Marianne looked around, spying.

"Eli," she whispered, "shall we have a lump of sugar? We'll just take one each. We're not doing anything wrong, you know, 'cause I asked for more sugar for Mother Calla. You heard it yourself. But we'll hafta agree no one will get more than the other. And if we find a double lump, I got dibs on it. Keep that in mind! 'Cause I'm the biggest."

I always agreed to Marianne's suggestions, and she wasn't long in getting her hand under the towel in the basket. However, she found no double lumps, no matter how hard she searched.

Nibbling on sugar, we continued on with our basket, coming out onto the main road where it was slippery and slushy. Marianne had trouble in her smooth-soled boots, but I had spikes in my boots. After a while we reached the marlpit. There we put down the basket to catch our wind.

The ice in the pit was breaking apart and looked dangerous, melted water forming black spots on it.

"If I had wooden-soled boots, I'd dare jumping springboard," egged Marianne.

I went down and tested the ice with one foot. It creaked.

"As long as it creaks it'll hold," encouraged Marianne.

I boldly ventured out onto the slippery stuff. It creaked in the ice sagging under me and making cracks right across the pit. But Marianne was right: it creaked but it held. Only when I had reached over to the other side did I go through with one leg and get my boot full of water.

"Hey, you!" screamed Marianne. "Didja get wet? So I'll take another lump of sugar, then I won't tell when we get home."

Those were reasonable terms. Marianne took a lump of sugar, whereupon we continued on our way.

After a good half-hour, during which we had often rested and switched arms, we came to the avenue of poplars leading from the main road to the poorhouse. We put the basket down on the milk board by the side of the road and then stood a while gazing at the gray, gloomy wings of the building. Marianne's expression indicated that she was revolving great plans in her mind. Finally, it came: "Shall we go in and look at the Jesox? He's not dangerous at all. He has chains on. They keep him in the stable so he won't freeze."

The project was so stunningly great and bold that I was speechless.

The Jesox was in our imagination a fabled beast, a marvel that frightened and allured at the same time. I had seen him in my dreams, for they used to frighten children with him.

The Jesox was a bedlamite who for many a long year, how many nobody knew, had been kept in a pen in the poorhouse stable; "in the pen farthest in to the right," said Marianne, who knew everything. It was claimed that in his youth the Jesox had been a clergyman, but had gone mad from too much reading. Whether this claim had any basis in reality is not known to this day. But the following *was* known and certified: he ate however much he was offered; if a book were placed in his hand he read from the book without looking at it; his speech was a monotonous babble and rabble. It sounded roughly like "Jesox, Christox, paradox, Christox, Jesox, paradox, Christox, paradox."

And on it went. Everlastingly. You understood how he had got his name.

I was, as mentioned, speechless. Marianne climbed down into the hollow and broke off a slender willow switch.

"They say he behaves funny when you smack him across the hands," she said by way of explanation.

Then we took the basket and went down the avenue.

When we entered the yard we stopped and looked about shyly, but not a soul seemed to be out and about. In a window in the dwelling house, one of the few windows that were not stuffed up with sack shreds or paper, could be glimpsed pale, sallow faces. The stable doors stood wide open. We continued and had almost reached the stable when a gruff voice checked us.

"What are you kids up to?"

The superintendent had come out onto the steps. The scourge of the poor, he was called. He looked very large and stern.

"We just wanted to look at the Jesox," stammered Marianne.

"Well, that's all right," said the man, friendly now. "If it'll amuse you. He doesn't do any harm to anyone. Besides, he's securely tethered."

To the right just inside the stable were two horses in their stalls. They were chewing oats. They were doing just fine with fresh Christmas straw under them; and on the flags swept clean behind them were white dander streaks as proof that they had been well tended to recently. Beyond the stalls were the pens. And in the pen farthest in on the right. . . . We heard a monotonous murmur as we carefully approached it.

When our eyes had grown accustomed to the semi-darkness, we saw the Jesox's head above the pen's partition. It was a head of sheer hair and beard in thick, filthy tangles. His eyes appeared like two white, hazy specks. I suppose he was looking on high, at the filthy stable roof. And out of his mouth, a black hole in his beard where a whitish tongue moved as in spasms, there flowed a continual, droning murmur: Christox, Jesox, paradox. . . . From the rafters, draperies of grimy cobwebs fluttered about his head. Naked, scabby arms stretched over the partition with clasped, emaciated hands. The fingers with long, claw-like nails were wringing as if in agony over all the world's sins.

From the Jesox's pen there came a nauseating stench.

How long we stood there in silent trepidation staring up at the Jesox I don't know, but it was a long time.

Marianne pulled herself together first.

"Now I'll smack him," she said, raising the willow switch.

She gave the Jesox a light stroke over his fingers. His murmur rose to a whimpering, a twitching went through him, and the iron chains rattled inside the pen. It wasn't at all funny. It was indescribably gruesome. Marianne had tears in her eyes.

"Eli," she burst out, "we'll give him a lump of sugar. I feel sorry for him."

I turned around to take a lump of sugar from the basket. It had disappeared! Only the towel was left on the flagstones. Dumbfounded I looked around. The basket had vanished into thin air. Then I heard a crunching sound above me, looked up and found the basket hanging high above my head, held by a giant's hairy arm. Frightened, I cried out and rushed backward into the walkway. My cry drew Marianne's interest from the Jesox and she too became aware of the calamity: over the partition in the pen adjoining the Jesox's we saw the idiot who had taken the basket. He was gobbling and gulping with his whole big, red face. Just now he was on the point of putting away six Liljeholmen's Stearin Candles, wrapping paper and all. The blue paper was rustling around his jaws. Marianne started to cry in a fit of anger. She boldly raised her slender switch toward the idiot and screamed, "Let go of the basket, you idiot! Let go of the basket at once, I'm telling you!"

The idiot actually obeyed and released the basket. He grinned stupidly and started to lick his greasy fingers. But Mother Calla's Christmas basket was empty. The idiot had not left behind as much as you could put on your nail. Only idiots can eat any amount whatsoever.

Crushed by our misfortune, Marianne and I sat down on the flagstones and gazed at the empty basket. The Jesox's murmur now sounded menacing, rather like an ill omen. Who could have suspected that an idiot was confined alongside the Jesox!

"It was you who put the basket there," Marianne pointed out after a little while.

"Sure! Me who couldn't lift it alone," I grumbled in protest.

Soon Marianne nevertheless roused herself and proved what a practical little woman she was.

"We can't come to Mother Calla with an empty basket. That simply won't do," she acknowledged. "And there's no time to go home. By the way we don't dare say that we went to look at the Jesox."

Her eyes ran searchingly over the stable, stopping at the large fodder bin. She flew up.

"Help me, Eli!"

With our combined strength we succeeded in lifting the lid of the bin. There was plenty of oats in it. We scooped the basket full of oats. From a pile beside the bin Marianne took two large beetroots and planted them in the seed. Next, she spread the towel over the whole thing, stuffing it down well at the edges. Mother Calla's Christmas basket was packed once again.

Then we left the poorhouse poorer than we had come. The Jesox's mournful matins was ringing in our ears.

For a good way we still had the main road to follow, but when we turned off onto the field road toward the commons the going got heavier, the snow lying wet and untracked there. And the basket got heavier and heavier. It became as heavy as lead.

Mother Calla had caught sight of us from the window and was standing on the doorstep when we arrived. Marianne whispered to me, "Now don't you say a word, Eli! I'm biggest."

Mother Calla reminded you of a stunted fir tree in a fair wind as she stood there on the step. Age and rheumatism had bent her, and her head hung deep with care. As little as we were, she seemed to look at us obliquely from below the way a troll looks at the sun. Now she welcomed us.

"God bless your mother, children! It's simply too much!"

The old woman wiped a tear from her eye with the left hand, stretching the right out for the basket. I winced in anticipation of the coming catastrophe. It failed to appear. Marianne spoke.

"Mother Calla, you mustn't peek at the basket before we're gone. It's supposed to be like a surprise."

Wise Marianne!

Mother Calla took the basket, weighing it in her hand with many praises. We wanted to leave at once, but there was no doing. We mustn't spoil Christmas! So we followed Mother Calla into her low cottage. The basket was placed under the folding table inside the door.

Inside she had prepared for Christmas as best she could: the dirt floor was freshly sanded and nicely patterned; the spittoon was filled with juniper twigs; Adam and Eve on the polished black stove had whitewashed, ample clothing; damp spots on the walls were concealed by pasted-up newspapers with pictures; the loom, which occupied half the room, was covered with a sheet that made it look like a church.

Mother Calla fussed about. She put more peat in the stove. She stirred the kettle with chicory coffee and put it on the fire. She took out a box with old rags and stockings and out of the depths of the box drew two dry saffron rolls and a piece of loaf sugar. The sugar she split with iron tongs into two pieces, one for Marianne and one for me.

While we lapped the bitter coffee, Mother Calla showered blessings and thanksgivings over the basket with oats and beetroots in it. The saffron roll expanded in my mouth; I felt that it was the widow's mite I was nibbling. For the first time in my life I had a practical application for my conscience.

I have little or no memory of the way home. But I do know that Marianne and I didn't look back.

On our return home Marianne gave a report and was most talkative. We were to say hello and many thanks. Especially for the blood sausage and the candles. We were to hope that everyone was hale and hearty. We were to . . .

"Where's the basket?" Mother asked.

I cowered like a mouse before the cat. It was all over now. But Marianne was equal to the occasion.

"Mother Calla asked to borrow the basket for a while," she said. "We can always get it later."

"What does she want with the basket," wondered Mother. "She's starting to get old, Mother Calla."

The Christmas tree had to be trimmed. Mother brought out boxes with candleholders, flags, cotton, silver garlands, and gold paper. But neither Marianne nor I could generate any enthusiasm. The gold and the glitter failed to captivate our eyes. The smell of sealing wax failed to tickle our noses. Downhearted, we each moped in our corners, not daring to look at each other. Mother grew anxious and took our pulses. Had we caught a cold? Did we have a fever? No, our pulses were normal.

When darkness had fallen I stole up to the attic where it was gloomy and spooky. In normal circumstances I wouldn't have ventured there alone in the dark. But from the attic a ladder led to the uppermost loft and from the loft window you had a view out over the commons. I had to go up there. Something moved in the pitch dark loft and I was so scared that I was about to die. But it proved to be Marianne. She was up there ahead of me, driven by the same thought.

We huddled together by the window side by side, spying in the direction of the commons. We held a hope against all reason: that candles should miraculously be lit in Mother Calla's cottage. But the whole commons was indiscernible, dark from the evening's darkness. Marianne started to cry; she sniffled aloud and I also burst out in tears. Between sniffles we stammered to each other. Our tongues pitied Mother Calla, but the source of our tears was the fear of punishment.

A child knows quite a lot about the way justice functions, and we knew that unmade confession is half penance. And in the same instant we had the same impulse. We had to go to Mother and confess to her; Mother was the way out, and later she would speak to Father. We groped our way down the ladder and dashed from there down the stairs, each of us struggling to be first. On the stairs Marianne pushed me, and I grabbed hold of the handrail where a splinter ripped open my left index finger. I was so beside myself that I didn't feel the pain; the blood flowed and I paid it no attention.

We found Mother in the bedroom and threw ourselves upon her, crying aloud. We bored our heads into her knees. It took her more than a little while to calm us down and get a comprehensible word out of Marianne. Eventually she learned how we had lost Mother Calla's Christmas basket and how we had lied. I held up my bleeding index finger as an extenuating circumstance.

To our relief, Mother was more flabbergasted than annoyed or angry. First she washed my finger, bandaging it and patting me consolingly on the head. Then she sought out Father and they held a short conference.

She packed a new basket, supplying it more amply than the former. Among other things, she added two extra candles to a whole package of Liljeholmen's. And then Father harnessed the racing sleigh and drove with the basket to Mother Calla.

The tree was lit and the table set when he returned. Christmas dinner was an hour late, but our appetites were so much the better. We ate lyefish with Skåne-style mustard, ham and stewed kale, and rice pudding with cream, cinnamon, and sugar. Boel, seventy-three years old, got the almond in the pudding. We prattled with her about her good luck: when would she get married—and to whom? She laughed at our taunts until the tears ran and she was close to choking. Mother had to give her a thump on the back.

At last pastry twists with raspberry jam were served. Marianne was impatient, eating only jam (though quite a lot of jam) and hurrying the rest of us along.

Mother and Boel cleared the table, and Marianne and I helped them officiously. We were in a hurry, for the Christmas presents were always distributed from the dining-room table.

Finally the moment arrived, and before our eyes lay the sealed packages with ribbons, bows, and verses. Marianne and I had happily forgotten all about Mother Calla.

Advent in the Thirties

«Advent på 30-talet»

EYVIND JOHNSON

SWEDEN 1940

Swedish novelist Eyvind Johnson (1900–76) received the Nobel Prize in literature in 1974. Johnson contributed significantly to the breakthrough of the modern novel in Sweden, considering each of his works as an experiment with the dark and bright sides of human existence. Three of Johnson's post-war novels have been translated into English: Strändernas svall *(1946;* Return to Ithaca*),* Drömmar om rosor och eld *(1949;* Dreams of Roses and Fire*), and* Hans nådes tid *(1960;* The Days of His Grace*).*

AS THE OLD WOMAN IS LIGHTING HER LANTERN, AT the very moment the match sputters across the striking surface, she suddenly thinks about how unreasonably nice things have become. She thinks about it, with the same joy, every evening when she has to go out and give the pig its supper, every time she needs to go to the pigsty or the woodshed in the evening. She thinks first of all—the happy feeling always comes in two stages—that they should have put electricity in the pigsty, too, and after that she thinks how nice, how clean, how incredibly convenient it is with electricity in the cottage. They have had it for four years, it arrived when one of their sons, Karl, was last home, and it still seems marvelous to her. The radio is a curious box, and you have to accept it as a gadget, a wonderful thing to be sure, but electricity is marvelous in such a different way. The radio with its fine voices and music is something that you are almost ashamed of, something that can stutter and irk, but electricity is something that you control in a totally different manner. Let there be light, and there was light by which you could work or read by. She thinks of it every time she lights the lantern: that they should have put it in the pigsty. And after that she is filled with satisfaction at having it in the cottage. She thinks about it on the front steps and on the way down to the pigsty and inside with the pig. She says silently: You'll have to make do with kerosene, piggy. But you still see good enough to eat. And in the dark, too, if you have to. You don't have too long to go now, she thinks about the pig. She likes it, you could almost say that she loves it—and since the dream of owning a cow never did come true. . . . She tried to figure it out but couldn't really make a go of it. You should be able to figure it out on your fingers or with paper and pen. One year they had no pig; that was 1912, when she was sick almost all year long. But over the years they had probably had well nigh forty pigs.

She opens the outer door to the pigsty, where the barrel with pig fodder is usually kept until it gets too cold in the fall; now it's been moved into the pigsty itself. When she lifts the latch to the frost-white inner door, the warmth strikes her. The inside of the door and the whitewashed walls glisten with damp in the lamplight.

The pig first gives out an introductory grunt, and after rising ponderously and ready for slaughter he comes up to the trough, and now the tone is more earnest. The old woman scoops pig fodder up out of the barrel, mixing it with the warm stuff she has in her pail. The vapor from the pigsty and the fodder is thick around her, rolling up in clouds as she stirs a few strokes with the scoop and pours it out. The pig grunts calmly and contentedly as he stuffs himself. She bends over into the pen and scratches his back.

"You fat lummox, you!" she says.

She would not have been able to remember all of them. But one year they had one that had a ridge of black bristles down the back. Of course it would make for inferior bacon, they said, but they hadn't noticed it. But he wasn't among the heaviest. One was very fat, but his legs became so weak that he couldn't stand toward the end. He should have had calcium, they said. But he was pure and fine on the inside. And one was vicious, wherever that came from. They had discussed the matter. But maybe it was inherited and incurable. For they had always been kind to the pigs.

"You fat lummox, you!" she says again.

Karl said that store-bought pork and the American stuff was inferior; the pigs got too much corn or whatever it was, and sometimes they got pork on board that tasted of herring, he said. It was probably some poor Norwegian fisherman who had sold his pig. She wondered, by the way, what that would taste like. Herring didn't taste so bad by itself. But maybe if the taste got mixed up in a pig's body . . .

One of the pigs was almost as smart as a human being, they called him Rosebud, but he wouldn't gain weight. He thought too much, said Niklas.

Niklas has now been sickly for a year and a half; this spring he'll be seventy. It's nothing dangerous, he's just tired, and then there's his stomach. It doesn't come from carousing: he's neither sipped up their earnings nor slept with snoose in his mouth. And the times he has been in somewhat happy spirits—when they were married, when Lina, the girl who died, was baptized, when Karl and Isak were confirmed (they had to lump them together, for Isak was left behind), and at old Isak's burial—he wouldn't fight then, but dance, and at the most a little arm wrestling.

She scratches the pig and thinks how good life has been. That Lina ended her days at seventeen was, looking at it now so long afterward, perhaps just as well; for one thing, she was disgraced, and for the other she had that birthmark on her face and had perhaps never got any real man. Isak became a lineman on the railroad down south; all his children were alive and well. And Karl went to sea with all that that involved, got to see the world and learn something. He was supposed to have a child down in Bohuslän, it was said; well, life was remarkable. He sent some cash home every Christmas and in between when convenient. And Niklas himself got six hundred from his state pension as long as he lived, and hopefully he would do so for some years to come. And the pig looked like he was doing well in his final hours; she guessed him at two hundred pounds. They usually put them down as late as after the second Sunday in Advent, but they managed to make headcheese, and the bacon was hung away nicely until Christmas, when they laid it in vats. Tomorrow was Saturday. Henrik Nilsson would come in the afternoon when he was free and slaughter him. He usually took two pounds bacon for his trouble and the bladder for his kids, so they could play with a balloon on Christmas Eve.

She raises the lantern with her scraggy hand and shines it on the pig. Happiness is a strange and singular thing. It fills her now, and she feels that it fills the pig, although he has to die. He's had a good life, the little there was, he's had good food, she has cooked the slops and stirred in coarse grits. The sty is warm and lovely in its way, if you didn't count the floor, but the pig hasn't been uncomfortable with that—for pigs are pigs. He's had straw to lie in and to pull onto the floor, and he's been as clean as a pig could wish, if he wished anything like that. She hopes he has an easy death. After death there's no use thinking. A pig doesn't die—he is slaughtered and becomes pork.

"Oi-iink!" says the pig and looks up at her; she fancies he is smiling.

The light glistens on the warm, damp, whitewashed walls and on the water drops on the ceiling. Now and then a drop, which has been hanging up there ripening, falls, accentuating this deep, still happiness.

She doesn't see him immediately, perceiving only that there is someone standing in the snowy darkness before the front steps. When she raises the lantern it shines on a man. She goes a few steps closer and wishes him a good evening.

He mutters something that at first she doesn't understand, then clears his throat and reformulates: "Kood evenink."

At the sound of this hoarse voice she raises the lantern even higher and examines him closely. He is dressed in an old, frayed overcoat, on his head he has a sports cap of about the same kind as Karl used to have, on his feet oxfords. His face was dark and tired and his beard a coarse stubble.

He takes off his cap and bows to her.

"Kood evenink," he says again.

His eyes gleam darkly at her. It's a hobo, she thinks, a gypsy tramp. She goes no closer, but stiffens up and asks, "What do you want?"

Niklas and she are alone in the cottage; it's over half a mile to town.

He mutters something again, making a new bow for her as if she were a rich councilman's wife, and utters, "Foodt."

His eyes implore, his eyelids blinking slowly with fatigue.

She considers whether he has lice. For lice she won't have, and say what you will, they've never been lousy, they've kept things clean and tidy no matter how poor they might have been when the children were small. But she couldn't make herself ask right off; it takes a little while before she says it.

"I don't suppose you have vermin?"

He doesn't grasp it right away, maybe he's not all there. But she points first at him and then at herself, scratching with her index finger up at her temple under her thick kerchief. He then shakes his head, although his response isn't too convincing.

"Wait here," she says, shining the lantern into his face once more and going past him up the front steps.

He hasn't understood, but hesitantly follows her.

On opening the front door she turns around and says once more, "You can wait out here, then."

Then he understands and goes down the steps.

She closes the door behind her, standing in the hallway deliberating. She doesn't lock the door. But at any rate she takes the Roman balance down from the wall and takes it with her into the living room. She puts it against the wall behind the stove and goes into the bedroom to Niklas.

He opens his eyes at her; she recalls in passing that she has to trim his beard tidy for Christmas.

"There's a man out in the yard," she says. "He wants food. But he looks curious and can hardly talk like folks do."

Niklas lifts the thin bony hand of an old man and slowly moves it through his tangled, gray beard. He is deliberating; they are thinking about the same thing.

"Have you taken the steelyard in?" he says.

"It's behind the stove."

"And the hatchet?"

She had forgotten the hatchet; it's standing in the corner between the hall door and the kitchen door.

"Take it in, too," he says, "give it here."

She brings in the little hatchet, and he takes it under the covers. They had heard so much talk and had read in the papers.

"What does he look like?" asks the old man.

"Not exactly hideous," she says, "but he is tattered and black as a gypsy."

"Does he look big and strong?"

The tall but worn-out old body creaks as he stretches and sits up in bed.

She has to think about it, she's not so sure about that.

"Well—sort of. But he looked like he hasn't had anything in him for a long time. He almost looked like he had consumption—and a hoarse voice."

The old man deliberates again.

"It's so close to Christmas," he says.

"Yes, it is," nods the old woman.

They think for a while.

"I guess you can give 'im a round of bread with sum'm on it," says Niklas.

She opens the door carefully. The man is waiting at the foot of the front steps. Standing ready in the hall, she shines the lantern on him and beckons.

"I guess you can come on in; it's getting cold outside."

The man hesitantly approaches, snatching off his cap well before he has stepped into the front hall.

She considered letting him stand there, but when she opens the kitchen door Niklas says from the bedroom, "I guess you can come in where it's warm and sit down."

The old woman points to the front door, which the man closes, and when she goes into the kitchen he follows her. She wipes off a chair with her apron, placing it near the kitchen window on the long wall. Niklas can examine him from his bed in the bedroom.

He sees his curly black hair, gray at the temples, his crooked nose, his heavy eyelids—his weary eyes are brown—his yellow skin under the coarse, bluish black stubble of his beard. Niklas thinks of Taters or Gypsies; they're almost the same to him. And how the fellow is eating!

The stranger holds the round, soft bread with margarine on it with both his slender hands. He stares at it, chewing with a kind of quiet voraciousness that seems foreign to this secure kitchen. He says not a word, just eats.

"You've been destitute a long time?" the old woman happens to say, but he doesn't answer, instead just looking inquiringly up. Then he seems to understand and nods between two morsels.

"Well, it's not so good all the time," says the old man from his bed. The stranger glances up and nods again. Then he seems to have remembered something: he stands up, bows for the old man in there, and sits down again.

The old woman fetches a bowl of milk; he lays the bread on his knee and drinks it.

"Maybe you'd like a plate of porridge?" suggests the old man.

There is porridge left over in the pot; they were going to fry it tomorrow for breakfast. The old woman ladles it into a plate, standing there helpless with it; but then she makes a bold decision.

"I guess you can come to the table."

She points. The man stands up. Now he is sitting at the table eating in silence. But not so quickly; he is starting to get full. Niklas moves restlessly in his bed out in the bedroom; he can't see him. But the old woman stands in the corner where the stove is, the steelyard behind her skirts.

"Maybe you'd like a cup of coffee, too?" she says.

He nods. The pot is warm, it's good coffee, she added grounds this morning. Niklas and she can drink evening coffee later, when the man has gone. The stranger drinks silently; he puts two lumps of sugar in and drinks from the cup and not from the saucer.

Then he rises from the table and bows to her.

"Would you like another cup?"

She comes with the pot, but he shakes his head and smiles a tranquil, warm smile. Before she had considered it she is pointing at the chair by the window and saying, "I daresay you could sit and rest a while longer, if need be."

The old man, who had been sitting tensely in bed listening—with one hand under the sheepskin cover—takes a breath. Now he sees that the stranger's face has become handsomer, it is probably the food and the coffee. He has got a bit of color in his cheeks and his look is not so frightened. But he looks tired, sitting hunched over as if he had no more strength in him.

"I expect you're without work, of course?" asks the old man.

The man on the chair doesn't understand immediately, but before the old man manages to ask him again he has nodded, "Yes, I em."

He has such a curious accent; he's not from this province, in any case.

"I expect you're from far away, of course?" the old man wonders.

The man has to hesitate again, then he nods.

"Far avay, very far avay."

"Where from, then?" asks the old woman.

He formulates the answer with difficulty.

"Oh. Nowhere. Very far avay."

"Nowhere?" she says, leaning forward and looking at him. She has the security of the steelyard behind her back, she can reach the cold steel with her fingers, and her old man grips a firmer grasp on the ax handle under the skin. But the man looks all right, all there. He isn't written up anywhere, then? Registered, she adds by way of explanation.

Perhaps he doesn't entirely understand what she is saying, but he replies, "I em a Chew."

That means nothing to them. Jew, she thinks, it was them that hanged Christ, our Savior, Amen, up on the cross. But then they had to wander around the world as punishment, or maybe it was only Jerusalem's shoe-maker, who is supposed to appear once every hundred years, as a warning to others. And once many years ago there had come a Jew here from the city, selling aprons and buttons and thread and suspenders; she couldn't remember it all. They carried on house-to-house peddling, the Jews.

She gets an idea. There is fear in her voice, but she has to know.

"You've got nothing to sell, then? Thread and garters and so on?"

"Sell?"

But then he smiles again and shakes his head.

"No, not sell."

"But surely there must be something you do?" held the old man. "What are you, actually, you yourself?" And the old man tries to be explicit to this foreign man, who has so much trouble grasping what people are saying to him. "What is it you do? I mean, what kind of work or so to speak handicraft or occupation?"

The man understands quite quickly; he smiles again, answering with hard-found words, "I em—I em—" he is searching, "I em a teacher ant a doctor."

"Good gracious, are you both a teacher and a doctor!" exclaims the old woman, staring surprised and suspiciously at him.

And the old man cannot keep his most natural thought to himself. "Then I guess you've been taken down a good peg or two, if I may say so."

A blush crosses the stranger's face when he grasps what the old man in the bed is thinking. His cheeks burn, his brown eyes flash in the blessed electric light and his hands are clasped nervously (exactly like a true Christian, the old woman thinks, but maybe he's repented and has been converted in Jesus' name, Amen, they say there are some like that?) and he stretches out his head and his thin neck and tries to explain.

He is not a doctor that cures anything; he is a doctor of books.

"Books?" says the old man. "Is there any future in being something as strange as a doctor of books? Yes, well, I guess I've heard about that sort. But—"

And once again the stranger tries to explain. He is a teacher but cannot stay in his country and perhaps he cannot stay here, either. He has to find work somewhere, anything at all, in order to be able to stay.

He relates a little for the old folks. They wince at the curious phrase: concentration camp. They had heard talk about it, they had read in the papers, but after all it's so far away, the country where they say they whip people who haven't done anything bad except that a long time ago they crucified our Savior. But, the old woman thinks, then it came as it was prophesied. They try to accustom themselves to his words and meet him halfway, and at last the picture is clear to them and is fixed in their heads. He is a foreigner, he was a teacher, they apprehended him because he was a doctor of books that had been prohibited and then—well, they beat him, no doubt. But he had been in the war as a young lad. He had seen so much.

"But I'd think you could have shifted for yourself," says Niklas reproachingly. "And been a doctor of those other books."

"Hush, Niklas," says the old woman, "perhaps you don't really understand!"

"Understand!" says the old man, "shouldn't I understand this: that if you're diligent and reliable and done your stint and been in the war, then I dare say you should have your rights!"

"Yes, of course," acknowledges the old woman. But then she hits upon it. "He does say that he's a Jew, and they're supposed to be prohibited, see." And she turns to the stranger. "Was it a Jew you said you were? A real Jew?"

He smiles wearily in the direction of her age-wrinkled face and nods.

And she gets another idea, it is almost like blasphemy, but she remembers something she has seen on a plate in a devout book once. The man sitting here in their kitchen looking like a tramp resembles, she thinks, Jesus Christ, God's only-begotten son, the world's Savior, Amen. She trembles at the thought as it breaks into her everyday notions; she clasps her hands without realizing it.

The old man expresses her innermost feelings in his own way.

"You look good and tired. If you don't have vermin, then I guess you could lie in the kitchen divan tonight. Besides, you can get things of that sort on you and not be able to help it. Once when we were building the railroad we got them on us, on all of us, in a barrack. But we washed our hair in soft soap and changed our shirts and drawers."

The old woman looks at him. Now both the old man's hands lie on top of the covers.

"If need be," she says, "then he can go wash himself and get a clean shirt before he lies down. For you still have enough so they'll last out your time."

The man sits down before them with closed eyes. But every time he is about to sink down he rouses himself up.

"Maybe he can lie on the divan cover tonight," she says. "Then—"

She gives a start; she has already, almost without knowing it, decided that she would let him stay here until he has really rested. Or until (she thinks this very dimly) the municipal officer from town has been here and questioned him.

She lets him lie down on the divan cover with a pillow under his head and a couple of old patchwork quilts over him. He falls asleep immediately.

Then she pours a cup of coffee for Niklas and takes it into the bedroom to him, and one for herself. She sits silently at the kitchen table brooding.

Niklas hasn't said anything about her decision, but still she has to excuse herself.

"Hey, Niklas."

"Yeah?"

"You know he could help Henrik with the pig tomorrow afternoon. Stirring the blood and scraping when we scald 'im. If only he's any good at it."

Niklas ponders the matter for a bit.

"Surely he must know something about that," he says finally with much gravity. "He's both a teacher and a doctor and has been in the war, and I reckon he got to learn one thing or another there. I remember well how it was when I did my stint."

She gets ready for the night. She closes the outer door. Suddenly she remembers something. She goes into the kitchen and gets the steelyard and hangs it out again. It might look bad if it remained there.

She turns out the light in the kitchen and goes into the bedroom. She ponders a bit when she has pulled the door shut. The lock is broken, nor has it been used in many years. And there is no hasp.

The old man looks at her but says nothing.

When she has turned out the electric light (it's so convenient, no blowing all your breath out, just turn a switch) and is about to crawl up to the old man in bed she wonders, "And—"

She was ashamed of calling it by its name.

"I put it under the bed," he says.

They lie silently a while, but then the old man hits upon it.

"They say that Jews aren't supposed to eat pork."

It sounds like commiseration.

"Yes," she answers, "but maybe it's not that way with 'em all. But blood pancakes no doubt agree with him."

Another while goes by.

"Hey, Niklas," she says. "Once as a girl I saw a plate or whatever it's called in a book. Him out there looks like—well, he looked like *Him*.

The old man remembers that she mentioned that picture long ago.

"Oh, well, there's so much in this world that can't be fathomed," he says.

And the old woman thinks, "'I was hungry and ye gave me food, I was thirsty and ye gave me drink, I was a stranger and . . .'"

*

The stranger turned up various places. The children had seen him on their way home from school or on the well-worn roads to the small holdings up toward the forest, and he had been inside several cottages begging for food in his curious language. Or he hadn't even begged, but simply stood by the door until the cottage's occupant had carefully and full of suspicion about lice invited him to sit and given him a sandwich or a plate of porridge. He was allowed to sleep on the floor or the divan cover or out in the cowshed, where there was one. During the three-day storm that came just before Christmas he poked his head up through the whirling snow here and there. They would see his face, red from the wind, whipped by the snow, on many paths. People who had been to the forest to cut down a Christmas tree had seen him, and he had stood outside both the shops downtown. They shook their heads and wondered. They didn't think he was a runaway convict—at least not of the ordinary kind—but knew instead roughly where he came from and how he was treated. In a number of places they had got him to talk. They would sit and drag the words out of him, and then they let him eat and sleep. His words were enlarged and modified in many ways, but by and large the picture was clear: he was a refugee. There was no animosity toward him—in any case, it was uncommon—but it still lay beyond their power to place him in a quiet corner. He was a person who had been hurled out into terrible unrest and couldn't stop: he was driven in circles by fearful powers out in the world that they had only heard about. If they had not seen him they might have thought differently in many quarters about people of his race. Some down in the village who kept one of the city newspapers knew with certainty that people of his kind were a danger to our country, forcing our own out and doing us great harm, and that the afflictions that men of his sort claimed to have suffered were partly freely fabricated and partly well-deserved. But when they saw him they couldn't think that way, no matter how they tried. He carried on no devilish game tainting the populace or converting it from Christianity, he ate and drank like an ordinary person, and there were no babies that disappeared in the district during his visit there. They felt that he was unfathomably, irreparably unhappy, a figure that no one could *really* help, and who couldn't help himself. In one place they had asked him to chop wood for his food and a place to sleep, and when he understood what they meant—they led him out to the woodshed—he stood there with the ax in his hand and smiled. He couldn't wield a saw so as to impress this woodland people. With an ax he did a little better, but he had told about being in the war for four years, from 1914 to 1918. In any case, his chopping didn't amount to much; he was no doubt too famished. But they couldn't say that he was lazy; he was willing, working until the sweat ran down his dark face. He was just so inexperienced.

And yet he was a teacher and a doctor. He had taught people about remarkable things and become a doctor of books. They had difficulty imagining this: somebody sitting around doctoring in books. Some tried to explain that this was a high honor and a mark of profound erudition — that not even every clergyman could become a doctor, indeed, not even all doctors had that high degree in learning, that final certificate, so to speak. He was, some said, obliged to wear a high hat with an emblem on it every time he appeared and held a lecture. This too was eagerly discussed during the weeks of Advent, even though there was so much to do.

In one place he stayed four days; they were slaughtering the pig and the old woman asked if he would join in and stir the blood. He went along willingly, and the old man and woman and the butcher talked with him a lot. There he told about his life, at least about most of it.

He was as dark as a Tater and a Gypsy, and the old woman had wondered if he could tinker; there was beginning to be an acrid taste in the coffeepot. He glanced into the pot, emptied out all the grounds (they didn't think so much of that since there was still strength left in the grounds), and scoured the pot with soap and water. But he didn't know how to tin. He stood there helpless with the coffeepot in his hands and looked anxiously at it. They rinsed out the pot with water and tried brewing coffee. It was weak, of course, for all the grounds were gone, but the taste wasn't so acrid. That returned only after a week, so they decided to have the pot tinned in the spring when the real Gypsies came. When they sampled the pig, the old woman wondered if he ate pork. Then he smiled back and took part in their meal; and he stayed an additional day and turned the meat grinder. He got blisters on his hands from it, although he had been in the war, and his sweat ran down. They offered him some slaughter soup when Henrik was there slaughtering the pig, but he left that alone when he had tasted what it was made of, pointing to his heart and shaking his head. He took snoose, but put it in his nose and sneezed like fancy folk. Nor did he smoke, again pointing to his chest.

While there he had to wash his entire body; they were afraid that he might have vermin. The old woman gave him one of the old man's home-woven shirts, it was large but warm, and the old man kept to his bed because of age, so they didn't have to save them. When she entered the kitchen with the shirt (she was probably also curious as to how he looked down to the skin) she got to see that he had large red marks, fresh scars on his back and arms. He smiled and explained to her in many words that they had struck him with dog whips and canes, those down there where he was from, people in his country. She touched the scars with her bony old finger and thought they were nasty. He had to move out into the light so that the old man, lying in his bedroom, could see them, too.

"That's nasty," said the old man. And the old woman looked up into the stranger's dark, unshaven face and pondered a long time.

Finally she said, "He comes in any case from Jesus Christ our Lord's people, Amen."

They wanted him to stay, but he went his way. Maybe I'll come back, he said. But perhaps I won't get to stay in this country.

They wondered why he couldn't get any work. He was still young, he himself had said thirty-seven, although they didn't really believe it, he might be about fifty, for he was completely gray at the temples. And every man who behaved politely and obeyed laws and decrees and paid his taxes and neither got drunk nor even chewed nor smoked tobacco surely ought to have the right to earn a living by the work of his hands or his knowledge, even if it was about things Egyptian. Though probably there was no peace on earth for him.

"I coult be expellt," he had said.

They pondered his words, arriving at: But surely he'll get to stay in some country, surely he can't crawl his way up to heaven or beyond this earthly round just because he was born of a Jew.

He didn't know; it was still undecided.

But in this country there were of course all sorts of things for him to do, if he wanted to. Or in America; they've gone there before. But now of course there were good times here, from what they say, they needed lumber and ore, which was sold abroad, and surely they needed people who sat in offices and could speak foreign languages and knew facts about the land of Egypt?

No, he didn't know how it would end. One day perhaps a sheriff would come and take him by the arm.

What would he do then?

He didn't know.

But in the Holy Land, then, if now he wasn't allowed to live in the country where his father and grandfather were born?

They thought of the mountains of Lebanon and the Sea of Gennesaret and Capernaum and the olive groves.

No, there was limited space there, too.

The city newspaper wrote that one had to understand what was happening down in his country. The people up in the backwoods sat around in the evenings trying to understand. They didn't do very well, although they thought and puzzled so it creaked in their noggins, just where intelligence sits, and moved within their breasts where all feelings have their seat. The people down in his country had all at once become even more furious and gone out on roads and paths and streets and broken the large windows in the shops and thrown all the wares out onto the road or street and been into their homes and driven them out and arrested and beaten them. They had burned their temples, big stone houses that almost looked like our churches, their synagogues, where they sat lamenting and calling upon their god, Zebaoth, or whoever it might be. And they wouldn't get any insurance back. But they had to pay large sums to the soldiers who had been there burning and stealing and breaking windows, and then they had to do repairs themselves with their own money, and when they had repaired what the others had broken they had to hand everything over.

The newspaper in the city wrote that one had to try to understand all this.

The people up in the backwoods read and pondered.

The newspaper in the city wrote that they had sent a man down there who had seen and studied how things really were. There was law and order on the streets, and cars and trains ran as they should. They had received our special correspondent, as he was called, so kindly and cheerfully that he was happy and felt at home. The large concentration camps, he wrote, were to be found, of course, but they existed to protect savage, Jewish criminals from the fury of the people. He had seen such a camp himself. And the prisoners, if you could call them that, looked happy and contented at being protected. All of them had replied that they were thriving and doing well, and it was better here than anywhere else. And that they got to learn so many useful things that they couldn't do before. They led a sound and healthy existence out in the fresh air. They all said the same, as if with one mouth. The newspaper wrote that all this about maltreatment was sheer nonsense. All the prisoners except those who had consumption looked sound and plump. But a number were pure criminal types. And one had to understand the people down there, who didn't want to see them out on the streets and market places. They were a free and happy people.

The people up in the backwoods read and wondered and tried to understand all of this. A man comes along and gives you a thrashing. In the first place, you should thank him for it and in the second place you should pay him for his trouble. Then he takes your cow, if you have any, or your pig, for you yourself are so knocked about that you can't take care of the animal. Then you should thank him for that. And then you should pay him for his trouble. Then they drive you out of your home. You don't get to stay anywhere, you get to try hanging in the air. And so that you may hang in the air, you should pay a copper. When they have given you a thorough thrashing, taken what you own, and driven you out onto the highway, you should pay them for their trouble.

One or two rose up, crumpling the newspaper and flinging it onto the floor and crying, "No, the devil take it!"

But the newspaper wrote that we must learn to understand and perceive and reflect and comprehend.

He goes around in his circle.

They look at him and give him food and let him sleep everywhere he goes. Or almost everywhere. Down in the village there are a few who have learned to understand and comprehend and perceive and reflect. They say, "Surely he can stay in his own country, in any case! And we have our own paupers to pay taxes for and to help."

But when there comes a tramp of another sort they say, "There are so many running around that won't work."

The stranger stands on the road leading everywhere and stares into the whirling snow.

One day the sheriff will come and lay his hand on his shoulder and say that . . .

Well, what will the sheriff say?

The White Church

« Tann hvíta kirkjan »

HEÐIN BRÚ

FAEROE ISLANDS 1948

The Faeroese writer Heðin Brú (pseudonym of Hans Jacob Jacobsen) (1901–87) wrote some of the earliest realistic descriptions, permeated with drama and humor, of the lives of Faeroese fishermen. Brú's greatest achievements are his short stories, with their sensitive understanding of village life and mentality.

WE CHILDREN HAD BEEN LONGING FOR SNOW FOR ever so long; sleds and sliding boards stood ready and waiting underneath the houses, but the ground was still bare. Every time a sharp squall rumbled on the roof, we ran out onto the street and held out our hands, catching some hailstones on our palms and putting them into our mouths; but no sooner had the shower stopped than it would all melt away, right up to the mountain terraces. But higher up the snow lay sparkling white. Then when the sun came out and the mountain stood gleaming red, we could go and tie lines to our sleds and go up the mountain; but we never got far before the next hailstorm drove us down again.

But then on Christmas Eve came a heavy snowstorm; the flakes gently descended, thick and soft, settling warily on all the grassland, on rocks and pebbles and housetops, muffling the sound of clogs and the footsteps of animals coming to drink in the farmyard. We little ones got scarves wrapped around our necks, put on our mittens, and sat on the doorstep to watch how everything was being covered up, running out at times and drawing lines in the snow, then sitting down again and watching how the flakes smoothed them out again.

The geese came waddling in through the door, dragging their egg sacks through the snow, stretching out their necks and chattering. "They're expecting a cold spell," said the old folks. Starlings and rock pipits flocked around the farmyard, settling for brief moments to shake their feathers, then flying up again. "The birds are expecting a cold spell," said the grownups.

As we are sitting there, the older boys come running through the farmyard to ask us to come up to the pasture and roll snow into balls. "We're going to build a church."

So we rolled balls of snow, first kneading together a lump in our hands the size of both fists, laying it down in the snow and rolling it so it grew and grew until we were no longer able to budge it, and the older boys had to come and take it, rolling it away and setting it up in the church wall. We rolled snowball after snowball, and the walls gradually rose, the snow melting in our shoes, our clothes dripping with sweat, but nobody gave up. Some trimmed the pieces, others set them in the walls, and still others removed the uneven spots and filled in the chinks. The grownups stopped on their way from house to house, chatting with us amicably and sympathetically; some men put in our ridge beam, gave us something to stand on when it got higher, others took knives and straightened out our window openings: the whole neighborhood was playing.

When twilight began to fall, the church was finished, with roof and steeple and all. The last thing to happen was that a man came with a copper mortar and hung it in the steeple. "You have to have a bell; all churches have a bell." And when the church bell rang Christmas in, the mortar rang as well in the white church. We all sat around in the snow listening to it.

When the supper fires started smoking, we went in for the evening.

Christmas morning brought hard frost and blue sky. The snow church stood gleaming white and frozen solid. The older boys lifted glaze from the stream and put it in the window openings, the teenage girls decorated the interior: here was the altar with a cloth on it, here stood the candles, and between the candles green heather, and a curtain in the doorway.

Later in the day the mortar rang, and we went, dressed up with hymnals in our hands, to the white church; highly excited about the great events we hurried on our way, panting so that our breath stood like a white fog in front of us, squeezing in at the door curtain and sitting down on the straw that was spread on the floor. The lights were burning on the altar and in the glaze windows. The boys sat quietly with their caps in hand; nobody spoke, after all they were in church; all eyes stared expectantly out into space, persistent children's eyes, wide open before what was to happen.—But what was going to happen?—Well, we hadn't thought about that; but we had built the white church, decorated it, and now we were here.—A while went by, and nothing happened. We looked up at the altar, at the roof, at everything else; our eyes were inquisitive but learned nothing. We leafed through our hymnals, closed them again, turned them over in our hands—nothing happened.

Then one of the teenage girls says in a low voice, "Somebody has to be deacon."

Nobody answers, only breathing can be heard, and rustling when someone moves in the straw.

Some grownup who had been listening at the doorway walks off quickly through the snow. "A deacon you'll get."

We all sit listening, nobody wants to rush off again before that which we're waiting for has happened. The girls whisper about starting to sing, squabbling about which hymn it should be and who should lead the singing. Then they are silent again.

Then the door curtain is drawn aside and the old deacon stoops under the low door frame and comes in, gray-bearded and bent with cane in hand, taking off his cap and groping his way between all the juvenile legs on the floor up to the altar, sitting down in the straw, drawing the hymnal out of his jacket pocket and leafing through it. All eyes stare at him, no longer searching around the room, no longer inquisitive, just quietly waiting.

The deacon gives the number of a hymn, letting a moment pass, then beginning to sing with the trembling voice of an old man:

> *Most gracious hour! when Christ came to his own,*
> *a hush fell over every reach of space,*
> *and life came flooding over cairns of stone*
> *that held this world's hoard of dead men's bones—*
> *Rise up and sing his praise, you pallid race.*

We all sang along with thin voices, enraptured. Outside grownups stood listening; we saw their silhouette on the glaze windows and heard men's voices joined with ours.

When the hymn is finished, the deacon returns the book to his pocket, puts his hands in his lap, and tells us the Christmas story, not out of a book, not once again from the mouths of others, but in new words of his own choosing. It seemed to the smallest of us that these events had taken place here in the village and that he himself had taken part. The flocks of sheep were grazing here just under the hills, and we knew the shepherds. He spoke not of asses but of horses standing inside eating hay and of cows standing and stretching to pull the hay from under the baby lying in the crib. The wise men were the doctor, the pastor, and the teacher. How could it be otherwise? The presents they brought had come from Tórshavn: something good to eat, something that spun around when you put it on the floor, one that made a noise when you blew in it, three such things. Hardest to grasp was this, that the baby lay in a stable.—The Virgin Mary was a stranger, and they invite her into the stable? Among us, strangers were invited into the parlor.

When the deacon is finished with the Christmas story, he sits down to talk with us. It was sluggish going at first, since the church silence was hanging over us, but little by little we recovered. The older ones talked gravely and soberly, trying to appear grown-up. We five-year-olds were silent, listening and wondering. The deacon called us over, setting us beside him in the straw.

"Now, little squirts, what should we talk about, eh?"

"About the angels! Do the angels fly down to earth to get a haircut at Christmas?"

"Why do you ask that?"

"Well, 'cause you can only get angel's hair at Christmastime."

"Why can't we see any angels down among the houses on Christmas Day, like the starlings and pipits, are they higher up in the mountains?"

"What's it like high up in the mountains at Christmas?"

The questions come pouring out, but it's a good thing that they don't need answering, for the next one comes on its heels.

Then the deacon stops us. "What it's like up on the mountains? Well, it's winter up there . . ."

Has anyone been up on the highest mountains at Christmas?

Well, the deacon had been there once, on Christmas Day itself. "And now listen.

"There was snow and frost when I set out. I put on my wool shoes and took a walking stick in my hand. For it's not easy getting up the mountain; the winter doesn't want anyone coming up to him, he defends himself, covering the cliffs with ice, whirling up snow flurries, and setting the wind to blowing. It was rough going upward, I had to dig in with my spiked stick; sometimes I took my knife and cut footholds in the ice; and the wind came rushing straight at me, trying to knock me off my feet, but I kept myself so low along the ground, pressing myself down into the snow when it blew hardest—and I happened to make it up.

"Oh, you should have seen all that winter had up there; well, I'll tell you this: winter is a crackajack at Christmas decorating. Atop the mountain crest the snow lay even and clean. The black sandy stretches, the dirty red marshes, the muddy puddles, all were smoothed over and gleaming white. And as far as the eye could see not a footprint in the snow, not a spoiling step made by any living thing; sun, mountain winds, and snow, and nothing else. Farther down were snowdrifts, where under every bit of shelter the wind had piled them up in long heaps, carved into sharp edges and smooth hollows. Then the sun shone on them, tinting the crests pale red and shading the depressions blue. The streams had stopped up, and mist from the waterfalls had frozen in midair, lying where it had fallen downward as beads of ice and rattling in the wind. The cliff ledges were gone, only snowy slopes going up and ending at the top in heavy crests hanging out in daring arcs, and out of the crests flurried powdery snow as light as down, which the wind steadily carried below through clefts among the snowdrifts. The waterfalls weren't their usual black gashes in the mountainside: they were glittering crystal gates in the white mountains, high halls of ice pillars bearing vaults of sea-blue glaze. Here inside one of these high halls I sat down, behind a long row of shiny blue glaze pillars. Then I saw that here was where winter kept Christmas; here was his huge church, here he had raised his altar for the high holiday. And while I was sitting, the sun came out and shone so that the ice pillars glittered like pure fire, and the mountain wind came and blew on the pillars, playing on them as on an enormous organ, blowing a deep resonating Christmas tune that was borne out to the crests, the snowdrifts, and the even snow at the top, a song of joy about creative omnipotence that each year overthrows darkness and raises up the light anew, each year bringing us toward sunshine and summer again. And as I sit listening to the sound, it seems to me that the streams, which are taken by force and bound by ice, join in, that all the life resting under the snow joins in this everlasting victory chant, for now the day is lengthening again, now the air is gradually warming, now we are returning to singing birds and the burgeoning earth.

"That's what Christmas is like up in the mountains."

The deacon takes his hymnal up out of his jacket pocket again. "Let us sing one more hymn, then I'll see about getting home again."

And angel hosts were rising up on wing,
their rush was like a thousand far cascades,
refuge of joy for every earthly thing,
each tongue the tidings then began to sing:
"Now life is won for us, and darkness fades."

The Legend of the
First Christmas Presents

« *Sagan om de första julklapparna* »

AXEL HAMBRÆUS

SWEDEN 1950

Since his debut in 1930 with the collection of tales Himlabågen
(The vault of heaven), *Swedish clergyman and writer Axel
Hambræus (1890–1983) published several volumes with homilies
and short stories that have won praise for their poetic tone and
delicate psychological insights.*

IT WAS THAT NIGHT OUTSIDE BETHLEHEM, WHEN
the angels had sung about Jesus being born. The three shepherds
had returned to their flock. They had a little sheep dog called Tip. He
guarded the sheep for them while they took a nap. And it was now the
time when they usually slept a while before the sun rose.

But they couldn't sleep at all. They sat talking with one another about
the marvelous things that had happened and how they had seen the baby
Jesus.

Then one of them said, "Such a poor child he was! And how poor
his parents were! I can't forget Joseph. He had such awful shoes. I don't
think I've ever seen such shabby shoes. Surely he's walked a long way
with them. I seem to recall that I've got a pair of shoes at home; he's
welcome to have them."

But the second one said, "I can't forget Mary. Did you see how her
cloak was tattered? I saw how she sat freezing in that drafty place, trying
to get the cloak around her shoulders, but it was too small, and it was
obvious that she was shy about it being tattered whenever visitors came.
I think that my wife has a cloak at home that she could have."

"Tattered?" said the third shepherd. "It wasn't tattered at all, it was
actually a real fine cloak. But didn't you see that she had had to rip half

· 141 ·

the cloak to shreds in order to get swaddling clothes for the little baby? I stood all the time looking at the baby Jesus. He had no real swaddling clothes, like those a baby ought to have, beautifully stitched and with red edging: they were his mother's cloak, which she had ripped apart in long strips and swaddled him with. But I seem to recall that at home in the clothes chest we've got swaddling clothes left over since my children were small. I'll give them to the baby Jesus."

And however the three shepherds talked this over, they agreed that they should go home and get the shoes, cloak, and swaddling clothes. And so they patted the sheep dog Tip and told him to guard the sheep carefully while they were gone, and then they were off.

After a while they were back with their things, and then they went in to Bethlehem.

But now there were no angels singing on high, and no light from the heavenly host to lead their way, and they had to walk in the dark, and when they arrived at the town of Bethlehem they were not sure of the way. Previously they had only seen a single road, and it led them straight to the stable, but now there were three roads, and they were all alike.

The first shepherd said, pointing, "I remember quite clearly that it was this way, the one going to the left. I recognize that house over there— we went past it."

"Then you remember wrong," said the second shepherd. "I remember quite clearly that it's *this* way that goes to the right. I remember a tree standing by the way, and I see it over there."

"No," said the third shepherd, "we should go this way, straight ahead. For there's a well, and we went past that well."

So the shepherds stood there quarreling a long while which way to take, and each of them was sure he was right. And so they decided to go each his own way, and the one who found the baby Jesus should return and tell the others about it.

And so they each went their own way.

The first shepherd went to the left. Past a house and one more and one more, and when he had then gone a piece he caught sight of the stable. He was so sure that he had come the right way that he wanted to run back on the spot and shout for his comrades. But he was a little curious. There was a light shining from the stable window, and he thought, "I can certainly go and look in through the stable window a little bit. I just want to see the baby Jesus, and then I'll run back to my comrades."

But when he looked through the window, there was no baby Jesus.

There was an old man sitting on a sheaf of straw, holding a tattered pair of shoes up to the light from the stable lantern. The shoes were so full of holes that the shepherd saw the light straight through them. And he heard the man sighing, "Oh, well, that's the end of these shoes, and I who have such a long way to go."

When the shepherd heard this, he completely forgot that Joseph was to have his shoes. He opened the door and entered the stable.

"I see that you've got such tattered shoes, old man," he said. "I've got a pair of good shoes here; if you want them, then take them."

"Oh, God bless you, my son, God bless you!" said the man, stretching out his hand for the shoes.

At that very instant the shepherd recalled that it was Joseph who should have had the shoes. But he couldn't take his present back now that he saw how happy the old man was with them. He stole out of the stable and went back to the fork in the road.

The second shepherd went to the right. He went past the tree and came to another tree and to still another, and when he had gone a piece he, too, caught sight of a stable. He thought, "I knew very well that I would go the right way. You should always go right; then you can never go wrong."

And he was so sure of himself that he went right into the stable. But then he saw that he had gone wrong.

There was no baby Jesus to be found. But there was a fireplace in one corner of the stable, where an old woman had made a fire from sticks and straw that she had picked up from the stable floor.

"Are you cold, old woman?" said the shepherd. For he was so surprised that he didn't recover in time to say something else.

"Am I cold?" the old woman grumbled. "Shouldn't I be cold in this miserable world, where there's nobody who takes pity on the wretched? Haven't I gone from house to house begging for a cloak to cover myself with, but nobody has given me anything?"

And the shepherd saw that the old woman was trying to cover herself with a cloak so tattered that her bony shoulders and skinny arms were showing right through the holes.

Then the shepherd completely forgot that Jesus' mother Mary should have had the cloak. And he took it and laid it across the old woman's shoulders. It was a soft and beautiful cloak woven from camel's hair and so warm that the most severe cold couldn't penetrate it.

And the shepherd saw how the old woman's face was transformed when she felt the comfortable warmth across her frozen back. A moment before she had looked really evil and ugly, but now she was almost beautiful, so happy was she.

"Oh," she said. "I had completely lost my faith in God, for I had been asking him so long for help but never got any. But now I know that he lives, since he has sent such a good person to me with this beautiful present." And she clasped her hands, calling out over and over, "Thank you, kind God! Thank you, kind God!"

But then the shepherd all at once recalled that it was Mary who should have had the cloak. What would he get for her now? And while the old woman was sitting at the fireplace thanking God, he stole out of the stable and returned to the fork in the road.

The third shepherd took the way straight ahead. He went past the well. And he went past one more well and one more. "This street could well be called Well Street," joked the shepherd, for he liked a good joke. And he went on a piece, and then he caught sight of a stable.

"To think that I still found the right way!" he said.

There was a light shining through a chink in the door, and the shepherd peeked in through the chink. It gave him quite a start of joy, for inside were indeed the three he was looking for, Mary and Joseph and the child, who was lying in the manger.

But when he entered he saw that he had still gone the wrong way. It was not Joseph and not Mary and not the baby Jesus. They were quite different people. And it was not even the same stable. He was just about to go away when he saw that the woman was taking her cloak in order to rip it apart for swaddling clothes for the baby lying in the straw, trembling with cold and without anything on its tender little body.

"Stop!" said the shepherd. "Don't rip the cloak apart; I come with swaddling clothes for your little baby."

"Who are you," said the man, "coming to us with such blessed assistance? We didn't expect our baby so soon. We were on the move and found no lodging. And we have no clothes for the baby."

But the shepherd never got to answer his question. He had completely forgotten that it was the baby Jesus who should have had the swaddling clothes. He took them from under his coat, where he had tucked them to keep them warm, and he helped the pale, trembling mother with her white hands to swaddle the little baby in the warm swaddling clothes. The woman wept with joy, kissing her little baby and laying it to her breast in order to give it food. But then the shepherd got shy and went his way.

Slowly he went back to the fork in the road. There stood his comrades waiting for him.

Silent and disappointed, they went back to their flock out in the fields. There the sheep dog Tip came toward them, wagging his tail in friendship. But when he saw that they were distressed, he rubbed against them and licked their hands.

And so they put new wood on the fire, wrapping their coats around them and lying down to sleep, after telling Tip to watch closely over the flock.

But when they woke up, they had all three dreamed the same dream. They had dreamed that Joseph and Mary and the child came to them. Joseph had the new shoes on and Mary the beautiful cloak and the baby Jesus the soft swaddling clothes with the pretty red edging.

When they told this to one another, they sat quietly a long while. Then the first shepherd said, "Maybe, anyway?"

"What, anyway?" said the second.

"Well, maybe we went the right way, anyway."

"Yes, maybe we did," said the third.

The Soldier's Christmas Eve

« Soldatens juleaften »

VILLY SØRENSEN

DENMARK 1955

Danish short story writer, critic, and philosopher Villy Sørensen
(1929–) is a leading exponent of modernism in Danish literature,
employing the seemingly naive tone of Hans Christian Andersen
in his analyses of the split between the life of the instincts and
the life of the intellect in modern man. Sørensen's works have
been translated extensively into English: Sære historier (*1953;*
Tiger in the Kitchen and Other Strange Stories), Ufarlige
historier (*1955;* Harmless Tales), *and* Formynderfortællinger
(*1964;* Tutelary Tales). *His account from Old Norse mythology,*
Ragnarok (*1982;* The Downfall of the Gods) *is the first volume*
in a series of retellings of Western mythology.

WHENEVER IMPORTANT BOMBS ARE TO BE
dropped, this is best done on Christmas Eve, for then the young
soldiers at the anti-aircraft guns are easily given to irrelevant thoughts, so
they don't spot the bombers at all, even when they are large and stately.
Such a bomber was flying high above the frozen sea, through the tender
snow of the heavens toward enemy territory. On the back seat a young
soldier was sitting with a bomb in his lap, and that bomb was so substantial that it could destroy the entire enemy country in an instant if it hit
the right spot. But the wind, which blows where it wills, can throw even
the heaviest bomb off course, and therefore the soldier who was most
skilled at parachuting had received orders to jump out with the bomb,
and so of course he jumped.

He had time to prepare his final words, for it was a long way down.
The airplane's virile rumbling good-bye was soon drowned out by the

wind screaming like an anxious woman, and the stars blinked in terror with their radiant eyes. The soldier wanted to fortify himself by thinking of the loveliest moment in his life, but suddenly he couldn't remember whether it was he himself or another who had experienced it. Moreover, he was interrupted—by beautiful singing in unison, growing closer and closer, and as soon as he managed to look around, a host of white angels came drifting down toward him. He looked angrily into their bright faces, but when he discovered that they were all alike, he began looking inquisitively at each individually, seeing to his astonishment that each was himself after all and not, as chance would have it, one of the others. He gradually started smiling at them, but checked himself when none of them was smiling back; they made only shy little grimaces around their red mouths. In their white faces the black shadows around their eyes were as distinct as the frames of eyeglasses. Perhaps they were mourning, good angels that they presumably were, at his near impending death, for when they had finished singing in unison they fell silent, looking at him with big blue and doleful eyes.

He wanted to make them understand that as a soldier he wasn't afraid of dying, and so tried to start up a casual conversation with them, since they were now going the same way, anyway, though he firmly resolved not to touch upon top-secret military questions.

"The stars sure are twinkling," he said, pointing at them with one hand, for now that he was falling the bomb felt lighter, and he could certainly leave it to one arm to hold it firmly.

The angels flew a long time, looking at one another, before they all answered in chorus through the mouth of the closest angel, "Lord, is it as we believe, that the light you bring to earth is stronger than even the radiance of the stars?"

"To be sure," said the soldier sullenly, for he could hear all right that the angels wanted to pump him—it even crossed his mind that they might actually form a camouflaged unit of the enemy air force. The greater was his surprise when he heard them raising harmonious notes of joy and saw them juggling with their wings, placing them against each other in supernaturally large angles, but when he saw them turning their feet in the air, hovering head downward, he saw himself obligated, as an experienced parachutist, to intervene. "It's unhealthy to fly head downward," he shouted, discovering almost to his fright that the wind had become so deferentially still that he didn't need to shout at all. "The blood sinks to your head and you can't maintain the right course."

At once the angels got their heads up and their feet down, flying on their best behavior alongside him, but their cheeks were full of shame.

"But we've been waiting for you so long," they said apologetically. "You who are to come from heaven to save humankind on earth."

The soldier winked shrewdly. "I've been sent from up there to annihilate a great empire," he said firmly, "and nobody will keep me from doing my duty as a soldier!"

"We know that already," said the angels singing, "the dominion of the evil prince will be at an end, hallelujah, hallelujah!"

"Hmm," said the soldier, "are you on our side?"

"Yes, Lord," exclaimed the angels with genuine astonishment.

"Hmm," said the soldier again. "Why do you talk about the evil prince when the enemy country is really a republic?"

"Infinite is your wisdom, Lord," replied the angels, "and we don't understand such difficult words, but we believe that whatever you do is always for the good."

"Really?" said the soldier. "Frankly I'm glad. I've not really thought about whether it is good or evil, for you see I just have to do my duty as a soldier. But if I do a good deed by dying—why, then, I can actually die peacefully."

"Yes, Lord," said the angels quietly, "we know that you must die together with the thieves in order to save mankind, as you already once had to die before you ascended to heaven."

"I had to die?" repeated the soldier offended, for he was still living and therefore couldn't believe but that the angels were speaking ironically about air force soldiers. And then his temper ran away with his one arm, so it struck the nearest angel's cheek, hard, and when the angel immediately turned the other cheek, his arm struck it even harder.

"Air force soldiers are living young people," he said reprovingly, but then his furious glance discovered that the stricken angel's cheeks had swollen up to two big hideous blood boils, and since he was keen on first aid, he pulled at once a tube of salve out of his pocket with the single hand he had at his disposal, expertly smearing it on the angel's cheeks, which once again became white as snow and red with delight.

And the angel flew over and kissed him on the cheek, so he had to dry it off with a peevish motion of his hand, while all the other angels broke out into an exultant chorus of thanks, "Praise, eternal praise be to He who does wondrous deeds!"

The soldier's mouth was filled with fearful barrack oaths, but the oaths got stuck and grated in his mouth. How could he say a reproachful word to them, didn't they look so innocent in their blue eyes, didn't their voices sound so childishly happy that they couldn't possibly say anything with evil intent? It's probably some angelic jargon, thought the soldier, just as we have our own jargon within the air force. You could certainly hear that they hadn't discovered gunpowder, but then you probably don't become an angel, either, if you have your intellect intact. "Let's be friends," he said, "there's no fun in squabbling, and of course they say that God regards not the brain, but the heart!"

But instead of shaking his outstretched hand as a sign of lifelong friendship, they bowed their heads and turned their backs on him, and even though that was where their pretty angel wings were, it seemed to him to be impolite. He clenched his outstretched hand into a fist, menacing them and shouting, "Maybe a soldier isn't good enough for you, you angels of peace; why, you'd be rejected by every draft board!"

The angels did not reply, they wept, loud and sniffling, so the soldier once again had to repent his harsh words, although he could not shift to a gentler tone of voice immediately. "Well, surely it's understandable if my nerves are a little on edge at the moment, but forgive me, forgive me!"

"Oh Lord, forgive us our trespasses, we look at you and our eyes ought to shine like suns. But tell us, have we become cold right down to our hearts from flying so long between heaven and earth in all kinds of weather? Why won't God acknowledge us any more, why has he locked the door to his heaven, why does he never let us bring joyful tidings to mankind any more? Is he sending you, his son, to earth because he can no longer use us?"

The soldier got so giddy from hearing these words that he would have fallen if he weren't already falling. Floating down a while in awkward silence, he tried to ignore the angels and did spot a few familiar constellations, but the stars were still blinking so nervously that he couldn't retain their image, and the angels were flying close around him, looking him straight in the eye imploringly. Then his heart began beating much more softly than a man's heart really should, and troublesome tears stood in his eyes—just now when the warmer though still chilly air gave him to understand that he was approaching the earth and had to orient himself.

"Go away!" he shouted.

"Forgive us our disobedience, Lord, but you mustn't, oh you mustn't forsake us without giving us a sign that we can bring to your Father. Then maybe he will take us into his good graces again!"

"Let me go," he screamed, for the hysterical angels wouldn't let him fall of his own accord, but held onto his arms and legs, conveying him horizontally across the nearby earth.

"Let me be; I'm getting off course!"

"Lord, hear us weeping over our sins—but Lord, this time you don't really have any use for the big ball that you're holding in your hand, now that you're coming to the earth as a grownup—couldn't we bring that to God as a greeting from his child?"

"I'm going crazy," stated the soldier coldly and objectively, for he wanted to keep a clear head, but in the next instant everything that was loose and could move in his body began to stir, and so as not to succumb to the agitation in his body he had to burst out laughing, he laughed and laughed so the angels, who didn't understand laughter, stared at him with large, anxious eyes, until he could manage to answer, albeit repeatedly interrupted by laughter. "Oh, you angels of peace, you touching creatures, yes, just take this big ball here, bring it to my exalted father if you know where he dwells, tell him that he can have it as a Christmas present and that he may do with it what he wants if only he doesn't drop it—now don't play ball with it on the way; carry it as gently to his lofty dwelling place as if it were a sleeping baby that mustn't be awakened!"

Then shining suns were lit in the celestial eyes of the angels, and their lips kissed the soldier's now free hands. Without quarreling they divided into two flocks, the one conveying the slumbering bomb up to God the Father, the other conveying the trembling soldier down to earth. "The snow is cold and slippery; you could fall and hurt yourself badly," they said, apparently without putting very much faith in the parachute on the soldier's back. Gently they set him down on the white field without touching the snow themselves—they had, of course, bare feet, but the soldier wore sturdy army boots.

"Good-bye, good-bye—and thank you!" the angels shouted with joy, flapping their wings vigorously in order to catch up with their colleagues who were on their way to God. The soldier listened to their song; when it had ceased he bent over and put cooling snow onto his forehead. When that didn't help, he threw himself full length in the snow, which immediately turned to sweat.

"What have I done?" he groaned, "I've made a present of our only ABC-bomb to the first God who comes along—the fear of death made me see beautiful visions, and fool that I am, I believed in the visions— now I've come down to earth again, but what's become of the bomb?—

the bomb was real, after all, and not a vision—or was the bomb just a vision, since I'm still alive?"

He stood up to look around, for one sees farther standing than one does sitting, and he saw enemy guns aiming at the heavens not far off, and although they were adorned with evergreen branches and Christmas decorations in honor of the evening, he took fright and was about to flee. But behold—a figure was already standing before him. To judge from its restless shape it was a human being, but no human features were visible; everything was concealed behind something that was now a dark mist, now a trembling light. A hope of deliverance grazed the soldier's young soul, for the stranger did not have the bearing of a soldier; perhaps it was a peaceful old farmer who wanted to grant him shelter. The soldier, who didn't speak the enemy tongue, gestured with arms and legs in order to make himself understood, but then the stranger suddenly spoke his own tongue, not perfectly, of course, he faltered and stammered, but with a touching, soft accent, "Merry Christmas, soldier!"

"Will you help me?" exclaimed the soldier happily, running up toward the stranger, but he fell over a clump of ice and remained lying on the ground, having only the strength to lift his head, when he saw the old man's eyes shining so warmly that his own heart enlarged, ripping the uniform to pieces over his breast, and still he didn't feel the cold.

But now he was addressed in a foreign tongue—or was it his own that was just pronounced all wrong?—his speech sounded so familiar, so well-known, and it scraped the bottom of his childlike soul and was still not understood.

"I'm not so proficient in languages," said the soldier, "I don't understand what you said."

"You understood it once," came the answer sadly, and now the soldier understood and still suddenly thought that he had understood more when he understood nothing.

"Then listen, soldier, in your own tongue, you have touched my heart by sending the angels up to me with a Christmas present—"

"Oh, God," the soldier whispered wonder-struck, pressing his knees against the sharp ice until they were bloody in order to be kneeling even more, and he forgot that he was a soldier and cried like a baby and could say nothing.

"From of old I have a present for you which you would never accept, for you're better at giving than at receiving presents. Shall we now exchange, oh, man? You give me your capable bomb, and I'll give you the eternal truth that I hold concealed here in my right hand."

Out of the dark light stretched a gently clenched old hand; it didn't look like it contained much, but the soldier believed, truly believed that God the Father was speaking the truth.

"The eternal truth," he stammered humbly, "but that's really all too much—what I gave you wasn't worth so much. And to be quite frank, it wasn't me that thought of it, but your own angels, I haven't deserved to get it at all."

"I beg you, beloved son, do not reject it, bring the truth to mankind, whom I miss, and they will once more acknowledge me!"

The young soldier looked in wonder at the trembling hand that was stretched up toward him although he was kneeling, as if the stranger had also sunk to his knees although he was God the Father himself.

"Father," said the soldier, "thank you for this great favor, but—won't you please keep your truth a little longer and bring me to safety, first? After all I'm in enemy territory, and what might not happen if it fell into enemy hands!"

"You eternal human," came God's loving voice, but when the soldier with a smile raised his head, God had vanished. Before him in the snow lay the hard, lonesome bomb quivering like a large, trembling heart.

Born of a Maid

« Jomfrufødselen »

WILLIAM HEINESEN

FAEROE ISLANDS 1960

The works of William Heinesen (1900–91), Faeroese novelist and poet writing in Danish, mingle comic and tragic elements in human life against the magnificent setting of Faeroese nature. His imaginative power is fully released—combined with a grotesque sense of humor—in his masterpiece, the novel De fortabte Spillemænd *(1950;* The Lost Musicians).

THE NORTHERN ATLANTIC CAN SOMETIMES IN THE middle of the darkest winter behave quite summerlike with calm sea and mild weather, and around noon the low sun can have a curiously large and penetrating radiance. *Halcyon* was what the fable-happy seafarers of ancient times called such summer weather at wintertime; then the kingfisher, halcyon, would brood, and in its brooding season the storm gods held a period of rest.

Such was the weather at sea between Iceland and the Faeroe Islands at the end of December 1919, when the steamer *Botnia* suddenly in broad daylight struck a drifting mine. It was a half-submerged mine; the lookout didn't see it before it was so close that it was useless to sound the alarm, he heard it scrape against the side of the ship, and for a few ice-cold seconds he was raised out and above time and place and was wholly and utterly back home with his young wife—he was only twenty years old and newly wed. But then nothing happened after all—the mine was inoperative, and perhaps it had sprung a leak since it was under the water surface. The ship headed quietly on, the waves flashing merry lightning in the bright sun. He thought that they would have done so in just the same way if the ship had gone down, the sun would have shined on and the world would have gone on.

A few days later, when the *Botnia* was about eighty nautical miles east of the Faeroes, the kingfisher's brooding season was over, and the three thousand Oceanids whom Neptune had begotten with his wife Tethys plunged into their mischievous amusements, which consist of doing harm to harmless ships. It is sweet tickling in their ears whenever stacked service slides down a tilting buffet and falls to the floor, they hoot like children in a Ferris wheel whenever poor passengers, gray in the face and with beads of frigid sweat forming on their forehead, wander into the indescribable hell of seasickness, and they are on the verge of convulsive laughter whenever the green and foaming seawater comes in heavily across the deck, eliciting agonizing sounds from the trembling iron hull. However, they are altogether happy and contented only if shipwreck overtakes the craft, and nothing can make them fume like the sight of sober and vigilant seamen or of passengers who are not affected by the paralysis of seasickness, but sit disrespectfully up in the smoking saloon with their toddy glasses and blazing cigars.

Quite specifically, the sea-god's malicious daughters must have hated Thygesen, the aging skipper of the *Botnia*, whose baggy red face was always hanging full of a certain depraved hilarity, of a similar lavish sort as that which heralds a sneezing fit, and which also seemed to include the forces of nature. The first mate, Strange, a solemn person, didn't like this perpetual carefreeness of the captain, either; he found it unhealthy, in all likelihood stemming from advanced hardening of the arteries. There was no reason in the world to laugh at weather like this, with a wind force of ten and a forecast of even higher gales, and that in waters just as full of drifting mines as a bowl of rice pudding was of raisins. The ship had lain hove to for eighteen hours, and their chances of getting home on Christmas Eve were already ruined. Strange envisioned his wife and three little daughters sitting and staring crestfallen and without joy into the candlelit Christmas tree—if they had even bothered to light it.

In heavy seas the cabin sections of the passenger steamer are turned into sick bays; here there is a sharp and abominable odor of bile and everted bowels, of emesis basins and camphorated spirits, and from the cramped staterooms emanate quietly desperate lamentations and loud invocations, mixed with coughing and stifled gurgling sounds. Seasickness is assuredly no fatal disease, but still it opens the door to a snake pit of agony, bringing, in a caricatured, perverted form, a foretaste of that death and destruction that finally awaits us all, and its victims carry on not much differently from the damned in Dante's *Inferno*, even if they are rather less communicative.

In such conditions inhuman demands are made of the stewardess (or *jomfru*, as she is called, *maiden* as well as *maid*); it is actually insisted that she do miracles and save souls. The stewardess in second class, an Icelandic seventeen-year-old, bravely did as she was able through most of a day and a night; then she too collapsed and became a patient, and the cries of the sick for mercy were left unanswered. Ørnfeldt, the waiter, who had otherwise been sitting comfortably in the empty dining saloon playing dominoes with the sole passenger up and about, had to lend a hand. That didn't please him at all. He tried to bring life back into the languishing girl.

"You can't do this to me, Maria!" he said, admonishing her. "A stewardess can't let something as silly as seasickness worry her. Why it's no sickness, it's just pure imagination!"

The girl lay fainting away and didn't answer. The sweat was sitting in dense beads on her brow under her wiry, sandy hair. She had light eyebrows like a calf. She was fully clothed and quite abundantly muffled in skirts and scarves and tomfoolery.

"You could throw off some of all the things you've gone and wrapped yourself up in!" said the waiter. "I've never seen such a getup!"

He made an irritated snatch down into all this foolish clothing stuff. She was lying motionless with eyes shut and mouth open.

"What the hell!" he said, his voice thickening with amazement. "Are you in *the family way*? Well, I'll be damned if she's not in the family way! Goodness gracious sakes alive! Isn't that a mess! Coming here on board . . ."

Maria stirred vigorously, trying to get free of his purposefully probing hand. Suddenly alert, she pushed herself up and glared at him.

"Go away!" she said.

"Just why so high and mighty, Maria?" he said, showing his teeth in an agitated smile.

Maria's face became distorted, she bit her lower lip, and suddenly she cracked the gaunt and knuckled back of her hand into the waiter's face. He clutched his nose, getting blood on his hand.

"Why dammit I'll . . ." he said, getting hold of a towel. He moistened it and began to cool his bleeding nose in front of the wall mirror.

Maria wept loudly with her mouth open for a moment, like a child, but suddenly she eased herself out of her bunk and was gone.

"Just you wait, you harpy!" he shouted after her, laughing menacingly. "I'll straighten you out for sure!"

"Well, that's a lovely ruckus," said Mrs. Davidsen, the stewardess in first class, as she began to undress Maria. The girl had been washed by a wave on deck and was almost drenched. She was shivering and her teeth were chattering.

Mrs. Davidsen had stern gull eyes and a deep furrow down her forehead.

"Then how far along are you?" she asked.

"Eight months," said Maria.

"Mercy sakes!" said Mrs. Davidsen. "Look, drink this; it'll warm you."

"Into the ninth," Maria added in a whisper, with her eyes closed.

"You're crazy," said Mrs. Davidsen. "Lie down here and rest."

"I don't need to rest," said Maria. "I'm feeling just fine now."

"The hell you are," said Mrs. Davidsen. "We'll have to see about getting this mess straightened out. I'll talk with the steward."

"Oh, no!" pleaded Maria.

Mrs. Davidsen disappeared and returned with the steward. He looked at the girl and shook his head.

"I've come across this kind of thing once before," he said. "The balloon burst, then; we had to go through the whole business."

The steward was an older, fatherly man with a polished bald head and a drooping mustache. He lifted Maria's clammy hand.

"Does it hurt anywhere?"

She shook her head.

"Seasick?"

"No. I'm fine again now. I'll go back . . ."

"Ørnfeldt's been indiscreet toward her," explained Mrs. Davidsen.

"Let Amanda take over second cabin," said the steward, "he's sure to stay away from her."

"Are you engaged?" he said, addressing Maria again.

"No."

"Has he left you in the lurch?"

"Yes."

"Why have you run away from home?"

Maria lowered her eyes without answering.

"You don't seem to be all there," said the steward.

"I'm feeling fine again now," said Maria. "I can manage my work okay!"

"See if it works out," said the steward, addressing Mrs. Davidsen. "Keep an eye on her."

Late the next day the storm abated somewhat and the ship gradually started to advance; the anemometer fluctuated between seven and nine.

In this way more than a day and a night passed, Christmas Eve Day arriving without their reaching the point where they could see the coast of Norway. At noontime that day the weather worsened, the wind growing to a full storm. The froth from the foaming waters stood in across the ship in violent showers. But the sky was clear, and between the salty cascades the low, red sun was shining, imparting to the walls and ceilings a magical and fiery glow that seemed infernal.

There were only four passengers above deck in first class.

They were sitting astride the bolted-down chairs in the smoking saloon, their arms hugging the chair backs. Three of these saloon riders were Icelanders: a doctor, a watchmaker, plus the renowned poet Einar Benediktsson. The fourth was a Faeroe Islander, the marine engineer Gregersen, a little deformed and bearded man with a gentle and continual smile in his aging faun face. The Icelanders sat with their hands squeezed around their whiskey glasses. The Faeroe Islander was a teetotaler. To the doctor's chair was lashed a little straw basket, in which a rectangular bottle of Mountain Dew tottered about with clumsy movements, like a baby in a crib.

The noise of the storm and the ship's frenzied lurching made conversation difficult, but the watchmaker was entertaining the company by singing. Balthazar Njálsson had a good singing voice, but it was never put to use except in a circle of close friends and under the influence of stimulants, and even if his repertoire was limited, still it was choice: it consisted of the old hymnist Hallgrímur Pétursson's powerful passion and funeral hymns. Balthazar, who was a clergyman's son and had studied for the clergy himself, had rejected all religion as immoral, but he was still fond of the old hymns and knew them by heart word for word. His two countrymen sang along in places they remembered.

The Faeroese marine engineer listened attentively, looking in wonder at the three singing fellow tribesmen. The two, the poet and the doctor, were strapping fellows to look at; the first supple and stately and with a penetrating fire in his eye, the other as stout as an ox and as swarthy as a mulatto. The watchmaker was slight and pale, with fine chiseled features in his beardless face. His attire was dapper and meticulous, a cutaway coat and white shirt front and collar, whereas the other two were in bathrobes and morning slippers, day-old stubble on their long-awake faces. About Einar Benediktsson everybody knew that beside poetry he carried on politics and large-scale commerce as well, and there were wild and funny rumors going about that he had sold earthquake zones, gold mines, and the northern lights to rich English speculators and eccentrics.

It was beginning to get dark, and the waiter came to turn on the lights, but the poet wouldn't hear of it—he wanted to enjoy the long twilight and the phosphorescent afterglow of the rush of the waves. The doctor handed the waiter the empty bottle in order to get it replaced, and while the evening was slowly setting in and the storm raging on, sovereign and senseless, the Icelanders continued their admonitory hymn singing.

> *Death must affront profoundly*
> *each that to life is born.*
> *Dost thou suppose that roundly*
> *thou canst its summons scorn?*
> *No, thou too art invited*
> *to join the feast of gloom,*
> *and dost await, benighted,*
> *for dust to be thy doom.*

In the course of that evening the storm grew to hurricane strength. An incessant surf engulfed the ship, the hull writhing and groaning like a woman in labor. Under a violent breaker two lifeboats broke loose and were swept overboard, and the remaining boats had to get an extra lashing. Around eleven the front cargo hatch worked loose—here they had to act quickly, men in oilskin struggling out into the dark with tools, lanterns, and ropes, the first mate Strange leading the way, his eyes ferocious as a wild man. The repair work, which in calmer weather would have been a mere trifle, turned out to be a long and furious struggle with giants; two of the crew would have been swept overboard if the first mate had not been so prudent as to have them tethered to the capstan with strong ropes.

When Strange came up to the bridge, deed accomplished, the skipper stood with a furtive, spicy smile, as was his habit.

"What the hell is the captain grinning at?" asked the first mate angrily.

"Am I grinning?" said Thygesen, roaring with laughter.

The first mate turned away, muttering something about *stark raving mad* and *irresponsible.*

"You're good, you are, Strange!" remarked the captain, seeming to fight off a new attack of laughter and sneezing.

Below in the passenger section the distress had gradually increased to the obviously catastrophic; several of the patients didn't have the strength to cling to the edges and sideboards of their berths, but were flung out onto the floor, getting bumps and lumps and bleeding skin abrasions or falling in a faint. Women and children howled to high heavens in terror. Their fear was far from unfounded. The steward, waiter, and ship's boys had to come to the aid of the overburdened stewardesses. In the middle of it all, Maria felt sick again. Mrs. Davidsen feared the worst and brought her to her bunk; but a little later the obstinate girl was on her feet again.

Up in the smoking saloon the four rode out the midnight hours astride their well-anchored chairs. Among the steady light bulbs on the ceiling the cigar smoke stood still or moved in easy circles, quite unaffected by the ship's dramatic movements. The wall clock had stopped, time had stopped and couldn't be bothered any more; a demonic timelessness prevailed in the empty and well-lit saloon, while the rapacious beasts of Ragnarok snarled and bellowed frantically in the twilight outside.

Balthazar had finished his hymn-singing and sat giving himself up to the enjoyment of a cigar. He thought that it was now the poet's turn to entertain the company. The doctor thought so, too, and Einar Benediktsson was not a man to leave good and literature-thirsty countrymen in the lurch. He emptied his glass, closed his eyes in recollection, and with a gentle but rapt voice began to recite his great ode to the ocean, the almighty, the cradle and grave of life.

> *How visions and shadows are powerful in your dominion!*
> *I see you when darkness for days envelops the daybreak.*
> *You then heave your breast to the height of the cliffs on the*
>   *coastline.*
> *Immense the obscurity filling the stoup you are raising,*
> *your brotherly toast to the sky, hailing gruff and cloudy!*
> *The coastlines you shroud in with lobes of deathly pale breakers.*
> *It's then that a sorrow finds voice in the clefts and the caverns.*
> *Then specters ascend in the glimmer of phosphorescence*
> *from deep-sea graves long forgotten, with wordless lamenting.*
> *There rises a bottomless sigh from abodes of the dead!*

The waiter came to change the bottle.

"Turn out the stupid light!" said Balthazar.

"But you don't want to sit chatting in the dark, do you?"

"Einar's poem shines better in the dark!" said the doctor.

The light was turned out, the glasses having been filled beforehand, and the long, uplifting hymn drew its broad dragnet through the darkness, borne by the poet's emotional, but calm and slightly bashful voice, until at length in the concluding stanza it rises up on large wings and greets the day.

> *Like marveling children, whose sorrow and joy you nourished*
> *with shells or with snails on the beach from your teeming bosom,*
> *we stand in the soughing of your all-powerful pinion—*
> *bountiful, beautiful ocean, lacking a heart.*
> *Mirages and loomings and faraway mountainous islands,*
> *me your succession of mutable images follows.*
> *Your breast may be cold when you bare your dazzling cleanness,*
> *and if I'm compelled to invoke you and get no answer—*
> *all that your glass-surface gathers to glittering oneness*
> *is lifting itself in my mind like a sun-drunken wave!*

The glasses were emptied in silence. There was a long lull. "Now it's your turn, Björn!" said the poet. "We must all do our bit to dispel this deranged night!"

"Me?" replied the doctor with a gruff voice. "I've got neither voice nor spirit, I only know how to slit open people's bellies and sew them up again. No—but can't we have a merry song? Surely our Faeroe Islander will want to give us a *ballad*?"

"It's hard to sing ballads without dancing!" came the faun's pinched voice out of the dark.

"Then we'll dance!" said Einar Benediktsson. "Turn on the light!"

Balthazar eased himself carefully down from his chair, but never got his footing and scudded helplessly across the floor. The doctor also tried to get over to the switch, but was overtaken by the same fate. The darkness echoed with the two victims' laughter and curses.

"Stay where you are and hold on tight!" commanded the poet. He had lain down flat on the floor, ingeniously trying to crawl on his stomach over to the switch, but he too started to slide, landing over under a table at the opposite end of the saloon.

Meanwhile, the marine engineer, Gregersen, had begun with his ballad, marking time by beating the heels of his shoes against the chair legs. With a delicate but piercing voice he chanted the old jocund "Bluster Ballad" about the emperor Charlemagne and his twelve peers in Russia, who are about to succumb to the heathen King Hugon's necromancy, but thanks to their courageous perseverance and the intervention of divine powers victoriously overcome the enchantment: Villum flings a gold bar through a wall ten yards thick, Engelbret dives into a vat with boiling lead and comes up again unscathed, Earl Olav has his will in the maidens' hall a hundred times, with a single blast in his horn Roland blows every hair from King Hugon's head, and finally Archbishop Turpin directs a torrential flood across the heathen kingdom, which would have fallen prey to the inundation if the magnanimous emperor Charlemagne had not through invocation of the merciful god of the Christians got the deluge stopped . . .

The fallen Icelanders joined in with the sonorous refrain of the ballad from their resting places in the dark, while they held tight to table and chair legs.

> *They sally out of Frankish lands,*
> *a worthy maid in saddle—*
> *blow the horn of Olifant at Ronceval!*

A little past midnight the storm began to moderate; the wind shifted to the north; stars were lit over the harried sea, where long ribbons of foam lay like the glittering of silver chains over the heavily breathing ground swells.

Out of Mrs. Davidsen's cabin came muffled screams, mixed with the cries of anguish coming from the seasick. The stewardess squeezed the young girl's hands.

"You mustn't be afraid, Maria," she said gently. "I'm here with you, and there's also a doctor on board."

"I'm not afraid," whispered the girl, bringing Mrs. Davidsen's hands up to her parched lips. She opened her eyes and sent the stewardess a feeble little smile. "Do you think this is *it*? Maybe I've just been lying the wrong way. Now I'm feeling just fine again!"

Mrs. Davidsen sat staring straight ahead. Suddenly she bent over the young girl's bunk and said softly, "Hey, Maria—when I had my first child, it was just like it is with you now. I was seventeen, too, and alone and abandoned, would you believe it?"

Maria raised herself up on her elbow, searching for Mrs. Davidsen's eyes.

"Did the baby die?" she whispered anxiously.

"No."

"Was it real bad?"

"No."

The girl sighed and laid herself down again.

"It was a boy," said Mrs. Davidsen. "He's fifteen now."

"And then later," said Maria, "so then you got married?"

"Yes. Not with the boy's father. And only for a short time."

Maria was dozing off. "I think I'll sleep a little," she said.

"Yes, you do that."

But a little later the girl broke down again, lying in her bunk writhing desperately. Mrs. Davidsen called for one of the boys and asked him to go up and fetch Dr. Helgason.

"Tell him it's important. It's a *birth*!"

The boy stared open-mouthed at her.

"Now look alive, Johan!" said the stewardess. "There's no time to waste."

"Let me take care of it, instead," said the steward and disappeared up the stairs.

Out of the maid's chamber there suddenly came a horrible cry of terror: "*Mama!*" And after that a hoarse and dreadfully wrenching sound, a witless animal roar.

The two boys looked at each other wide-eyed. Johan held his clenched hands up to his mouth, biting his thumbnails; his light blond hair stood around his head like terror's halo. Robert, who was a few years older, bared his teeth in a stiff smile.

"Hell yeah!" he said like a grownup. "That *hurts* like hell, that's something you just know!"

Up in the smoking saloon the light was lit and the marine engineer, Gregersen, was sitting in lofty loneliness playing solitaire. The three Icelanders lay stretched out, each on his own sofa. They were sleeping soundly. The steward approached and shook the doctor. Dr. Helgason squirmed a little and turned over to the other side. The steward tried to make himself heard, but without success. Gregersen came to his rescue.

"There's a woman who's about to have a baby!" they shouted into the drugged man's ear. "There could be human life at stake!"

"Perhaps two human lives!" added Gregersen.

"What's up?" shouted Einar Benediktsson. The poet had leaped up from his sofa and stood scratching the back of his head, seedy and baring his teeth. His eyes became like glowing coals when it was explained to him.

"Björn is dead drunk!" he said. "Come, we'll undress him and take him out onto the deck!"

It was an easy matter getting the clothes off the lightly dressed doctor. After that the three men dragged the stout and luxuriantly hairy, gigantic frame out into the ice-cold air on the weather side. The doctor made some attempts at bracing himself up, he laughed deeply and bewildered, but at once collapsed again and had to be held to keep from falling to the deck.

"Get a bucket!" said the poet, and when the steward hesitated, he bellowed into his ear, "Dammit, man, fetch a *bucket*, I said!"

The steward got hold of a pail of water and handed it to the irate poet, who instantly chucked the contents onto the doctor's head, without worrying about whether the other two also got some ugly spots on their clothes. Now Björn the bear came alive; he let out some bellows and started to shiver and snort.

"What the hell?" he groaned. "*Stars?*"

"Christmas stars!" shouted the poet. "A child shall be born of a maid! You're to help it into the world, and that at once, on the spot! Now do you understand?"

The doctor was led back to the saloon and rubbed with a bath towel, he snuffled and sputtered, but all at once he coughed soberly and with wrinkled brow; cured, he got into his bathrobe and hurriedly followed the steward.

Quietly and quite privately the poet drank a large gulp from the bottle. Mr. Gregersen went back to his solitaire. The watchmaker had awakened. He was sitting on the sofa with both hands pressed against his abdomen. He looked like he was suffering a lot. The poet filled his glass. "Look here, my friend!" he said gently.

He added, addressing Gregersen, "Balthazar is ill. He's going down to be operated on."

"Is it serious?" said the marine engineer, pushing the cards together into a pile.

"Cancer!" said Balthazar with a sigh, raising his glass in a greeting.

It was no easy birth; Dr. Helgason had need of all his art.

Mrs. Davidsen assisted him with hot water, towels, and medications from the ship's medicine cabinet. It looked critical for wee Maria, her frail body writhing before heaving waves of pain, like a vessel in distress. Mrs. Davidsen, who was otherwise used to a little of everything, was about to swoon at the sight of all the blood flowing over the doctor's energetically working hands. The young girl had no more voice left, a ghastly, hoarse rattle was coming out of her throat; she had bit herself on the tongue, dark red liquid was trickling from the corners of her mouth.

"Shouldn't she have an injection?" asked the stewardess. "She's feeling terrible."

"No," said the doctor. "Not yet."

Outside in the corridor the two ship's boys stood listening to the alarming sounds forcing their way out of the maid's chamber. Robert stole a peek in through the chink of the door. He hastily turned away and ran as if for his life up the stairs. Johan followed him, smitten with his panic. He found him in the deserted pantry.

"What is it, Robert?" Johan asked astounded.

"Who the hell asked you to come here and pry?" said Robert. "Can't a guy ever be left alone anywhere?"

"Do you think she'll die?" whispered Johan.

"Of course!" said Robert, turning away. "Of course she'll die. There was nothing but blood, all over the place!"

"What are you two swabs doing here?" came a voice behind them. It was Josef, the cook. He was standing in the door to the galley with a lit candle in one hand and a hymnal in the other.

"And then you don't even say 'Merry Christmas'!"

"Merry Christmas!" said the boys both at once.

The cook put the candle down, stuck the hymnal in his pocket, and pulled out a bottle of stout.

"I think it's a bit stiff," he said, taking a gulp of the black ale, "I think it's a bit stiff no one here on board, not a single living soul, is bearing in mind what evening it is this evening, or rather night! Damn it all, they're all of them going about like heathens and whited sepulchers—God forgive my mouth. Not as much as five minutes, for instance, has been spent on a Christmas carol! The first mate, who is otherwise such a thoughtful man—I don't understand him. But hell's bells—forgive my mouth!— it's a holy night, maybe the holiest in the whole almanac!"

The cook sat down on a stool. He took another swig from the bottle and pulled the hymnal out again. His brown eyes were red-rimmed; they had the same color as the dark, sticky ale.

"But since I've now got you two here," he continued while leafing through the book, "then we can just take and sing a verse, just one single little verse, couldn't we, of this one here: Silent Night, Holy Night!"

He gave the boys a pleading look. "Well, it's not for *my* damned sake—I've already sung it down in my cubbyhole. It's for your own sake. Come on!"

He started to sing by himself, in a drawling voice. The boys watched him bashfully.

"Beg your pardon?" the cook interrupted himself. "Don't you know the tune? Are you heathens, then? May I ask? Come on, hell's—pardon me! It goes like 'Hours fly, time goes by'! Why every nitwit on earth knows that verse, or what? Really now, that's the limit!"

He slammed the book shut and lit a cigarette.

"As you wish," he said. "Now you've been warned."

He had another gulp of ale, took some long drags from his cigarette, and sent the two boys a bittersweet look. Some spasms crossed his pasty cheeks. He screwed up his eyes and said in wringing the cigarette between his thick lips, "It's not for me to *preach*, that's not my business, but you two curious lubbers still ought to try thinking a little about *the eternal*. Life is short and dirty. It's no lie that it's a vale of tears! Well—what the hell do we all exist for? Tell me that! To eat and drink? To whore with muckraking bitches? To kill and eat our fellow mortal creatures, the animals, who in so many ways are much better and much more honest than we are ourselves?"

The cook emptied his bottle and worked himself up, red blotches standing out on his cheek flesh; he crushed his cigarette stub out on the sole of his shoe, chucking it into a trash can.

"Really!" he said. "For what's the difference between an ordinary sin-sniffling human sop and a pig? May I ask? What difference is there between a girl and a sow? Both just as hungry and lecherous, with the same kinds of flesh and flanks and tits and blood and bile and piss! Sin, my boys, sin, it weighs down all creation!"

The cook had tears in his eyes. He continued, his face awry with emotion, "Well, just don't you think now that I imagine that I'm an exception! But still I'm trying to do my best to repent so as not to go straight to hell! And if you don't do the same—hey now, where are you going, Robert?"

"Out to throw up!" said Robert.

"Me, too!" said Johan.

The cook gave a heavy sigh and lit a new cigarette. He shrugged his shoulders and said to nobody in particular, as if he were talking to the emptiness in the bright and scoured pantry, "It's the usual thing. That's what you get for your good will."

Below in the stewardess's cabin the woman in labor struggled for her double life. Sweat and tears poured down her cheeks like rain on a windowpane, and her screams for help no longer had any sound. The powers of destruction and creation clashed mercilessly in the cramped cabin, fighting their eternally implacable struggle for the world's dominion.

"But couldn't she have a shot?" asked Mrs. Davidsen pleadingly.

"Not yet," said the doctor.

The steward, the waiter, and the two boys were standing out in the corridor. They strained their ears and kept quiet. A little later the first mate appeared in the stairway, with somber eyes in his weather-beaten, bearded face.

"It seems so quiet here?" he whispered inquiringly.

The steward shrugged his shoulders without looking him in the eyes. The two boys stared at him with shifty terror in their eyes.

Up from the kitchen regions came fragments of loud and bleating singing.

And when from earth our praise can rise
forever new up to the skies
and gladly it rejoices,
our alleluia, although dim,
is joined by blissful cherubim
with myriads of voices.

It was the cook singing. The first mate's face took on an ominous expression. Josef was obviously drunk, and in that condition to sing *hymns*, and on the most holy Christmas night itself—no, that was simply going too far! It shouldn't be tolerated!

The first mate disappeared up the stairway, his face dark red; he could be heard quarreling with the cook, which apparently developed into violence, the service fell to the floor, and Strange's castigating voice could be heard, "It's goddamned serious enough, you idiot! My mother died when I was born!"

But now there came muffled voices from the stewardess's cabin. Water splashing. Something sounding like a hollow slap. And then suddenly a brittle, coughing sound as from a little, cracked clock, a sound rapidly rising to the vehement and inconsolable crying of a baby, sharp and piercing like a fine-spun metal wire.

"Ho, ho!" said the first mate, who appeared on the stairs once more. "So they've nabbed our stowaway after all!"

A little later Dr. Helgason stepped out of the cabin door, stiff and sweaty of face and with a blood-soiled undershirt. He rushed with hurried steps over to the men's room.

"How about the mother?" asked the first mate.

"Everything's all right!" replied the doctor. "It's a boy."

"Well, I'll be!" said the first mate, whose voice was quite drunk with laughter from relief. "Then he was born lucky indeed—on Christmas night itself!"

The steward uttered a loud and heartfelt yawn. The two boys avoided looking at one another.

"Strange gave Josef a well-earned clout earlier!" Robert remarked. "Did you hear it?"

The sky was overgrown with clouds again. It was snowing heavily, but the storm had moderated and the sea began to calm down. The steamer hooted in warning out into the dark cavern of Christmas morning.

"What's up with you, Strange?" Captain Thygesen asked. "I do believe you're *grinning*?"

"Me?" said the first mate. "Oh well—sure, sure."

"Well, don't hold yourself back, whatever you do!" said the captain caustically. "Why every once in a while you've got to be allowed to be a bit *stark raving mad* like that!"

"Well," the first mate passed it off.

"And *irresponsible*!" added Thygesen, sniffling with amusement.

The first mate let the old man have his fun. That was his business.

The snow shower thinned out. The lighthouses on the Norwegian coast were beginning to be visible. A cloud the shape of a huge ostrich laid a gold-glittering egg: the morning star!

The first mate went back to his cabin.

"Peace on earth, good will toward men!" he thought as he sat there before the photographs of his wife and their three little daughters. He felt some remorse at the thought of the slap he had given the cook. It was a bit hard. But that's how it always went with poor Josef. He invited it. He was an intemperate and quarrelsome person. But surely he was also a struggling soul at bottom.

Strange decided to go below and see if the cook was still up. It was Christmas morning and peace on earth. He wanted to make his peace with Josef and not let the sun come up upon his wrath.

Yes, the cook was still up. He was sitting in his cabin staring lonesomely into space with leaden eyes and the closed hymnal in his lap. Before him on the folding table stood three lit candles, flickering solemnly under an enlarged photograph of an anxious old woman. It was no doubt Josef's mother.

"I come to ask you to forgive my temper earlier," said the first mate, settling full of friendliness on the edge of the cook's bunk.

"Can't be forgiven!" replied Josef without looking him in the eye.

"Stuff and nonsense," the first mate passed it off. "Can't we as Christian brethren . . . ?"

"No!" the cook cut him off. "For you're a Pharisee and I'm a publican. The publican and the Pharisee aren't brethren. I'm a penitent sinner and you're a whited sepulcher. You can go to—pardon me!—with your drivel about Christian brethren!"

The first mate shrugged his shoulders and stood up.

"Well, whatever you say, Josef," he said. "Whatever you say. Good morning and *Merry Christmas!*"

The cook didn't answer. He had put his hymnal aside and was sitting with his face hidden in his hands

Down in the maid's chamber the hot-tempered baby's crying had died down. Mrs. Davidsen had washed and swaddled the little boy and laid him at his mother's breast. She poured eau de cologne into a saucer and set it on fire, cleansing the air.

"Johan!" she called out into the corridor. "Robert! Aren't you coming in to wish us luck and a merry Christmas?"

"Oh, go fly a kite!" muttered Robert, disappearing up the stairway.

Johan quickly followed, but midway up the stairs he stopped and thought twice. Suddenly he thought it was a shame for Mrs. Davidsen that she should have called in vain. Mrs. Davidsen was a battle-ax, but that was easy to understand if it was true what they said: that her oldest son was a scalawag and had been in the clink. He slipped into the stewardess's cabin and stood bashfully by the door. It smelled strangely exotic and sweet here. He couldn't help thinking of the Christmas carol's "gold, frankincense, and myrrh so pure." The young mother didn't notice him. She lay staring into space with bright, vacant eyes. Her reddish hair was combed tight against her head. Her face was quite without color—spirit-like. With a shiver he thought that she had indeed also been close to death. She had still not quite returned to this world. The downy back of the baby's head was clearly outlined against her bosom, which was almost indistinguishable from the white duvet cover. Over at the washstand stood a pail with something gray-violet and veined in it, looking like entrails. He happened to think of the cook's words about the girl and the sow, and a shudder of sorrow and disgust passed through his mind.

"Well, that's how you yourself once lay at your mother's breast," said Mrs. Davidsen. "And it's not so long ago at that. Fourteen years?"

"Fifteen!" said Johan.

She gave his light, bristly hair a little tug.

But now footsteps and voices were heard outside in the corridor. It was the doctor and his friends from the smoking saloon.

"How's it going?" asked the doctor, bending down over Maria's bunk. "All right?"

She nodded, almost imperceptibly and without looking at him. She just lay there staring into space with a brilliant, but blurred and sealed gaze.

"Ah yes," said the doctor with a low voice. "A new human being! It's just as remarkable every time you experience it!"

He continued, with warm voice, while stroking his stubby chin in meditation. "Isn't life really praiseworthy? So tireless! A wealth of new possibilities! Who knows—maybe a new *Snorri* is lying here! In any case—a new human being, a new soul, a steamy mirror, the beginning of everything. . . !"

He made an embracing motion toward the others. "Come!" he said. "Shouldn't we bow in awe before new life? Before the ancient and eternal vision of mother and child?"

The poet kneeled down by the edge of the bunk and lowered his head. The marine engineer, Gregersen, followed his example, smiling and with folded hands. The watchmaker and the doctor remained standing, but with their heads bowed, too. Mrs. Davidsen turned away and hid her face in a towel.

The young mother still lay staring into space without seeing anything. She was breathing evenly through her half-open mouth, while with her pale hands she gingerly held the baby to her breast.

Afterword

BO ELBRØND-BEK

CHRISTMAS MARKS BOTH THE HIGH POINT AND THE turning point of the year. From ancient times it has been an important time of transition; the winter solstice, the dark days done and the bright days to come, was celebrated by bringing to life the myth containing the central elements of the interpretation of life, in order thereby to renew one's self and society. With the introduction of Christianity the heathen festal traditions nevertheless gained a new divine content.

Much later Christmas stories (of which a few are briefly discussed here) became an entertaining and interpretive part of the tradition. In our selection of texts we have stressed that Christmas, appreciated on many planes, should be integral to plot and theme. Much literature relating in itself to Christmas is generally not regarded as traditional Christmas stories. This is not just a question of genre, of its usually being impossible to select a suitable passage, for which Henrik Ibsen's drama *Et dukkehjem* (1879; *A Doll's House*) can serve as an example. The action takes place at Christmastime, when a new person is "born" or emerges in the female protagonist, Nora. This new identity in which she becomes aware of herself and takes responsibility for her life in society simultaneously means a break with the prevailing patriarchal norms that have repressed her and kept her personally dependent upon others. With her realization that she must leave her earlier conventional existence behind, she finds a more authentic life, which Ibsen implicitly equates with the birth of Jesus.

But no matter how close the authors are to the Christian message as presented in Protestant Scandinavia, as a rule they find useful the archetypal conflict between light and darkness, life and death. This is true both at the personal level, where a child's birth simultaneously represents a rebirth, a renewed contact with the inner child in the persons involved as well as among the audience, and at the social level, where the Christmas gospel holds out hopes for a better, more complete life here on earth. But even though miserable social conditions shattered these hopes earlier, in as much as fulfillment in this present life was crushed or denied as far as the lower classes were concerned, still, the utopia of the kingdom of God was no less effective. The creation of the Social Democratic–dominated welfare society abolished the elemental hunger and poverty that was— and still is—built into the antihumanistic social models that refuse to see the poor, the needy, the weak, and the outcast as parts of a collective. It is nevertheless an irony that exactly the Scandinavian societies—which are among the most highly developed in the western industrial world with regard to the quality of life—have simultaneously become the most secularized, despite individual differences.

Many Christmas stories give their authors occasion not only to tell a good story but also to manifest an evangelical sympathy and solidarity with the weak in society, be they poor and outcast, women and children. In more than one sense Christmas can be described as the holiday for children. Sophus Schandorph's humorously pointed "Christmas Eve in the Henhouse" tells how an outcast, the true scum of society, in this case a fatherless proletarian boy, possesses in spite of everything the surplus that is needed to create a society far more genuine than that illusion of a temporary solidarity created by the hierarchical bourgeois society once a year.

Within its negative course of events, Amalie Skram's "Karen's Christmas" also includes a social utopia. The young, poor maidservant is, like the Virgin Mary, somewhat at a loss to identify the father of her child. But this is simultaneously a passion story whose closing picture forms an unconsummated and for that very reason appalling Pietà. But the story is neither harmonized nor resolved in an edifying manner by Christian idealism, seeing that the attribution of a positive view lies quite outside the story's basically religious horizon. Its tragic end, partially inspired by Hans Christian Andersen's fairy tale "The Little Match Girl" from 1845, contains both a sharp protest against prevalent conditions in society and a dream of a more humanly decent life.

This tendency toward social realism does not dominate William Heinesen's "Born of a Maid," which forms a secular pendant to the Christmas gospel. During a hurricanelike storm in the North Atlantic, young Maria gives birth to a healthy baby boy. The story, which is masterfully told with warm humor, concludes with a doctor, a poet, a watchmaker, and a marine engineer on board, bowing as did the wise men from the east at the sight of the mother with her child, in awe of the mystery of life, the wonder of childbirth—and the redemption of the mind. For the nonbelieving humanist, life is holy!

Hans E. Kinck's wistful short story with the symbolic title "Before the Candles Go Out" is a penetrating psychological study of the influence of a social milieu. A middle-aged couple that had married late because they had both been marked for life in childhood by their respective parents' loveless and unhappy marriages, unconsciously re-create that pain and disintegration whose expression was forbidden to them as children. But their four-year-old daughter, with her symptoms of a nervous stomach, finally unites her parents. Gathered at the sickbed, the child becomes the catalyst that enables the adults to articulate their earlier pain—thereby restoring the healing link to the inner child.

Hans Christian Andersen's ironic self-interpretation in "The Fir Tree" portrays, just as the title character in Mozart's opera *Don Giovanni* (1787), instability and longing. While still quite small, the fir tree dreams about happiness and splendor everywhere else but where it has taken root. When it is chopped down at Christmastime, it has to leave its childhood surroundings, just as Andersen left his hometown of Odense to find fame at the tender age of fourteen. That painful separation falls like the blow of an ax, with which the fir tree's growth is stunted. The tree looks forward to the glory and splendor of Christmas Eve, but with completely unrealistic notions. Already the next day the Christmas tree is put up in the attic, and eventually, like Don Giovanni, it goes up in flames when it is used as fuel under the wash kettle. With this the bittersweet story is irrevocably over—and the tree's self-scrutiny has come too late, but hopefully not too late for the audience. Andersen himself, the first proletarian in Danish literature, knew better than anyone else the poetic and human costs that made him homeless in the life that he was continually reduced to observing as an outsider.

Christmas has traditionally brought "peace on earth" for Christians; even in wartime, weapons have been stilled when Christmas was rung in. Johannes V. Jensen's harsh tale from Himmerland, "Christmas Peace," deals with a signal breach of this peace, as a felon nicknamed the Tinker, an implied reference to his profession as a thief, provokes a showdown with his neighbor, Peat-Christen, and is killed in self-defense. The homicide, of which the authorities acquit Christen, is the culmination of the Tinker's self-destructive relationship with society. In reality the two families are equally poor, but ideological interpretation and reinterpretation results in an abyss between them from a social point of view: Peat-Christen supports himself and his family by honest means as a dirt farmer and day laborer, whereas the Tinker's perversion of his talents results in inarticulate rebellion against degrading social conditions, which brings him into conflict with the law, local society, and the authorities.

In Eyvind Johnson's "Advent in the Thirties," we stand at the brink of an incomprehensible catastrophe. A poor old peasant couple, with scant knowledge of a world filled with conflict beyond the backwoods, are confronted with a tired and starved Jewish refugee who has narrowly escaped the German Nazi concentration camps. The confrontation with his alien and unhappy fate gives the local inhabitants an opportunity to take a critical attitude toward the anti-Semitic propaganda of one of the clever, big-city newspapers, according to which the alleged afflictions were partly fabricated and partly well-deserved. Against this view, the author, who was one of the earliest and most persistent Scandinavian writers to attack Nazi tyranny with its racist teachings and anti-intellectualism, makes the ethical demand of his contemporaries for love of neighbor in a binding way, as the sheriff and district attorney informs the Jewish refugee that . . . "Well, what will the sheriff say?" The answer thus depends in the final instance upon the reader, for no one can avoid responsibility for decisions affecting the common good!

As staged by the poet-philosopher Villy Sørensen, the struggle between good and evil is seen in the light of the cold war. With Socratic irony he tells the story of "The Soldier's Christmas Eve." The gullible angels of peace think that the soldier is Christ come again. Like some kamikaze pilot, automatically obeying every order no matter how criminal, he has been dropped over enemy territory to ensure that the bomb reaches the correct target. Mankind's Faustian aspiration for truth and light has thus led to the creation of the most terrible weapon of annihilation, which threatens to pollute and destroy not only the more or less imaginary enemy, but all of humanity. The author's pessimism is clear in the soldier's encounter with God, when the soldier, swayed by his image of the enemy, refuses God's fondly meant Christmas present, for fear that it will fall into enemy hands, whereupon he is left behind with the bomb ticking down toward death. Fallen humankind, abandoned by God, angels, and humans, stands alone and isolated because in its divided, alienated condition it is incapable of finding the way to life, truth, and itself, which is what God symbolizes.

The confrontation between those of yearning faith and those of little faith is developed in a different direction in Selma Lagerlöf's poetic "Legend of the Christmas Roses," which is about the lost paradise. Abbot Hans imagines he has created an exotic garden that is as close a substitute, even an approximation for paradise, as humanly possible. However, it is in the wild forest that the miracle happens, when on one Christmas night the abbot and a lay brother witness the forest turning into a most radiant paradise in celebration of the birth of Jesus. But the lay brother, believing it is the Devil confusing their senses with his phantasms, disrupts and ultimately destroys the revelation because he is incapable of distinguishing between paradise and hell, evil and good. The forest will never again celebrate the hour of Our Savior's birth. Yet as a paltry reminiscence of the great Christmas garden, the Christmas rose still blooms at Christmastime.

Springing up and blooming amid the harsh, dark winter symbolizes for Selma Lagerlöf the triumph of life over death. And reading or listening to this and similar visionary stories at Christmastime continues to take place in the trust that our purified hearts may become as children again, which is the condition for our being able to bid the *new* year welcome.

Bibliography

GENERAL

Dawson, William Francis. *Christmas: Its Origin and Associations.* London: E. Stock, 1901; repr. Detroit, 1968.

Harrison, Michael. *The Story of Christmas.* London: Odhams Press, 1951.

Hole, Christina. *Christmas and Its Customs: A Brief Study.* New York: M. Barrows, 1958.

Meisen, Karl. *Nikolauskult und Nikolausbrauch im Abendlande.* Düsseldorf: Schwann, 1931; repr. 1992.

Miles, Clement A. *Christmas in Ritual and Tradition.* London: T. F. Unwin, 1912; repr. Detroit, 1968.

Rietschel, Georg. *Weihnachten in Kirche, Kunst und Volksleben.* Bielefeld & Leipzig: Velhagen & Klasing, 1902.

Tille, Alexander. *Yule and Christmas: Their Place in the Germanic Year.* London: D. Nutt, 1899.

SCANDINAVIA

Bø, Olav. *Vår norske jul.* Oslo: Norske samlaget, 1970.

Bø, Olav. *Årshøgtidene i norsk tradisjon.* Oslo: Universitetsforlaget, 1980.

Bringéus, Nils-Arvid. *Årets festseder.* Stockholm: LT, 1976.

Celander, Hilding. *Nordisk jul.* Stockholm: H. Geber, 1928.

Eskeröd, Albert. *Årets fester.* Stockholm: LT, 1953.

Feilberg, H. F. *Jul,* 1–2. København: Rosenkilde & Bagger, 1962 (2nd ed.).

Hodne, Bjarne. *Gledelig jul! Glimt af julefeiringens historie.* Oslo: Universitetsforlaget, 1982.

Olsson, Marianne. *Julen för 100 år sedan.* Göteborg: Tre tryckare, 1964.

Piø, Iørn. *Julens Hvem Hvad Hvor.* København: Politiken, 1977 (3d ed. 1984).

Piø, Iørn. *Bogen om Julen.* København: Sesam, 1990.

Acknowledgments

Peter Christen Asbjørnsen, "An Old-fashioned Christmas Eve," originally published in Norwegian as "En gammeldags Juleaften" (*Den Constitutionelle*, 1843) and reprinted in *Norske Huldre-Eventyr og Folkesagn* (Norwegian fairy tales and legends), 3d ed., 1870.

Hans Christian Andersen, "The Fir Tree," originally published in Danish as "Grantræet" (*Nye Eventyr* [1844; New tales]).

Amalie Skram, "Karen's Christmas," originally published in Norwegian as "Karens Jul" in the Copenhagen newspaper *Politiken* (1885), and reprinted in *Fire Fortællinger* (1892; Four stories).

Sophus Schandorph, "Christmas Eve in the Henhouse," originally published in Danish as "Juleaften in Hønsehuset" (*Fra Isle de France og fra Sorø Amt* [1888; From Isle de France and Sorø County]).

Karl A. Tavaststjerna, "Christmas Matins in Finland's Barkbread Country," originally published in Swedish as "En julotta i barkbrödets Finland" (*Kapten Tärnberg och andra berättelser* [1894; Captain Tärnberg and other stories]).

Hans E. Kinck, "Before the Candles Go Out," originally published in Norwegian as "Før lysene slukner" (*Vaarnætter* [1901; Spring nights]).

Johannes V. Jensen, "Christmas Peace," originally published in Danish as "Julefred" (*Nye Himmerlandshistorier* [1904; New Himmerland stories). By permission of Gyldendal.

Selma Lagerlöf, "The Legend of the Christmas Roses," originally published in Swedish as "Legenden om Julrosorna" (*En saga om en saga och andra sagor* [1908; A legend about a legend and other legends]).

Frans Eemil Sillanpää, "A Farm Owner's Christmas Eve," originally published in Finnish as "Erään talollisen jouluaatto" in *Maan tasalta* (1924; At ground level). "A Farm Owner's Christmas Eve" is translated from the Swedish translation ("En gårdsvärdinnas julafton") by Bertil Gripenberg. By permission of Werner Söderström Osakeyhtiö Publishers and Printers.

Gunnar Gunnarsson, "At the Bottom of the Snow Ocean," originally published in Danish as "På bunden af snehavet" (*Dag tilovers* [1929; One day to spare]). By permission of Gyldendal.

Jakob Sande, "A Legend," originally published in Norwegian as "Legende" (*Straumer i djupet* [1935; Currents in the depth]). By permission of Gyldendal

Norsk Forlag.

Fritiof Nilsson Piraten, "The Christmas Basket," originally published in Swedish as "Julkorgen" (*Småländsk tragedi* [1936; Tragedy from Småland]). By permission of Albert Bonniers Förlag.

Eyvind Johnson, "Advent in the Thirties," originally published in Swedish as "Advent på 30-talet" (*Den trygga världen* [1940; The secure world]). By permission of Albert Bonniers Förlag.

Heðin Brú, "The White Church," originally published in Faeroese as "Tann hvíta kirkjan" (*Flókatrøll* [1948; Shaggy sheep]). By permission of the author's heirs.

Axel Hambræus, "The Legend of the First Christmas Presents," originally published in Swedish as "Sagan om de första julklapparna" (*Med färglåda och slungsten* [1950; With paint box and slingshot]). By permission of Gunnar Hambræus.

Villy Sørensen, "The Soldier's Christmas Eve," originally published in Danish as "Soldatens juleaften" (*Ufarlige Historier* [1955; *Harmless Tales*, 1991]). By permission of Gyldendal.

William Heinesen, "Born of a Maid," originally published in Danish as "Jomfrufødselen" (*Gamaliels besættelse* [1960; Gamaliel's obsession]). By permission of Gyldendal.

CPSIA information can be obtained at www.ICGtesting.com
Printed in the USA
LVOW07s1821270714

396253LV00004B/295/P